FEVER HEAT

FEVER HEAT

BY HENRY GREGOR FELSEN

Octane Press, Edition 1.0, September 2025
Dell Publishing Co. Edition, 1954
Fawcett Publications Edition, 1961
GP / Books Edition, July 1990
Felsen Ink Edition, 2013

ISBN: 978-1-64234-133-1
ePub ISBN: 978-1-64234-191-1
LCCN: 2024951949

On the cover: Cover art used with permission of Bantam Books
(Penguin Random House).

Designed by Tom Heffron
Copyedited by Faith Garcia
Proofread by Larice Addamo

octanepress.com

Octane Press is based in Austin, Texas

CHAPTER 1

THE GUY SHOULDN'T HAVE PASSED ME the way he did because it made me mad, and it's not good to get mad behind the wheel. It leads to what I was doing when he pruned me—driving aimlessly from one side of the United States to the other, wondering what I was going to do when I ran out of gas money.

The road had been straight, and I'd been cruising along in overdrive at an indicated seventy-five. I'd seen the guy come up from behind, and if he wanted to travel faster than I was going, that was his business. Until he made it mine, too.

I led as the flat ended, and we had a hill to climb. A hill with a blind right turn at the top. As soon as I felt the grade under my tires, I kicked down into direct drive to keep up my revs and my pace. I checked the guy behind me and saw him take a couple of quick, nervous jerks toward the center line. I didn't speed up for him or slow down. I drove my own speed, figuring that once we were up the hill and around the turn, I'd wave him by if the road was clear.

Then he did it. Just as we hit the yellow no-passing line. He pulled out and started past, racing toward that blind turn at the top of the hill. And just about that time, a cattle truck poked its big nose around the turn, coming down the hill.

Maybe I was slow because I was used to professional drivers. It took me a big second to realize that the guy wasn't going to back off and duck in behind me. He was going to try passing if it killed him, and me, and the load of steers on the truck.

I knew he couldn't make it, cursed him for a fool, and backed off, so he could cut in ahead of me. When he went by, I saw him look at me, spit out a dirty word, and go for my front end.

I hit the brakes as he looked over his right shoulder and cut across my left fender, trying to shave it and scare me off the road. Then he was past, and pulling away, and I was after him.

A race driver who takes up a challenge on the highway is like a fighter who lets himself get sucked into a barroom brawl. It's dumb, it doesn't pay a dime, and you can ruin yourself. But I wasn't a race driver anymore. I was an ex-race driver. And I was mad.

I took after him.

I don't know why he picked that particular way to choose me. Maybe he noticed the signs of a track-weary stocker. Hubcaps missing, a body whose rippled and battered skin showed the wounds of competition and the effects of being under the hammer too many times. Maybe he saw where the big 22 I used to carry had been painted out. Maybe he saw all that and wanted to do it the hard way, on a hill with a turn.

Whatever it was, the minute the guy went past, I was after him. It was as though his passing car had ripped away the apathy I'd felt ever since I hit the road to nowhere. Suddenly, I was alive again, and mad.

Stupid? Sure, it was stupid. But the second my foot went down,

I was in a race. And a race is a race, whether it's at Langhorne, Darlington, Gardena, Daytona Beach, or Highway 6.

I moved up.

The guy ahead of me was driving an Olds. Faster than my Hudson Hornet on the straight, and more lightning from a stop to a start. But he wanted to race around turns, and that's where I had him by the shins.

I watched him. When he saw I was after him, he opened up and almost stood the Olds on its ear going through a hard right turn. I slid around behind him, in the groove, and came up on his tail. I was close enough to see him take a quick look in his rear-vision mirror as I closed in, then the Olds coughed a little smoke as he floored it.

There was no hurry. I was mad, but I wanted to teach him a lesson he'd never forget. A lesson about passing other people on hills and turns, and cutting in too soon. I teased him. I moved in closer, until I was almost breathing down his neck. He kept looking in the rear-vision mirror to see what I was doing. When he did, I was close enough to see that he had a fat, round face and egg-like eyes. There was a dark suit jacket hung up on a window hanger on the right side of the car. I guessed the sample cases were in the trunk.

I pushed him, and he was easy to push. It's an old racing trick, and it can make even a good driver blow up once in a while. He hit into turns with his tires screeching and his front end dipping like the bow of a small boat. I stuck with him, pushing, making him go faster than he wanted to go, or should have gone.

I stayed on top of him until he got rattled and tried too hard. He began taking the turns faster, rougher, and I dropped back a little. I was still close enough to crowd him, but with room to swing away if he got panicky and braked wrong on a turn and rolled. Because I wanted him to roll.

A nice game for a grown-up man to play. Sporting thing for a pro to do to an amateur. Proud deed to recite to St. Peter. There had been a time, not too long ago, when I did my bit beginning at ten thousand feet. It began gracefully, and then out of the steep turn, I would roll on my back and point down. That's the way a dive-bomber went. Slightly upside down. When you were hanging by your safety belt, you had the right angle, and you went for your target. And when you leveled off, you were at eight hundred feet, flying through the smoke and dust of other bombs, bouncing back into the sky like a rubber ball.

Some guys never pulled out. They had what the psychologists call "target hypnosis." You look so hard at where you're going, you go into a trance and keep going until you hit. But that never bothered me. We were flying close support for the army troops outside of Davao in the southern Philippines, and bombing was a chore to be performed every other day. There were no enemy aircraft and practically no ground fire. It was just a long, dull flight to a dive and then back home again. Impersonal, routine. Nothing to get wound up about and nothing to unwind against.

But it had been different on the track.

Different when the guys you were fighting were wheel to wheel with you, when you ate their clods and breathed their fumes and smelled their burning rubber. Especially different when the sound of your engine winding out became the ugly sound of Thelma's mocking laughter. Because she knew you were a prisoner of the race, and she knew where you were and what you were doing, but you didn't know about her. And after what she had done once and got away with, she liked to tease and keep you in doubt. Hoping you'd get so wild you'd kill yourself. But you didn't oblige. You had death on your mind, all right, but it was for the guy ahead of you who suddenly became the one she'd cheated with or, for all you knew, was still cheating with. And every time somebody got too close, it was the same thing, until you'd been thrown off all the tracks. And here you were trying to kill again, on the highway. Because it was a race, and a race brought it all back.

The Olds was climbing toward ninety again when I was ready. I had my plan worked out, and I was ready to make it work. Even if it killed us both. That Olds was my target, and I had to go in on it. *Had* to. Whenever my turn showed ahead.

It hadn't taken me long to figure out the guy's driving habits. He went like hell on the short straights, waited until he was almost in the turn to brake hard, then picked up his speed coming out. It wasn't bad, but it wasn't good. It got him around the turns, but it was rough on his brakes, and they were beginning to show signs of fade. I kept my foot off the brake. I'd seen so many turns I could judge them at a look. Coming on a turn, I'd back off the throttle a little so I could hit it fast but with plenty of reserve horses to pull me around. That way I'd get into the turn fast, with the revs up, just a little slower than it could be taken. When I got in, I tromped it, and there was the power I needed to pull me around. It's the way to take turns when you know your car, and a way to die if you misjudge how much power you'll have to call up on the turn. But I knew how much I had, and when.

I set the guy up by faking a couple of passes on the left. I'd move up on him, and when I did, he played it true to form. He moved in front of me. I grinned and nipped at his flanks again, pulling him over to the left to block me. He began to worry more about me than the road.

Then I saw my chance. A wide curve to the right. It was time to move in for the kill.

We roared at the turn, and I faked to the left again. When he pulled over to block me, he was going into the turn and got caught on the outside. He started around on the rim in a big, wide arc. The kind that rolls nice new automobiles on their thin, shiny tops. I kicked the Hudson and took the straight line across the turn, starting sooner and staying on the inside. I had him.

In a way, I knew what I was doing. In a vague, remote way. But all I lived for at that moment was the turn. I was riding hard behind a golden hood ornament with all my brains in my right foot. It was target hypnosis, and that green Olds was my target.

The Hornet screamed as I put my foot in it and went into the turn with everything it had. I slid up next to the Olds and stayed there, coming around fine while the other driver was fighting to stay on his wheels.

I didn't give him a chance. He wanted to come around and ease toward the right side of the turn, but I was inches away, and he couldn't. I kept him on that wide turn, drifting into him, forcing him to the left, so that the inertia building up would fly him into the cornfields.

All in all, it only took a couple of seconds. The guy hung on to his wheel as hard as he could, smart enough to keep his power on while he used light brake. I hadn't figured him to be that smart. But when I looked across at him, the fat red face looked like a dough ball, and his pouty lips were skinned back from his teeth in a grin of fear. He had the same expression you see on a cat's face when it is surprised by a dog. Wild, desperate, and afraid.

Seeing him afraid did it. I didn't want to kill him anymore. In the split second it takes to see a dozen mental images at once, I lost my hatred and my hypnosis. He wasn't a mean-faced, nasty bastard who had pruned me on a hill. He was somebody's flabby, hard-arteried husband or Daddy who squinted down a thousand miles of concrete a week to make the groceries and the dolls or the footballs. A puffy, repulsive-looking road bully whose boss was probably chewing out his rump to cover more miles, and whose wife and kids would cry if he didn't make it home.

Maybe he was a bachelor. It didn't matter. The image of home and kiddies hit me hard as only a bachelor can feel it. And that saved him. I didn't edge him off the road.

I cut down to the inside of the turn, making my beefed-up running gear squeal in protest, and pulled ahead. Then the Olds tore loose.

The left rear wheel lost its footing on the concrete, and the tail of the car whipped toward the ditch. I've got to give the guy credit. He didn't give up. Maybe he was too scared to do the wrong thing. Watching in my rear-vision mirror, I saw him kick up a storm of dust and stones as his rear wheels went off the road. He seemed to hang there for a moment, and then with his wheels churning, the tread caught and he came out of the skid, shooting across the road toward the opposite ditch. The tires howled again, laying black tracks on the concrete. The tail of the car bounced as it went off the road again, but his speed had been cut. He spun half around on the loose dirt and came to a jolting halt. He'd made it. Then I was gone.

By that time, I'd quit racing with him and was racing against something else. Racing against the road, the howl of the engine, against the strange hot country I was driving across, against myself.

The guy in the Olds stayed back, and I lost him in a couple of minutes. But I drove as though I was on the last lap of the Mexican Road Race. Foot to the floor, engine winding out, whipping past cars, tractors, and trucks. The speedometer needle climbed to the top peg and snuggled there. The tach read too many rpm for too long for a mill that had howled around too many tracks too many times. The wind tore at the open window to my left. I stared down the white highway, seeing the rising heat waves dance off the concrete, and smashed into them.

I don't know how long I drove like that. When my foot goes down, I forget everything, even time. I can't remember what I passed, or what the road signs said. I came to slowly, like from out of a dream, when I could sense something going wrong. I flashed a look at my temp gauge. It was all the way over to the right. I winched and eased off, coming back to normal, letting my fingers relax, feeling my right leg trembling. I moved my body forward, feeling my back soaked with sweat. And as the world made sense again, the let-down set in.

A guy had passed dirty on a curve, and I had tried to kill him the no-hands way. I'd been crazier than he was, passing on another turn, forcing him out where he'd have hit anybody coming from the opposite direction. Maybe a woman with a car full of kids, or a farmer in a truck, or a bus. Because I couldn't control myself when I was in a race. Because I was what the other drivers used to call me—to my face: "Nuts."

And, after it was over, tearing along at top speed, wasting gas, beating my pooped pistons to death, going like hell to nowhere. Because of a blonde who had walked out and left all the memories hanging in my closet. A blonde named Thelma with a kiss as warm and moist as the south wind, who even had the mechanics sneering at me before she was through. And the harder I tried to be the track terror, the more they sneered and the crazier I drove. Until they got tired of putting up with a homicidal nut who used to be a driver. Until I had to go.

I began to worry about how far I'd have to go to find a place to fix the car. I could hear a slight pinging, and I wanted to get stopped before the boiling water dropped below the level of the valve seats, and I earned a cracked block for my trouble. That was all I needed. To wreck the ear before I sold it.

So, I took it easy. In a little while, the guy in the Olds showed up behind me, but he stayed back. He could have passed me. I didn't care. I'd won my point—whatever it was. But he stayed back. Even he knew I was nuts.

The next town had been dropped at the bottom of a long hill. Like a lot of Midwestern towns, it had been built along a river, where there would be trees and shelter. I didn't look at it with any particular interest as I approached. I figured to stop long enough for repairs and shove off again. It was just another place with houses and trees and two or three white church steeples. Like a million other places where a couple of thousand people become neighbors and never do figure out why they live in this town instead of another one just like it.

I laughed at the place just before I drove into it. It was called Town. And there was an old wooden, bullet-riddled sign along the highway that read:

WELCOME TO TOWN

Speed Laws Strictly Enforced
At All Times

And that was all they called the place. Town. Nothing in front. Not Johnstown, or Hilltown, or Horsetown, or any other Somethingtown; it was just Town. Somehow, I liked that. It was straight and to the point.

I noticed something else on the way in. On my right, near the river, there were tall poles with lights and a small grandstand. It might have been the high-school football field, or where Town's puberty league gathered to play night baseball. But it wasn't. It was the town's dirt track. Probably they called it a quarter-mile, but it looked longer, more like three-eighths to me. I felt a knuckle grinding in the pit of my stomach. It was a racing town.

There were a couple of new car agencies with garages in Town, but I didn't stop at them, and for the same reason a strange whore doesn't check in at the YWCA. I hit the back streets of Town and found what I was looking for, my own kind. An unpainted concrete block building with a sign that read *Bill's Garage.* And alongside the garage, in the weeds, were a couple of battered Fords converted for jalopy racing. This was it. This would be home.

I pulled to a stop under a tree, in the cool shade. I got out stiffly and lifted the hood. The big six-cylinder engine was making noises in its throat even after I'd shut it off. I left the hood up to hasten cooling and stretched. There was no hurry. My car and I both needed a rest. I had a pretty good hunch my water pump had gone sour, but nobody works on a red-hot motor.

I went inside the garage. There was an office section with a battered wooden desk, a typewriter under a dustcover, and a beat-up adding machine. There should have been messy stacks of letters and bills and circulars and a couple of naked calendars, but the office looked neat. It didn't look busy.

I wandered through the office into the main section of the garage. There was a big coal stove in one corner and a couple of work benches, spongy and black from grease and oil. I looked at the tools hung neatly on the wall over the benches. They were a top pro brand, but there were hardly enough left to fix a bicycle. The place didn't even have a pit. There were four jacks in a corner that they used when they needed room under a car.

Nobody was in this part either. And more importantly, there wasn't a single ailing automobile in for repairs. In this day and age, when garages are busier than obstetricians, that seemed kind of funny. I thought the place might be out of business, but if that were true, the doors would have been locked.

I looked out of the back door. There was a shed behind the garage, and the junk was there. I looked it over. A lot of iron, and most of it track iron. Old blocks, heads, parts of front ends. Bent wheels, bent axles, bent driveshafts. Busted radiators. The stuff looked as though it had been pawed over a thousand times. Most of it was shot. Racing's unrotting corpses.

I walked around to the front of the garage again, lit the brand of cigarette that is smoked by 82 percent of the race drivers and 28 percent of their mechanics, and looked over the jalopies.

They were standard hybrids stripped for action. One had a '36 Ford coupe body painted blue. The other was covered by a '32 Ford Tudor shell, painted red and yellow. Both had all the glass out, lights off, mufflers off, and hoods off.

I looked at the Tudor. The body had been in so many rollovers and collisions that it was butter soft. All that held it together was the framework of welded pipes that covered it. The cage that kept the driver alive.

There was an unpadded metal bucket seat, no floor, no "interior" of any kind. Just the seat, the framework of heavy pipe, and a heavy surplus oxygen tank, mounted in brackets behind the driver's seat, for a fuel tank. A rusty, empty-socketed instrument panel, a hook to hold the gear shift lever in second. A rear-vision mirror. A safety belt.

That's the way they look after a few races. Battered, beat, junky. Like they had been gutted by fire and smashed by trains. But they were built that way on purpose. The driver needed a place to sit down, and a wheel to hold, and a frame to protect him. A twenty-dollar body to be hauled around by an engine that probably costs five hundred.

On impulse, I got in. The doors were still chained shut, so I got in the usual way, through the open top. I lowered myself into the uncomfortable bucket seat, gripped the ancient steering wheel, and tried the car for feel. It felt lousy. Like sitting in an empty beer can with wheels.

I rested my hands on the wheel and stared ahead through the glassless windshield frame. It was a sample of the competition cars in Town. It might be a place to pick up a few extra bucks. Most of the cars were probably driven by gas station kids in their spare time, and there would be some easy money for a while until some fool kid got in the way and stayed there.

I shook my head. No, I'd promised myself I'd never go back. The guys had been right. I didn't belong on a track. Against good drivers, I was dangerous. On this track, against local boys, it would be murder.

Uh-uh! Fix the water pump, climb into the Hornet, and shove. Drive until busted, sell the Hornet, start walking. Be a sailor or a waiter. Swing a pick, push a broom. Be anything but a driver. A killer.

I bent over the wheel of the jalopy, sighting over the exposed engine, remembering a hundred races at once, and hurting inside. "Rrrrrrrmmmmmm," I growled, dreaming. "Rrrrrrmmmmm!" Hands and feet moved as I re-lived lost moments. The green flag dropping, the snarl of gunned motors, the dust from spinning wheels. "Rrrrrrrmmmmmmm!" The fight for position, the traffic jamming into the first corner. Looking every which way at once. "Rrrrmmm!" The quick check in the rear-vision mirror to see if it was safe to cut toward the inside. "Rrrr . . ."

The rear-vision mirror was filled with a girl's face. She was standing just behind the car, watching and listening. She should have been laughing at the sight of a grown man playing racer in a junk jalopy. Only she wasn't laughing. She was standing behind me with her arms folded, the fingers of one hand digging into the opposite arm. Her eyes were wide and staring. It was a beautiful version of the look I had seen on the red-faced guy just before he spun off the road.

Our glances met and locked in the rear-vision mirror. I gave her a silly, guilty grin and winked to chase my embarrassment. Her mouth tightened, as though she were going to be violently ill. I had the feeling that I was getting the same look a rattlesnake in her bed might get at the exact moment she discovered it wasn't a stocking.

CHAPTER 2

I REACHED UP AND PULLED MYSELF OUT OF THE CAR through the opening in the top. By the time I hit the ground and looked at her again, the horror was gone from her eyes, and in its place was a searching, curious look that didn't make any more sense than the other. The way she looked at me with her head tilted to one side and her eyes taking me in point by point, I had the funny feeling that she wasn't surprised to see me. That she had been expecting me, and now that I had arrived, she was checking to make sure I was what she had ordered.

She wasn't a kid. I figured her to be in her late twenties. She had light brown hair and was wearing a yellow summer dress and a white shell necklace. She had brown eyes, a nose, and a mouth. The way they were assembled, she was pretty. She wasn't fat and she wasn't skinny, but a nice dressful of in-between, with a woman's bosom, a woman's hips, and a girl's waist and legs.

So, this was the bookkeeper. That explained the neat office and the calendar with a dog picture called *Man's Best Friend*, instead of the one called *Reaching for the Soap*. Whoever Bill was, he probably didn't care whether he had any business or not, as long as he had this cute one around to talk to.

The girl's level, searching look disconcerted me. I tugged at my cap. "I wasn't trying to steal your jalopy," I said. "I need repairs. You open for business?"

She didn't seem sure. "It all depends on what you want done. My mechanics are out right now."

"I can fix it myself," I said. "All I need is a part or two and a few tools." I nodded toward the sign of the garage. "That is, if Bill doesn't mind."

She looked from me to the Hudson cooling in the shade. "If you're in a hurry, it would be all right to do your own work." Her voice was soft, pleasant, and remote. She was all business—with one exception. The way she kept studying me as though I were someone she ought to know.

"I'd rather," I said. "I don't like strangers fooling with my car. I'll pay labor costs anyway if you think Bill might feel I'm cheating him."

She turned away, so I couldn't see her face. "He won't," she said, walking toward the garage.

I followed, a pace behind her out of habit. I never like to lead on the first lap, even on foot. "How do you know?" I said, just to be talking.

She stopped, turned, and moistened her lips with the tip of her tongue. "I'm Bill," she said.

"You don't look like Bill," I said, taking the opportunity of that repartee to look her over from head to foot. "Last time I saw Bill, he was an ugly red-headed guy with buck teeth."

She didn't smile. "Bill was my husband." She kept looking at me, as though I should know something about it. "He died last year."

I looked down at the cigarette in my hand, very much aware of how the smoke curled from it. "I'm sorry."

"You didn't know," she said.

"Now you run the place," I said, as though I'd made a big discovery.

"I try to. *As* you can see, I'm not exactly swamped with business."

I tried to brighten things up. "I stopped when I saw the jalopies outside," I said. "I'm kind of a racetrack guy in my way. Did your hus— Did Bill race the cars outside?"

"Yes, he did." She answered very carefully.

"You don't, though. I mean, they don't look in running shape."

"No, I don't. My husband was killed at the track last year. He left me the garage, but I don't sponsor racers."

"I can see why," I said. "You know, you didn't look exactly pleased when you saw me in that Tudor. I can see why."

"That's the car my husband was killed in," she said. "When I saw you in the car, I was frightened. There was something about you that looked like . . . he used to."

That explained the look she had worn and the god-awful feeling that came over me. Not that I'm any more superstitious than any other green-hating driver, but this sounded like a straight tip from beyond the grave. I'd violated one unwritten law by being an uninvited stranger in another man's bucket. I'd taken a dead man's seat and had looked like him. If that wasn't a warning to stay off the track for good, nobody ever had one. I looked at the girl as though I half-expected her to dissolve into frothy bubbles and float back to where she came from through the ceiling.

But when I looked at her, she remained in the flesh, and pretty, smooth, tanned flesh it was, too. It was . . . homey. She seemed like the kind of girl who belonged at the cottage door when you got home at night. Not the racetrack girlfriend type. The wife type.

"Maybe that explains it," I said.

"Explains what?"

"Why you're empty."

She nodded. "I don't understand it. It's all right for a woman to work in a garage, but people seem to think it's wrong for her to own one. They don't seem to trust me."

"How about your mechs?" I asked.

"I have two," she said. "Fred's really retired, but he comes around when there's any work just to help me out. He liked Bill. He's helpful, but—well, some of the work is just too much for an old man to handle."

"What about your other man?" Whoever he was, I suddenly didn't like him because he had to be younger than Fred.

"Oh, Ronnie's all right," she said. "He's Bill's younger brother. He's only twenty, and all he's interested in is building hot rods. But he tries to help. I think he wants to show that he can take Bill's place."

I looked at her shoulders, the soft line of her neck, and the creamy skin that just began to swell out when it disappeared into her dress. Twenty. I'd been twenty once. I didn't doubt that Ronnie wanted to take Bill's place. The punk.

"Where are they now?" I asked, wondering why in hell I was feeling upset because a kid I didn't know might want to make love to a girl I hadn't known for ten minutes.

"Probably out to lunch."

"One of them ought to stay."

"One used to," she said. "But there's not much point to it anymore."

I spun the tail half of my cigarette into the gravel beyond the open door. "I've got a busted water pump," I said, getting up. "If it's all right with you, I'll run the car in now and get to work on it."

"It's all right," she said.

I closed the hood on the Hudson and drove it into the garage. When I got out, she was leaning in the doorway to the office, watching me. I noticed she had put on fresh lipstick, and it made a little knot in my stomach.

"I see you're from California," she said.

"That's right." I hunted for the wrenches I needed.

"Do you like it out there?"

I bent over the motor. "It stinks."

"Oh?" She sounded disappointed. "I've never been. From what I've heard, it sounds nice."

"It's all right if you like living in the midway of a cheap carnival," I said. "A wonderful place to settle down if you plan to raise two-headed kids to show the tourists."

She laughed. "You sound bitter."

"I'm not," I said. "I just don't like people who louse up the scenery. You got a drive pin that will fit this pump impeller?"

"Why don't you look for it yourself?" she said. "You told me you don't like to have strangers fooling with your car."

She didn't say it sassy. I grinned and rummaged around the parts shelves. I was beginning to feel right at home. It was damned pleasant having her stand by and talk while I worked. A touch of the cozy, domestic-type warmth mechanics seldom find in garages. But I didn't find the part I wanted. All she had was a collection of oil filters, a few carb repair kits, spare headlights, and a sad assortment of windshield wipers, spark plugs, off-breed piston rings, and similar junk.

"I don't want to complain," I said, "but you can't run a garage with this stock. Who does your buying?"

She shrugged. "Who buys? Most of this was left by my husband. It's what we haven't used. We had a lot more, but I guess we sold everything good. The other race drivers used to come here until everything was gone. But why replace when there isn't any business?"

"The drivers were business," I said.

"They're all on the books for too much now," she said

I stared at her. "You mean you let the track characters have *credit*?"

"They were all Bill's friends," she said. "I needed business."

"They gave it to you all right," I said. "Friends like a buzzard is friend to a dead steer."

She looked disturbed. "Don't you think they intend to pay me, eventually?"

"They intend to," I said. "And when you go broke, they'll all be sorry they didn't."

She walked toward me and stopped by the front door of the car, resting her elbow in the open window. "You don't have much faith in human nature, do you?" she asked.

"On the contrary, I have a great faith in human nature," I said, swallowing a nasty word as I skinned my knuckles. "I have a deep and abiding faith in the knavery of man. I always expect the worst, and I am seldom disappointed. But let's get back to you," I said. "What's going to happen to this place? The way you're going now, there's no future in it. Even if you starve slow."

"Oh," she said, teasing, "I'm sure someone will come along and cheat me out of it."

I straightened up and looked the place over slowly. It was a good place. Somebody would get it, and somebody would make it go. The right guy in this spot . . .

"Did you ever think of selling out?"

"No!"

I was surprised by the vehemence of her words. She'd almost said it defiantly. For the first time, I noticed that along with her prettiness, there was a look of tension about her. Like she was holding something in. An uneasy quiver went over me. I'd met tense girls before. One minute they were aloof, and the next minute they were hanging on to you for dear life, kissing and gasping and turning pale and half-fainting. This one too?

"But if you can't make it go, you'll lose it," I said.

"I'll find some way to keep open."

"You must love the garage business," I said.

"*I hate* it."

I looked around for a back door. She sounded nuts. She looked so nice, too. Dangerous to play with. I concentrated on dismantling my water pump. To my surprise, the girl moved closer and leaned against the front fender of the Hudson. Then tension and strain were gone. Suddenly, she was relaxed, friendly, and girlish again. "I have a reason for wanting to keep the garage open," she said. "Bill loved the place so much. As long as it's open under his name, it's as though he isn't all dead. I suppose that sounds silly to you."

"No," I said. "It sounds nice. If a guy knew he had a wife who felt that way about him—"

We were both silent for a moment, thinking our thoughts. And we were close. I can't explain how or why, but it's the way it is when some people meet. You can know some people for years and never get friendlier than a nod, and others you can meet for the first time and feel you've known them all your life. This girl and I had only been together a few minutes, yet I felt it was the beginning of something, even though I planned to be on my way when I'd repaired my water pump. Maybe I felt that way because I wanted something to happen. Wanted to have a fresh, warm girl to put my arms around and red lips to kiss. I wondered what she wanted. What she felt.

They say sorrow and grief are close allies of passion. The guys around the tracks used to say that if you could get a woman crying, no matter what the reason, she was as good as in your arms.

"How'd your husband get killed?" I asked.

"On the track."

"Somebody hit him?" She seemed to draw up into a smaller person. "I don't know. I wasn't there."

"Didn't anybody say how—"

"I didn't ask," she said stiffly. "I don't want to talk about it. If you don't mind."

She was stirred up all right, but not in the direction of tears. And I'd been hoping she would get weepy and need a firm shoulder for support. Evidently, she had it so bad, the tears weren't her answer. No, no tears. Just an empty old garage that she kept open like a priestess sticking with the temple of an abandoned religion. It was kind of noble and hopeless—and pointless.

"I'm sorry," I said. "I didn't mean to stir up old hurts." Well, I was nuts in my way, and I guess she had a right to be nuts in hers. I liked her better for it. It gave us something else in common.

"I'm sorry I snapped at you," she said, smiling. "But Herbert, a friend of mine, is always nagging me to give up the garage and— well, it's a sensitive point with me."

She looked around the empty garage with a little puzzled frown. "People are funny," she said. "I hated the garage even worse when Bill had it. He was the leading stock car driver in this part of the state, and the garage was always full. People are like that around here. They're race crazy. Bill was a hero, and they liked to have a hero work on their cars. He tried to live up to what they expected of him. Now they don't come here anymore. And now that he's gone, and business is gone, I wish it could be again. It can't happen, but I want it to. But it can't be. Bill can't come back, and without him here, there's no business."

"Justifying," I said, "my faith in the natural meanness of the human being."

She made a face at me. "I feel sorry for your wife," she said. "Having to live with such a pessimist."

"Don't bother," I said. "There isn't one to feel sorry for."

"Then I feel sorry for the woman you marry," she went on, half-teasing again. "The way you suspect everybody else in the world of being evil, you'd probably feel the same way about your wife. You wouldn't trust her either. You'd . . ."

I slammed the hood down as hard as I could and tossed the wrench away. "Look, ma'am," I said, "one of the reasons I left California was on account of too many lady preachers. I don't like the cornfield variety any better."

She stepped back as though I'd slapped her, turning beet red. "I'm sorry," she stammered. "I was only making talk. I didn't mean anything. I'm sorry if I was too personal. You see, I'm alone here most of the time. I don't talk to many people, and when I start . . ." She looked as though she were going to cry.

I touched her for the first time. "Come on," I said, patting her arm just above the elbow. "It's not that bad. I'm a little jumpy from too much driving and not enough sleep or food. You didn't say anything wrong."

It wasn't that I couldn't stand a woman's tears. I can. I've seen a lot of women bawling because their dear ones were wrapped up in a lot of wreckage on a corner, or because they wanted to go to the movies, or thought they ought to have a new hat. One of the few good times I had in California was when Thelma cried so hard she couldn't talk back.

"It's over," I said. "Now that we've insulted each other, don't you think we could exchange names? It sort of makes us old friends, doesn't it? What's your name?"

"Sandy," she said. "Sandy Richards."

"Pleased to meet you," I nodded at her. What I wanted to do was bow, for some sudden, silly reason.

"What's your name?" she asked.

"Jones," I said. "It used to be Manikaveteovski, but my old man simplified the spelling when he came to this country. Asa Jones. I'm usually called Ace." Most of that was true. Only around the tracks, they didn't call me Ace. They called me *Nueces*, which is Spanish for nuts.

"Pleased to meet you," she said.

We were both searching for words when a car drove up outside and stopped. It was a new Chrysler, a soft blue under a thick film of dust. Dry mud barnacles clung to the lower surfaces. A farmer got out and slammed the door.

Sandy looked at me. "Oh, dear," she said. "Here comes a customer, and I'm all alone. I wish Fred and Ronnie would come back."

"Maybe you can stall him until they do," I said. "Well, I'll get back to my car while you talk business."

The farmer didn't go into the office. He behaved like most guys shopping for repairs. He came into the main section of the garage first, snooping around to see what other cars were there and what was being done to them. He came up behind me and looked over my shoulder. I didn't say anything, and neither did he. Finally, he cleared his throat.

"Boss around?"

I nodded toward the office. "In there." He grunted and walked away. He was big, with a face like an unshaven brick. About fifty, wearing a gray shirt with long sleeves, a pair of gray work pants, and barn shoes. Thick through the shoulders, smelling of animals and grain juices and sweat.

She was waiting for him in the doorway. "Can I help you, sir?"

"I come to see about getting my car fixed," he said.

"Certainly," she said, trying a professional smile. "What seems to be the trouble with it?"

The farmer looked her over. "That's what I brung it here to find out."

"Our mechanics are out right now," she said, trying to sound professional. "If you want to wait, or leave your car, I'm sure they can get at it this afternoon."

The farmer rubbed his chin with the back of his hand. "Yeah," he said unenthusiastically. "But I'd kinda like to know what I'm gettin' into before I leave the car. If the boss can give me an estimate . . ."

She tried patiently to explain. "I can't give you an estimate until the mechanics have looked at your car."

The farmer shook his head. "Well," he said, "I guess I'll be back later, maybe." Yeah, he'd be back all right. I don't know, it wasn't any of my business, but I couldn't keep out.

"Just a minute, Mister." I walked toward the farmer, wiping my hands on a rag. "What'd you say your trouble was?"

The farmer looked at me, then at Sandy, and back to me again. He couldn't figure out what was going on. Neither could I. I don't know about Sandy.

"You a mechanic?" the farmer asked. His eyes swung to my car, and he took in the California license.

"In a way," I said. "Want me to look at your car?"

"I seen some other garages," the farmer said. "They told me I needed a ring job."

"Let's look at your car," I said. "Ring jobs cost money." I started out, and he followed, curious but not hopeful.

He started the motor, and I listened and looked around, and then I looked at the dash. The oil pressure was too high. The motor sounded tight enough. I had an idea. 1 signaled for him to shut it off.

He got out of the car looking angry. He'd been through this before. "Well?" he demanded.

"I can sell you a ring job if you want it," I said. "But if my hunch is right, I think I can take care of you for about fifty cents."

He looked at me for a moment, then leaned over and spat on the ground, rubbing the place with his shoe. "What's your idea?"

"I'll tell you if I'm right," I said. "Just take a chair for a couple of minutes. Talk to the boss, if you want to." I jerked my head toward Sandy, who was standing by the garage door, watching us. The farmer walked over to her, and I went for a few tools.

The farmer came out again when he heard the car running.

"Ready to roll," I said. "Fifty cents."

He walked past me and looked at the dash. The oil pressure was back to normal. He turned around and looked at me. "What was it?"

"Your oil pressure relief valve was too tight," I said. "That's all."

The farmer reached into his pocket and pulled out a handful of change. He picked out a half-dollar, hesitated, and fingered another one. I waited for him to offer a dollar. He scowled at the money and made a noise like a bull belching. "What will that come to?" he asked.

"Fifty cents," I said.

"Ought to be worth more than that," he said, letting the second half-dollar slip back with his other change.

"Half a buck will do it," I said. "Just remember, any time you or your friends need honest work done at the right price, you send them down here to Bill's Garage." I grinned. "You tell them how they get taken care of at a garage run by a woman."

"By God," the farmer said, crushing down the seat as he got behind the wheel, "I'll do that very thing. And you'll see me again anytime I need work. Ring job! Wait till I tell them people off!"

The farmer drove away, and I turned to Sandy with a big grin on my face, ready to flip her the half-dollar. She wasn't grinning. Her lips were tight, and there was an angry, humiliated look in her brown eyes.

"I suppose you think you're real smart, pulling a trick like that," she snapped.

"Wait a minute," I said. "I don't get it. You want business, don't you? I got you some."

"What kind of business? It's easy enough for you to pull your trick and move on. But what am I going to do when other people come around expecting the same thing—and I have Fred and Ronnie to depend on. Don't you see? It will make me seem a bigger fool than ever."

"I'm sorry," I said. "I just wanted to help."

She looked at me the way women look when they see a new hat in the window and wonder if it's worth trying on. There wasn't much to look at. Not quite six feet of rangy man body, dressed in wrinkled khaki trousers, tan billed cap, and a light tan poplin jacket worn over a tee shirt. A long, thin nose, a chin somewhat on the lantern side, high cheekbones, cat-green eyes almost hidden by a perpetual half squint. Like a million other guys you find under cars when something has to be fixed.

"Mr. Jones," she said, and there was the framework of a gently teasing smile at the corners of her mouth, "I don't want you to think

I'm prying, and be insulted, but are you by any chance looking for a job?"

Suddenly, it seemed to be disgraceful to admit being out of work to this girl. "As a matter of fact," I said, "I'm not. I'm on my vacation."

She made a little gesture of defeat. "It really doesn't matter," she said. "I couldn't offer you a job anyway. I couldn't afford to pay half of what you'd get anywhere else."

"Probably not," I agreed.

"I suppose I'm silly," she said, staring at my left shoulder. "But for a few minutes, everything seemed . . . different. I've been coming here day after day, watching business fall off until there was nothing left. I didn't see any way out. When I saw the way you handled that farmer, it was like old times, when Bill ran the garage. He always knew what to do. And people listened to him. You have that same quality."

"In the Marine Corps, we called it command presence," I said, grinning.

"Maybe." She looked past me. "I didn't think of it that way. I just knew again what it meant to have a man around who knew what had to be done—and did it."

"Yeah," I said, looking at the outline of her hip as the wind blew her dress against her. So, she liked to have a man around who knew what had to be done and did it. A pretty little widow with all kinds of sweet memories.

"You know," I said, "I'm like you. I don't like to be somebody's employee, either. Actually, I'm not on vacation. I'm scouting around. You know how sailors always want to leave the sea and buy a chicken ranch. Well, my dream has always been to find a nice little garage where I could be my own boss. Or be somebody's partner."

A fast decision? My life had been built on split-second decisions that paid off in death for a wrong guess. I was on the move, looking for something, somewhere, to make me stop moving, even for a little while. Maybe I'd found it in Town. A rundown garage to play with for a while. A tense, pretty little widow who would be grateful. Not a bad lash-up for a month or two—or three. Until I'd worked both for enough money to get moving again.

"I don't know," she said doubtfully. "All I have is the building, and even that won't belong to me until I pay it off with Bill's insurance money."

"The risk isn't too bad," I said. "You supply the building and the tools, and I'll do the work. We'll split fifty-fifty on the net take." I grinned at her. "Don't get the idea that every farmer is going to drive away from here with a four-bit job. But we may have to lose a little at first until we get known as a place where good work is done cheap."

She gnawed her lower lip. "I don't see why it shouldn't work, she said. "If you can afford to live for a while until the money starts coming in."

"I'll manage somehow," I said. "I'm not long on cash, but I'll get by. I can sleep here at the garage if I have to. In fact, I could sell my car and use the money from that to live on, although we need to buy some tools and supplies. We could make it go, Sandy."

It wasn't that easy. Maybe she had some idea of just how inclusive the partnership might be, and she didn't want to be rushed.

"I don't know," she said. "It seems too important to decide in a moment. We hardly know each other—"

"Right," I said. "And the best way to get acquainted is over coffee. Why don't we go have lunch and talk some more? If the idea doesn't hit you, no hard feelings. Okay?"

"Okay," she said. "Fair enough."

We walked past the two Fords, and she stopped by the one in which Bill had been killed. "Only one thing," she said firmly. "I won't listen to the idea of sponsoring any racers."

"Who asked you to?" I asked, taking her lightly by the arm.

"You look the type."

"Me?" I laughed and tried to make it sound convincing.

"I'm not altogether stupid about racing, even if I don't like it," she said. "I saw your car. It was used in stock car races, wasn't it?"

"The *car* was," I said. "I bought it from the driver before I started east. I was his mechanic, and I knew it was a good car."

"Then it's settled? No racing?"

"You couldn't bribe me to get in a race," I said, and I meant it, for reasons of my own. "But let's get down to business. The first thing I want to do—if we go partners—is to sell my car. It's a cream puff. Still has that new smell, and it's owned by a mechanic who never drove it over thirty-five miles an hour."

She laughed, and there was more than amusement in the sound. It was a relaxed, carefree laugh that went beyond my tired pleasantry. I looked at her, and her face had a serene, taken-care-of look on it. She thought she hadn't made up her mind yet, but we were partners.

CHAPTER 3

WE WERE BACK IN THE GARAGE AGAIN, taking inventory. Not of what we had, but of what we needed. The partnership deal had been settled, and now Sandy was perched contentedly on a high stool with a pencil and pad, while I paced the garage and told her what we needed. The more I looked through the place, the plainer it was that it had been picked clean. I stood in the middle of the garage and squinted at Sandy through the streamer of smoke that spiraled up from the cigarette in my mouth. She looked up from her writing.

"You look disgusted, Ace."

"I'm mad," I said. "The buzzards. Didn't Fred or Ronnie keep track of the tools? You've been picked cleaner than a preacher's piece of chicken."

"The fellows used to come in to borrow tools," Sandy said. "I didn't want to turn them down."

"All we have to do is round up the stuff that belonged to Bill, and we're in business," I said. "You tell me who took the stuff and I'll get it back."

I looked down at a couple of wrenches in my hand. I noticed that both of them had notched handles. I went over to the bench and looked at more tools. Every one had the same funny little tent-shaped mark, like the sign over a ladies' john in China.

Bill hadn't been an idealist. Just for fun, I picked up a discarded coil that had been tossed into a box. It carried Bill's brand. The same with a couple of other parts. Good old Bill. He was paving the road.

"Forget the tools I listed," I said to Sandy. "We'll get back the ones you already own—with interest. Make a list of parts now. We ought to stock up on water hoses. Hoses blow fast, and they're easy to sell to anybody. Then we want a dozen good used radiators, all kinds of gaskets, and a flock of rebuilt jugs—I mean carburetors. And repair kits, too. Wouldn't hurt," I rattled on, "to have a supply of alky conversion kits for the carbs. Then—"

"Then nothing." Sandy's voice crackled. I looked at her with all the innocence I once had. "What's wrong?"

"Don't try to fool me, Ace," she said scornfully. "Don't you think I know what you're doing? You're planning to work on racers. I can tell that from the parts you want. And you promised."

"This is your lash-up, Sandy," I broke in. "If you don't want to run any cars on the track, that's up to you. But let's face facts. Those track characters used to come here for their work. We want them back. We might like to get the shiny trade, but we have to start where we can. Once we get going and build up our good trade, we can give the jalopies the deep six. But right now, they mean eating money."

"I don't want that kind of money," Sandy said in a low, tense voice.

I swore silently at Bill's ghost. Every time racing was mentioned, Sandy seemed to turn to stone.

"If we don't get it, somebody else will," I said.

"Even so. I don't want to encourage a thing that killed my husband."

"How many guys quit racing since they quit coming here?" I asked. "I'll bet not one guy. They find a way."

"Let them." She was as cold as ice.

"We might as well quit right now," I said.

"You don't understand," she said, shaking her head.

"I understand this," I said. "You let me build the business the way it has to be built, and Bill's garage will hum. If we turn our backs on the only business we can get right now—I might just as well be on my way."

This was it. A lot of things depended on her answer. Personal and professional.

She looked at me, and there were little beads of sweat along her upper lip. "We'll try it your way, Ace."

"That's the girl," I said. "And we'll only fool with the racing crowd until we can afford to drop them. Okay?"

"Okay." She still wasn't sure, but she was going along. All she needed was the right guy to tell her what to do and when to do it.

Another car approached. When I heard the deal pipes and the roar as it picked up in second, a block away, I had a hunch it was Ronnie. I listened as the car came close, racing in second, then howling and backfiring as the driver backed off the throttle and let his compression brake him down. The noise slid up to the garage door in a shower of gravel and stopped.

"Sounds like our staff has arrived," I said to Sandy. She nodded. I could see she was trying to figure out a way to break the news to her faithful retainers that they had another poppa on the Salt Lake Line.

When they came in, they were about what I had expected to see. Fred came in first. He was a dumpy little dried-up old man with narrow shoulders and a little pot belly that he carried under his dirty blue shirt, like a stolen melon. Wherever his skin showed, it was grimy, not with recent dirt, but with the accumulated grime of years, like the ancient rust on derelict ships. He carried his head pulled down toward his right shoulder, and there was a tight, sour look on his face, as though somebody had shoved a lemon in his mouth and sewed his lips to the bad taste. When he came in, he had one finger in between his shirt buttons, scratching his stomach. He was hatless, and his white hair was tangled as though he hadn't combed it since the day he was kicked out of high school. His eyes didn't change expression when they saw me. There wasn't any to change.

Ronnie strolled in behind Fred. He was a big boy, with a toothpick in his mouth. He stood a good six feet and was built like a blocking halfback. He was wearing a faded denim shirt, tight-assed denim pants, and black engineer boots. His shirtsleeves were rolled up to show a pair of powerful forearms, and the neck that rose above his open shirt collar was short and thick. A big boy. A big man.

A big man until you looked at his face. A big face, but petulant in a childish way. Full lips, almost in a pout, and dark eyes that carried a chip in each pupil. Dark hair cut in a butch, showing a big, round, stubborn head.

Fred kept walking until he was standing alongside my Hudson. He stopped scratching his belly and used the same finger to scratch under his chin. A conservative, Fred, who didn't change tools just for the sake of change. He examined the car carefully, but from a certain distance. He blinked slowly and meaninglessly, like a chicken trying to sleep standing up.

Ronnie glanced at me casually, with a mixture of hostility and indifference, and made for Sandy. He came up behind her and slid his hand under her hair, so his fingers rested on her neck. "Hi, Sand," he said, the toothpick rolling in his mouth, his fingers working slowly.

She shook him off. "You don't have to touch me every time you say hello, Ronnie."

He sensed I had something to do with the rebuff. His face darkened, and he looked at me again. "You want something?" he demanded.

I pushed my cap back on my head. "Yeah," I said. "I want you to get back from lunch by one after this. Right now, I want you to grab a broom and clean this place out. After that, you can wash and polish my car. If you're smart enough to do that right, I might let you do some mechanical work."

Ronnie swelled up like a bullfrog trying to get rid of a gas bubble. "What the hell," he said. "What's this about, Sand?"

"Ronnie and Fred," Sandy said, "I want you to meet Mr. Asa Jones. He's going to be my new partner in running the garage. He's from California."

"I don't get it," Ronnie said, glaring at me. "This guy wasn't around when we left. How'd it happen so fast? What's the big deal? Who is he? What's he want with us?"

He stood with his feet planted wide, nostrils flared, and chin out, ready for a fight. Fred sat down on an empty gas can and began building a cigarette.

"It's like this, son," I said. "Miss Sandy here and I are going to be partners. We're going to bring this place back to life, and that means work. If you want to work here, you'll get a chance to do everything you're smart enough to do. But you'll have to do your share of the dirty jobs, too. If the work or the pay doesn't suit you, you're free to go somewhere else."

I turned toward Fred. "The same goes for you, Fred," I said, scattering my shots. "I need you here, and so does Miss Sandy. We both hope you'll stick and help us make a go of this place."

"What are you payin'?" Fred asked.

"Scale," I said. "But there's one condition."

"Yeah?"

"We don't have a lot of money," I said. "Most of that has to go for stocking the place. I'll pay scale for the actual work you put in, but I can't pay for the time there isn't any work. I will later, if we make out."

Fred licked his cigarette and stuck it in his mouth, in one corner. "Suits me," he said. "I got nothing to lose. I'm just hanging around anyway."

"You, Ronnie?"

He still didn't know the palace had been carried. "My brother used to own this garage. I guess I've got something to say about it." He looked like he wanted to fight.

"You've got something to say, all right," I said evenly. "And you can start out by telling me how come every tool that's worth a good god damn is missing. You tell me that, and I'll have some more questions. I want to hear you talk. Maybe you can tell me why you let everything your brother built up go to hell."

That hurt him the way I meant it to. For a minute, I thought he was going to cry or throw something at me. But he knuckled. "I can get the stuff back," he said. "It was just borrowed. I know the guys who have the tools."

"Good," I said. "Let's go get them back."

"Okay," he said, still mad. "The next time I see—"

"Tell me, Junior," I cut in. "When's the next race date?"

"Tonight," he said. "And don't call me Junior."

"All right, Senior," I said, dropping my cigarette and stepping on it. "Let's go."

"Go where?" He wasn't about to move. "All your buddies will be working this afternoon," I said. "They'll be getting ready to race. They'll be using our tools. We'll go get 'em now, when they need 'em." I didn't wait for him to answer and moved toward the door. "We'll be back later," I said to Sandy. I turned toward Fred. "Go over that list I made with Sandy. If I forgot anything, add it."

I walked outside and waited alongside Ronnie's rod. It was a typical small-town hop-up. A '48 Ford coupe, black, with white sidewalls, dual pipes, and lowered at the rear. A minute later, Ronnie came out. We exchanged hard looks, and then he got behind the wheel. Now that I was alone with him, I began to soften him up.

"Where to?" he asked sullenly.

"The rounds," I said. "Well hit everybody that's sitting on Bill's tools. Then I need a new water pump for my car."

He grunted and started the car. He spun his wheels on the gravel as he wheeled it around in low, then slam-shifted into second. When he was in high gear, I looked at him out of the corner of my eye.

"Smooth," I said. "You drive for anybody at the track?"

He shook his head. "Can't. I'm only twenty. I won't be twenty-one for two weeks."

"How about then?" He scowled and burned rubber taking a corner. "Sandy doesn't want me to."

"I heard," I said, "that your brother was top dog on this track."

"On any track," Ronnie said, staring over the steering wheel. "There wasn't anybody around here that could touch him. He was leading point man on every track in this part of the state. He really could run." There was a lot of pride in Ronnie's voice. "Bill would go into the turns deeper than anybody else dared before he backed off. That's where he won his races. On the turns."

"That's where they're all won," I said. He looked over at me, curious. "You been around tracks much?"

"You saw my Hudson," I said. "Used to belong to Commodore Tucker. Know who he is?"

"Who doesn't?" Ronnie said, beginning to look excited. "NASCAR champ, AAA champ. Won the last Mexican Road Race . . . you knew *him?*

"I kept his cars running," I said. "That one I'm driving is the car he used when he won that last big race at Gardena."

"It looked beefed-up," Ronnie said.

"It is," I said. "When we get back, I'll show you how. Maybe you can help me sell it. I'll need the dough for the garage."

His grin faded. "Oh," he said, mad again. I waited. He'd tasted the bait, and he'd be back. He took a deep breath, shoved his madness to the back of his mind, and came back to the topic he lived to think about.

"I'd like to drive the track," he said. "I've tried to talk Sandy into running Bill's cars again, but she won't."

"You'll be old enough in two weeks," I said. "Of course, I wouldn't blame you if you didn't want to drive. After what happened to your brother—"

"I'm not scared out, if that's what you mean."

"Nobody could blame you if you were," I said. "After all—"

"I ain't scared," he shouted. "It's Sandy. She won't let me run."

"Run for somebody else," I said, feeling like the serpent that offered Eve the apple. "A guy that really wants to run will find a way."

"I want to," he said. "The guys around here think I'm scared on account of what happened to Bill. I'd like to show them that there's another guy in our family who can run the wheels off 'em. Boy, if it wasn't for Sandy—"

"She doesn't own you," I said. "When you're twenty-one, you're a man. Or should be."

"It ain't that simple," he said, looking trapped.

"You give me the right driver," I said, "and I'll give him horses nobody around here has ever heard of."

It was like catnip rubbed on a kitty's nose. He grabbed the steering wheel hard and shook it. "Boy, if Sandy would only let me run."

"Maybe she will," I said cautiously. "You work with me, and I'll see what can be done. But it won't be easy."

He was already seeing himself on the track. "What's the deal?"

"Well," I said, "I'll have to act like I don't want you to race. I promised Sandy we wouldn't run a car. But I'll tell her that if we don't let you drive for us, you'll quit and drive for somebody else. And I'll say it would be better to have us looking out for you than for you to be with strangers."

"Yeah," Ronnie said. "It ought to be simple." He looked over at me with a friendlier gleam in his eye. "Maybe you taking over the garage isn't such a bad idea after all."

"It will work if you play it the way I tell you," I said. "You have to act like you're fed up, if Sandy's going to believe us. Don't hang over her like an orphan calf sucking on a sugar tit. If you act like a kid, she'll treat you like one."

"I don't want to make her mad," Ronnie said, wavering.

"She won't be," I said. "You're Bill's kid brother, aren't you? Well, show her that the kid's a big boy now, see what I mean? The way it is now, she runs you like you were ten years old."

"Will you back me up?" he asked.

"Do what I say, and you'll be running on the track this summer," I promised. "But don't let Sandy catch on that we planned it that way."

"Man, man," Ronnie muttered as we turned into a driveway where three guys were working on a battered yellow coupe with a blue 66 painted on the sides. "This is almost too good to be true."

Yes, it was. The last thing I needed around the garage was this horny young hand. With him out of the way, I'd be able to work on Sandy. I didn't know how long I'd hang around Town. Until the easy money started coming hard, probably. And during the few months it came easy, I was afraid I'd get lonesome if I had to sleep by myself.

Now that young Ronnie was all set to quit in a big, loud voice, all I had to do was be there to hold the door open for him when we let him go.

CHAPTER 4

THE THREE GUYS WORKING ON THE COUPE didn't look up when we stopped. They were hanging over the engine, greasy and mad. Ronnie and I watched them from five or six feet away. You can't get too close to guys working on a racing car. Right away, they hand you a wrench or make you help lift.

They were typical race boys. All in their twenties, smeared with grease, with tired red eyes and needing shaves. Lean, angry men who wanted to run when the green flag dropped.

The coupe squatted under a tree that had a block and tackle rigged to a big horizontal limb. Parts and tools were scattered around on the ground. I picked up one of the tools near me. It had Bill's mark on the handle.

"Having trouble?" Ronnie asked.

They stared at him. Finally, one of the men spat on the ground and wiped his mouth with the back of his hand. "I don't know what's wrong with the thing," he said angrily. "We've gone over every damn thing a dozen times, and it still runs sick. Ignition's all right, the carburetor's all right, valve springs are new . . . I don't know what in hell's wrong."

"It ain't run right since I took the fence last week," a second guy said. He looked the youngest of the three. A husky lad in a filthy undershirt, Western overall pants, and boots. There was a big scab on his left arm near the elbow, and a dirty, fading bruise on his chin.

The three were silent after this, leaning against the coupe, smoking cigarettes with hot, irritated movements. They were stumped, and mad.

"This here is Ace Jones," Ronnie said. "He's from California. He's gonna take over Bill's garage. Ace used to be the mechanic for Commodore Tucker."

Ronnie didn't bother to tell me who the three guys were. It didn't matter. Those things took care of themselves.

The oldest-looking guy threw away his cigarette and looked at the coupe. "No use running the goddamn thing this way," he said mournfully. He looked at the engine and called it every dirty name he could think of.

I walked over to the car and looked down at the engine. It looked like any other old Ford mill. The boy who drove it came up to me and said, "Want to hear it?"

I nodded. He tried to start it again. The most he could get was a couple of bad coughs.

"I could be wrong," I said. "But the way it sounds to me, I'll bet your cam's bent out of true. That would make the heel reopen some of the valves and foul you up."

"Hell," the driver said, "I'll try anything if I can get running by tonight. Come on; let's tear the son of a buck down."

"We don't have no other cam," one of the others complained.

"We'll get one," the driver said. He looked at me. "You got a track grind left?"

"I think so," I said. "If I'm not around when you come by, Fred will take care of you. You can pay him for it."

The driver wrinkled his nose. "Pay Toad?"

"That's what the guys call Fred," Ronnie said, seeing my look.

"Yeah," I said. "We'll have everything you guys need as soon as I can get the stuff. But it's all for sale when we get it. On cash terms."

"Well," the driver said, looking at the others, "we'll be around if we need anything."

"Good enough," I said. "Now, Ronnie and I'll just take our tools back with us, if you don't mind. You boys know the pieces I mean. They've all got Bill's brand on them."

"Don't be hard," one of the guys said. "We'll get the tools back to you."

"Pick 'em up, Ronnie," I said. "We're in the garage business, and we can't run without tools."

Ronnie went around picking out the tools that had come from Bill's. The three men watched him silently, without offering to help. When he had all he could find, he put them in the trunk of his car. His face was red with embarrassment.

"Well," I said, "glad to have met you fellows. See you at the track tonight if you get running."

They didn't even grunt. I got in Ronnie's car and waited for him to get behind the wheel. "One," I said. "Now let's go after the next guy."

"You made the guys sore," Ronnie said, looking worried. "I thought we were going after their business."

"They won't come to us if they've got all our tools," I said. "Don't you worry, Ronnie. Those guys want to run tonight. They'll be around. And they're like everybody else. They won't appreciate anything we do unless they have to pay for it. You'll see."

Ronnie swung the coupe down a side street. "I know another guy who's probably got a lot of our stuff," he said.

"We'll take him next," I said.

"His name is Loren Peale," Ronnie said, gunning his car through the ratty side of Town. "I don't even know why he tries to race. He never wins anything unless so many guys sour out that he picks up two or three bucks just because he's on the track."

"Ask any guy why he races," I said. "Nobody can give you a reasonable answer. Not even the front-runners. Look at all the guys who lose their shirts on slot machines or betting on the horses. The more they lose, the madder they get to play. It's the same way with racing. If drivers lived by logic, they wouldn't be drivers. Like you. Give me a good, sound reason why you want to drive on the track?"

Ronnie shifted his weight. "I don't need any reasons," he said. "I just want to."

"There you have it," I said. "That's why we'll make money with the garage. We'll have what the boys need to keep going."

Ronnie pulled to a stop in front of a house that was little more than a sagging, rotted shack. It sat in the middle of a weedy yard, crumbling like a decayed tooth. The windows were bare, and where panes had been broken, they had been covered with ragged squares of cardboard. A black stovepipe stuck out of one glassless pane, and rags had been stuffed around it to make it tight. The house had been built with a front porch supported by brick pillars. One of these had been knocked apart, and the porch sagged down and away from the house, ready to let go at any moment. Two dirty, half-naked kids were on the porch when we stopped. They were hitting each other with ragged cotton blankets for weapons. They didn't seem angry or to be fighting. They just stood facing each other and hitting each other with the blankets.

"Peale's kids?" I said to Ronnie. "Some of them," he said. "He's got three or four more."

"That Peale by the car?" "The short one is," Ronnie said. "The tall one is his buddy, Duke Ossman."

We got out of the car and walked up the dirt drive. I shook my head. Not out of surprise, but from seeing how true the types ran from one side of the country to the other.

Peale and Ossman weren't working on the car; they were polishing it. Their racer was a coupe, painted a fire engine red with silver markings. The number 21 looked as though it had been put on by Michelangelo. From radiator to rear bumper, the coupe gleamed like a showroom car. There wasn't a mark or bump that could be seen. Everything was tight, pretty, and shiny. Standing next to that tumbledown shack, it looked like a Rolls-Royce.

A pretty racer, with no scars. A car that made the crowd gasp when it appeared among the battered, tinny, junky-looking competitors. There was only one way a racing car stayed pretty and unmarked and shiny. That was by staying out of traffic. That could be done by staying ahead of the pack or trailing it. This guy hid his car's virginity in the dust.

Race night was coming up, and the car had to be polished. It had to look pretty. I didn't have to be told what it cost to keep the car shiny. One look at the house and the kids answered that question.

When they saw us coming, Peale and Ossman ceased their careful clean-up job and greeted us cordially. Ossman, a tall, thin man with straw-colored hair and clear blue eyes, tossed down his cleaning rag and filled a pipe for a smoke. Peale was pleased by the visit, but he stood next to the car, continuing to caress it with a soft rag while we talked.

I guess I've seen Peale's type around every track in the country, and in every other place where there is noise and excitement. He was short and almost dapper in the dirty work clothes he wore. His blue chambray shirt was tucked neatly into his trousers, and the way it fitted around his chest, I was sure he'd had it cut down, the way it's done in the Marines. The cuffs of his Western-type denims were turned up just a trifle higher than they're ordinarily seen, and the metal buckles on his boots had been shined. His shirtsleeves had been rolled back about two turns. He was tattooed, of course. But on his left wrist, there was a big, gaudy watch that must have cost $150, and on his right wrist, there was an ID bracelet with fake shiny jewels set around his name.

He was fairly husky and good-looking in a cheap way. He had a small, carefully trimmed mustache, and his hair was a little too long and combed into a duck's tail in the rear, like a Hollywood type. He had regular features, a straight nose, even white teeth, and flashing dark eyes.

"This is Ace Jones," Ronnie said. "He's going to help my brother's wife get the garage running again. Used to be the mechanic for Commodore Tucker."

Peale stuck out his hand. "Commodore Tucker? Looks like the big time is hitting Town. The real big time. I hope you won't be stingy with your know-how, Jones."

"It can be bought," I said. "That's my business."

"I'll be around," Peale promised, rubbing his car with the rag. "I usually manage to keep this little gem arcing, but I have my troubles like everybody else."

I looked at his little gem. It even had a complete hood covering the engine. A track geek wagon. His car was stripped inside and braced, but it was fancy. Padded bucket seat, canvas safety belt bleached white, and an instrument panel. In a frame-bashing hassle like jalopy racing, the smart guy has a place to stick the ignition key, a gas pedal, a stick shift, a clutch pedal, and a brake pedal that is often there for its ornamental effect only. But this character! He had a chrome speedometer, oil pressure gauge, temp indicator, and the rest of the stuff you carry on the family sedan. In addition, he had a big tach and one of those ornate gadgets that gives you a detailed report on the condition of every moving part from the valves to the loose rear bumper.

I looked over Peale's car with more than a casual interest, and the poor jerk was flattered. Then I got right to the point.

"I've bought into Bill's place," I said, "and we're in business now."

"Glad to hear that," Peale said, hitching up his wide, studded belt. "We need a good place for the Indys. Those damn outfits that run their own cars won't do nothing for you. Afraid you might cut into their money."

"Yeah," I said. Ronnie knew from my tone what was coming up, and he turned away to stare at the road. Soft, like any kid. "The point is," I said, "I can't do any work for anybody until I get back all the tools that were borrowed from Bill. I see a couple around here . . ."

"We're all through with them now," Peale said with honest light in his eyes. "I was just about to run those tools back this afternoon, wasn't I, Duke?"

Ossman continued to suck at his pipe, placid, relaxed, almost dreamy. Like a slender young Dutch farmer, giving nature an easy shot at making him fat. "Seems we were," he said, half to himself. The mild lie came out with a little puff of blue pipe smoke exhaust.

"As long as I'm here," I said. "I'll save you the trip. Ronnie, you help Peale round up the tools with our brand on them, will you?"

Ronnie did, with his head hanging. But Peale scurried around, falling over his feet in an effort to please. He'd associated me with the big time, and I couldn't do anything to make him feel bad. Not even what I said next.

He'd collected the tools and laid them at my feet, and he was looking at me with the expression of an insecure retriever who needs a pat on the head from his owner. He was all ready to roll on his back and let me tickle his belly with talk about the big tracks and the big names who ran them.

"One more thing, Peale," I said, looking thoughtfully at his car.

"Yeah?" He was anxious to please.

I put on a frown of friendly concern. "Well, I've been looking over the books, and I notice you're into us for a pretty big chunk."

Peale rubbed his face guiltily and shook his head. "Yeah," he said, trying to laugh about it, "I guess I am into you pretty deep."

He shook his head again, trying to look as puzzled as a policeman on a private-eye TV show. "You know how it is in this game," he said. "I haven't been in the money the way I hoped. You know how a jinx hits. It sticks for a while, and when it's on, you can't run in front if you run alone. I figure my jinx ought to be about wore out now, and once I get back in the money again, why, I'll take care of you. Fair enough?" Determined nod, honest look, slightly shaky voice.

"I can't buy it," I said. "Nothing personal, you understand, but I can't play favorites. What I told you goes for all the other guys on the books. I need cash to get going."

The poor sap looked trapped. What I was saying to him had the same meaning that loss of credit at a town's only bar means to a busted boozer. Dry mouth. Thirst for what was being taken away.

"Yeah," he said sympathetically. "I don't blame you at all, Jones. I'd do the same thing. Uh . . . how much am I on for?"

"I haven't had time to check it all," I said. "Seems to me most of the parts you got from Bill were on the books. You've used the parts, but I could take them back and call it square."

He turned pale. If I took back what he owed, he wouldn't be able to start, let alone run. I'd checked for Bill's little brand and found it on the carburetor, the intake manifold, and the heads. And there was probably a lot more I hadn't seen.

"I'll pay you," Peale said, starting to sweat. He rubbed his car a little faster, nervous and afraid. He looked around toward the house, as though looking for something he had that he could sell. All he saw was his kids, still blanket-fighting on the porch. "Just give me a couple of days. Maybe we can work out a deal. I could pay you so much a week on the back stuff and keep my credit good for what I might need. Could we work that?"

"Sounds possible," I said, acting as though I was doing him the greatest favor in the world. "Come and see me about it when you get it figured out."

Peale seemed cheered. "We'll find a way, won't we, Duke?" he said to Ossman. "We always have found a way to keep this baby running. Ain't always been easy, but we're always there, ain't we, Duke?"

Ossman knocked his pipe against the sole of his shoe and put it back in his mouth again to nibble at cold. His face didn't change expression as he bent down and picked up his polishing rag. It remained calm, detached, and remote. "I guess we are at that," he said to the rag in his hand. He began polishing his side of the car, his blue eyes fixed on the work, a strand of limp, straw-colored hair bouncing on forehead as he worked.

Back in the car, Ronnie let out a big breath, not knowing whether to admire me or hate me. "Jesus," he said, "you were sure tough on old Peale. He ain't got a dime. Where's he gonna get the dough to pay up?"

"Why the hell do I care about that?" I said. "Does the guy at the dice table worry about where the suckers get their dough? If they can't pay, they can't play with the bones. Same here."

"That finishes old Peale," Ronnie said. "We'll never see him again."

"Stick around," I said. "He'll be our first customer. He'll get the money somewhere. Maybe he'll draw straws to see which of his kids quits eating, or maybe he'll get the old lady out hustling the dough, but he'll have it for us. No matter how he gets it, he'll bring it to us and think we're doing him a favor by taking it, just so long as we keep him running on the track."

"Who do we put the screws on next?" Ronnie asked, squealing through a corner.

"Nobody just yet," I said. "We don't have to. By tonight everybody in town will know we're back in business and what we're after."

"That'll give 'em a chance to hide the tools they stole," Ronnie said.

"Don't worry. Right now, take me to one of the garages that runs a good car. I want to pick up a water pump."

After we got the pump, we drove back to the garage and carried in the tools. Sandy stared at our load and laughed. Fred picked his nose with his scratching finger.

"We've only hit two customers," I said. "By the time we get through the field, we won't have room for all our stuff."

Sandy handed me the list she and I had started. Added to it were the things Fred had thought of. A nice mixture of essentials and chromed stuff. Race-wise, too. Old Fred, or Toad, didn't need any diagrams.

While I studied the list, Ronnie walked around my Hudson, looking it over closely. He was humming to himself and in high young spirits. "Man, Ace," he called out. "I'll bet this wagon will really roll. How's about letting me take it down the road once?"

"I'll do better than that," I said. "You can demonstrate it for me to any possible customers."

Both Sandy and Fred looked a little puzzled by this sudden friendship between Ronnie and me. We'd left almost at one another's throats, and now we were volleying glad sounds across the Hudson's hood.

"Tell you what, Ron," I said. "You take Sandy and this list and see how much of the stuff you can get. On credit, of course. I'll pay in full as soon as I sell my car, to get us off to a good start. Meanwhile, Fred and I will stick this water pump on and get acquainted. Okay?"

"Anything you say, Ace," Ronnie said loyally. "Coming, Sand?"

He was acting too happy. I caught his eye and tried to take him down with a warning look. He winked back.

After Ronnie had left with Sandy, Fred and I went to work on the water pump. For a while, we didn't say a word. We didn't have to. The old goat knew what to do and when to do it. I began to have a little more respect for him. He was going to be mighty handy to have around.

We got the pump replaced, and I knocked off for a smoke. Fred sat down and started building another home rolled. He squatted down like an old engine part, looking just as worn and oily. When he licked his cigarette together, even his tongue looked dirty. Nothing that would ever wash off. Motor dirt had worked into his skin to mark him for life the way a coal miner's nose wears the indelible blue marks of exploded powder.

"I guess we'll make this place hum, eh, Fred?" I said.

He didn't seem to hear.

"Toad," I said.

He looked up. Squat, expressionless, grayish brown, you could almost see the jewel in his ugly head. "Toad," I said, "This place can go. We can make it go."

His cigarette sputtered and sizzled as he sucked in, and the spit fought the fire. It was his sign of attention.

"I'm thirty-four years old," I said, leaning against my car. "I've been looking for a place where I could settle down. I've been a tramp much too long. This place could be it," I said, trying to sound like the sailor home from sea. "With Sandy to keep books, you and me doing the work, and Ronnie taking care of the crap details, we can keep this place filled. There can be a living in it for everybody." Toad's lumpy cigarette had gone out. He fired it up again.

"I know I'm a stranger," I said. "And I don't blame any of you for taking it slow. After all, you don't know anything about me except that I'm moving in on you. But you give me a little time, and I'll show you I know what I'm doing. Sandy's had a bad year since Bill got creamed, and it will be worth something to see how she feels when we've built the place up for her."

I didn't want to prattle on, but he was making me nervous. I wanted him to say something. Finally, he did.

"Just like old times," he said, looking at me with a sour smile. "I ain't surprised you nosed out this place. Yeah . . . you're just like Bill."

I'd heard a lot about Bill by this time. That he was a top mechanic, a bold driver, a good guy, a straight friend, and admired by all for his sterling qualities. I wondered which of these old virtues were showing on me. I thought of how Sandy had, in effect, put her trusting little hand in mine because I had the same qualities as Bill when it came to getting things moving and making her feel taken care of.

I warmed to old Toad. He didn't say much, but he didn't miss much, either.

"Am I?" I asked. "In what way? What was he like?"

Toad pinched out his cigarette with stubby, callused fingers. "Like you," Toad said. "A no-good bastard."

CHAPTER 5

IT LOOKED AS THOUGH I WOULD have to get rid of Toad as well as Ronnie. But I was curious.

"I thought Bill was a swell guy," I said. "That's the word I got."

Toad spat. "He was. Bill was a hell of a good guy. He was a good mechanic, and he had a lot of friends. A lot of business—until he got track fever."

"Yeah?"

Toad rubbed his hand across his forehead and hunched deeper into his squat. "I don't have to tell you," he said. "You're marked with the same goddamn brand. You'll go the same goddamn way. Living for them two piles of iron. Turning away people because you're too busy getting ready for a race to mess with 'em. Letting everything go to hell just so you can get on the track."

"Bill did that?" I asked.

"I ain't telling you nothing new," Toad grunted. "You knew it the minute you walked in. You've got the brand on you."

"I thought things went to hell after Bill died."

"They just stayed to hell," Toad said with a cough-like chuckle. "I wouldn't want to tell you how many times I stayed in here all night workin' on one of them cars. Me and Bill. And Sandy in the office, tryin' to sleep with her head on the desk, and cryin' when she waked up because Bill wouldn't go home or take in payin' work, or hardly eat or sleep if one of the cars was sick."

"He really had it," I said.

"By the time he took that fence rail through his guts," Toad said, "the only people who come here for anything was the sad bastards who run their own cars. They never bought anything, and what they couldn't steal under the name of borrowin', they borrowed under the name of stealin'. Bill didn't care. He wanted to help everybody run.

"He'd work on some racer all day for nothin' minus thanks and send away anybody with a family car who'd pay for regular work. The night the Lord called Bill home in the third lap on the east corner, he was so deep in debt he couldn't have climbed out with a ladder. This place ain't as broke now as it would be if he'd lived. Sandy stood to lose it by the end of summer. Would've lost it nice and quiet and easy—if you hadn't of come in today. Now she's got it all to live through again, with a second damn fool who's no different from the first, except you're skinnier, uglier, and meaner."

"I told you," I said, "I was looking for a quiet place to settle down and have a nice, quiet little business. I aim to run a garage here, not a Salvation Army post."

"I knew it the minute I seen you," Toad said sourly to himself. "The minute I seen your face and the way you talked and the car you drive."

"You saw me get those tools back, Toad," I said. "That's only the beginning. We're going to hear music on the cashbox from now on in. How does that make me a no-good brother bastard to Bill?"

"Haw!" Toad hucked sardonically. His expression turned tight and acid. "We was all passin' away peaceful until today," Toad said. "I didn't do nothin', Sandy sat around growin' pale and thin, and Ronnie sulked for his keep. Settin' and watchin' the time go by. And what happened? I come back after lunch, and I find Sandy with a light in her eye and some color in her cheeks. And it's easy to figure what done that. Then you go off with Ronnie, and he's about to bite your head off, and when you come back, he's doin' a jig. And it's easy to figure that too, Jones boy. There's only one thing that lad wants out of life, and you offered it to him. Wheels on a track."

"Go on," I said. "You've got it all figured, haven't you, you dried-up old shite-poke."

"Yup. It ain't natural to make all that good humor in such a few minutes. It ain't honest. You work your tricks too easy, mister."

"You finished beating your gums?" I said. "Because if you have, and that's your say, you don't have to stay around on my account. I'll bet you were a hell of a big help to Bill. Why, you doddering old wart, you probably don't know any more about being a mechanic than a monkey knows about football."

Toad reached for his sack of Bull Durham. I got out the pack and tossed him a cigarette. He put his foot on the cigarette, ground it to bits, and rolled his own.

"Two is bad enough," Toad said bitterly. "Turning the trick with Sandy and Ron wasn't enough for you. God damn it, Jones, I was satisfied to sit around here and snooze all I wanted. Now you got to come around and rattle them damn wrenches and start them racing mills turning. I'm too old to stay up all night working on them damn motors! Too old, I tell you. Working my tail off in the pits and making them long runs to the other towns. Damn your miserable soul, Jones, you turned the trick with me, too. When the hell do we start?"

I sat down next to Toad and rubbed his tangled white hair with the heel of my hand. "You already know that, you spavined old fire horse," I said. "We've been started for three hours."

"I lived to see that day again," Toad said. "We ought to build up old seventy-two first. That's the Tudor. Only how the hell are we going to get past Sandy? She's death on racing."

"You leave Sandy to me," I said. "I'll take care of her."

"That goes without sayin'," Toad said. "But what's that got to go with racin'?"

"You're an evil-minded old goat," I said to Toad.

"No, I ain't," he said. "But Sandy is. Once I gave her a fatherly little pat on the backside, and she slapped my face."

Toad was all right. He was one of the breed. We'd both known it from the start. There was only one thing that bothered me. If we got rid of Ronnie, who would drive for us? Just sitting around the garage thinking about it was making me nervous. I had the wheel itch, and I had it bad, but I couldn't drive. That was one thing I had to stay away from. Too wild, too mad, too mean. If I didn't kill somebody else in my frenzy, I'd drive myself into the slot next to Bill. No driving. It would ruin everything.

"We'll build us the best car," I said, "and then we'll take the best driver."

"Ain't Ronnie going to run for us?" Toad asked.

"We'll power the coupe with a rubber band for Ronnie," I said. "Let's not waste sweat."

"The boy is a natural," Toad said. "It wouldn't take him long to learn."

"He'll get his chance," I said. "But we want the best driver we can get in that bucket. If Ronnie can do it, all right. If not, we'll get the man who can."

Toad gave his sour chuckle. He threw away his home-rolled cigarette, and reaching around, took my pack out of my shirt pocket. He stuck one cigarette in his mouth and another behind his left ear. "I suppose you want this back," he grumbled, looking at what was left of the pack.

I took the pack and picked the extra cigarette from behind his ear.

"Just as I thought," Toad said contemptuously. "So damn tight you could keep out water longer than a duck." He took the cigarette from his mouth and put it behind his ear, but a feeling of contentment expressed itself in the way he rested his back against the wall as he squatted on his heels.

Home. It took Toad to make me feel that I'd taken off my pack for a while. We'd work together day and night, and anyone watching us would think we hated each other's guts. Maybe we did. But that's the way it went when it was right. The hard talk, the strain of resentment, anger, and contempt that was background music to every spoken word. The racing world is put together with conflict, tension, and fear, and its citizens are each a tribe unto themselves. They make casual alliances that challenge death; they work themselves sick to keep an enemy in competition, but they have no courts in their souls for ambassadors, their language contains no elaborate compliments, and their customs are stark and devoid of any lush company manner foliage.

But those who understand the climate of this barren world are attracted by the very cruel conditions it imposes, and they can survive and enjoy the struggle. There are times, even in this hostile land, when a campfire is lighted, and only those who have learned to live in this cold and darkness and wind can appreciate its light and feel its warmth.

- - -

Ronnie and Sandy came back while Toad and I were talking tires. If we were going to run 72, we needed more changes than a new baby needs fresh diapers. We ran on four wheels, but when we drove into the pits, we were going to carry along a dozen more. Big tires, small tires, medium-size tires. Knobs, Ascots, baldies. A track was never the same twice; it changed between the first race and the last. The right tires at the right time meant being in the money—all other things being equal. The engine had so many rpm to deliver, so much torque it could supply. What we did on the track with those rpm and that torque depended on gears and tires. Especially tires.

Ronnie bulled in first, almost shaking the cement floor with his hurried, heavy step.

"I think I got a buyer for you, Ace. How much you asking?"

"Twenty-five hundred," I said.

Ronnie's face fell. "I figured around fifteen at the top," he said, looking embarrassed. "It's pretty beat up, and an off-breed at that."

It was beat up. It was a car that had started out in life as a nice, respectable club coupe. Now it looked like what happened to the young American schoolteacher who started out looking at religious paintings in the Louvre and wound up getting drunk in the Place Pigalle.

"Beat up," I said. "What the hell are you talking about? A couple of wrinkles on the fenders? That's a competition car. It's made to go."

"That's what I told him," Ronnie said. "He's looking for a car to race at the fairs. He can get a new Olds with a straight stick for about twenty-three hundred, but I thought—"

"Find your friend, Ronnie," I said. "Tell him not to make a move without consulting Jones. If he has that kind of money, we need him more than General Motors does. And what's good for Bill's Garage is good for Bill's Garage."

"He won't buy anything until he sees your car," Ronnie said. "He wants to know when he can see it."

"As soon as he brings his eyes around," I said. "Go get him." Ronnie ducked out. "Twenty-three hundred," I said to Toad and Sandy. "If we can get our hands on that kind of money, we can start expanding before we open."

Toad chuckled, trapping the sound in his nose. "If you get more than a thousand bucks, I'll admit Harry Houdini ain't dead yet."

Sandy checked through the office to see that everything was in its place. She moved easily, gracefully, with a faint touch of the efficient housewife in her manner. She looked at her watch. "It's getting late," she said to me. "If you don't need me, I'll leave now."

"Let me run you home," I said.

"It isn't far."

"Too far to walk as long as we have a car running."

We walked into the main section of the garage, and I held the front door of the car open for her. "It will be a tight squeeze," I apologized. She looked at the twin carburetor air cleaners I had mounted inside the car, under the dash, where they'd get less dust in a race. Then she looked at me with that funny come-to-me-go-from-me expression and got inside.

I felt relaxed and domestic driving her home. I played the little game of making believe she was my wife, and what we'd feel if we were both going home together. Stealing looks at her profile, the smooth skin, the full mouth, the soft brown eyes, and the rich glow of her hair. I decided I'd like the idea. Even though there were shadows under the eyes, and the head was held a little too straight.

Once in the car, Sandy seemed like another person. As though she'd left her garage personality hanging on a hook over the tool bench. Out of sight of the garage, whatever it was that kept her subdued and uncertain there vanished. Like she suddenly came out of the dark, into the light. She turned toward me, so that her knees were on the seat, and her back rested against the door. And she examined me with a frank, open interest.

"Anybody you've seen hanging in the post office?" I said.

She wasn't disconcerted. "I don't think so. Where'd you come from, Ace?"

"Out of the nowhere, into the here."

"Seriously."

"California."

"Is that where you were born?" She had a piquant, bright look on her face. Curiosity was doing wonders for her.

"Born in Kansas," I said. "A long time ago."

"You're not so old."

"The usual story," I said. "Went to grade school, high school, college, and war. I flew a dive-bomber in the Marine Corps. I got

into racing somewhere along the line and raced and raced until I
—well, until I got tired of it. Here I am."

"You drove . . . too?"

"Yeah. Do me a favor, Sandy. Don't tell anyone I was ever a
driver. Not even Ronnie or Toad. It's behind me, and that's where I
want it to stay. I want to be Ace Jones, the mechanic, not Ace Jones,
the ex-race driver. Do you mind?"

"Mind? I don't mind. In fact, I'm glad you told me—and glad
you quit. Until this moment, I was afraid you were planning to go
into racing. I didn't trust you."

"But you do now?"

"Uh-huh. If you feel that strongly against racing, I don't have
any suspicions left. But I knew you were a driver."

"Saw my crash hat and stuff?"

She laughed. "The moment I saw you. Don't forget I was married to a driver for two years. The very way you move, and talk, and
look at a car . . ." She looked down and pressed her lips together as
she remembered Bill.

"Then we'll keep my secret a secret," I said, wanting to get her
mind off Bill. "That gives us something in common, doesn't it?"

She nodded, picking up her smile where she had left it.

Sandy lived in a small, neat white house. I stopped out front and
turned off the ignition. She wasn't in a hurry to get out. I felt like a
kid on a date and wondered if she felt the same way.

"So, this is your place," I said.

"It's small," Sandy said. "But easy to take care of. Kitchen, living/
dining room, bedroom, and bath. What more does one person need?"

I had sense enough not to be obvious and say, "Another person."

"It's nice," I said. "Homey."

"Talking about homes," Sandy said. "What are your plans? Would
you rather live in a furnished room than the hotel? Would be cheaper."

"I'll bunk down at the garage for a while," I said. "There's time
to look around for a place."

She wrinkled her nose. "It won't be very pleasant."

"I'll be all right," I said. "It's got a roof. That's more than I've had over me a lot of times. The times I've slept in my racing car, or alongside it . . . you get toughened up following the tracks."

I fished for a cigarette and was about to put it in my mouth when I saw Sandy was holding out her hand for one. We both lit up, puffed smoke at each other, and relaxed a little more. She looked sweet with her legs tucked up under her. I could imagine how I looked.

"Wasn't it exciting?" she asked.

"At first," I said. "But it got old."

"I wondered why you'd want to stay in Town. There must be a million places that would be nicer to live in."

I shrugged. "It takes more than a climate or wide boulevards to make a town the place you want to live," I said. "It depends on people."

"There are nice people all over."

"You don't always meet them right away, like I did here," I said.

"Is that why you quit racing? Because of the people?"

I had to say it carefully. "There are a lot of reasons why I quit racing," I said. "When we know each other better, maybe I'll want to tell you about them."

"You make it sound mysterious."

"It's not mysterious," I said. "And it's not very pretty either." I felt my voice getting unsteady.

"Don't feel you have to tell me if it makes you feel bad," she said. "I don't want to pry."

"Don't get me wrong," I said. "I'm not trying to move in on you in any personal way you don't want. But I think someday I would like to tell you. I don't know yet."

"It's hard to keep things inside yourself, isn't it?" Sandy said. "But it's hard to say them, too."

"It takes the right person to tell them to," I said.

Sandy smoked silently, frowning at her cigarette. Then she

shook herself a little and gave me a bright surface smile. "I'd better go in, Ace. It's late." She opened the door and looked back at me over her shoulder. "I'm not having much," she said apologetically, "but if you want to take potluck with your partner—"

"I don't think I'd better, tonight," I said. "I don't want to start crowding you from the first minute."

"You wouldn't be crowding. I don't like to eat alone anyway."

"How about tomorrow?" I said. "Maybe we could have a little celebration dinner together. I don't want to eat and run, and we'll be leaving for . . . unless you want to come down to the track with us."

"The track," Sandy said. Suddenly her voice was dull.

"Yeah," I said. "We want to spread the word that we're open for business—and get back more of our tools."

"I don't want to go," Sandy said. Again, her voice sounded lifeless. She got out of the car and closed the door. Her face had changed. It wore a beaten, weary look. "I'll see you in the morning," she said.

I waited until she had gone into the house, watching her walk away with an easy, lithe step. Just before she went into the house, she turned to look at me. It was an accusing look, dark and strange. Then she went inside.

In a way, I couldn't blame her. All she'd get at the track would be a two-hour reminder of how her husband had been killed. Maybe that explained the depressing effect I had on her from time to time. Another driver, living while her husband was dead. Another man trying to take over the job that belonged to her husband. With every familiar sound and activity, another reminder that she was a widow, and Ace Jones was a stranger.

She had troubles, but she wasn't alone. I knew all about her ghost and how it haunted her. Wait until the weak moment when I trotted out mine!

— — —

When I got back to the garage, Ronnie and Toad were there with Ronnie's prospective buyer for my car. He was a slender, pale, gum-chewing youth in slacks and a sport shirt. His name was Joe, and he had the habit common to many small-town boys of ending his declarative sentences with a question. He was suspicious of me and my car.

"Joe," I said, "I hear you want something to run the tracks with."

Joe stuck his hands in his pockets and looked at me with a kind of leery, hangdog expression. "I might. But I'm more interested in street and road use, right now."

"Oh," I said coldly, turning away. "I thought from the way Ronnie talked you were looking for a hot car." Joe snickered nervously. "I am. But not a, a—" He didn't finish.

I looked around as though afraid I'd be overheard. "You raced much?" I asked.

He shook his head. "I ain't interested in jalopies. I'd like to get on bigger tracks with a late stock, if I race. I got a friend who races late stocks. I've had his car around a track. Not in a race. But I think I could drive one."

"Of course you could," I said. "Ronnie's probably told you about the drivers I used to work for, hasn't he?"

Joe nodded guiltily, as though admitting a private sin.

"The Commodore used to tell me there was only one way to race," I said. "Get out in front and stay there."

"I guess that's right," Joe said, hands still in his pockets as though I might charm his money out with talk.

"That's how he won 'em," I said. "Some of 'em in this very car." I paused to let the momentous fact sink in. "He beat the best drivers in the country—and the best cars—in this very car. And I guess if it was good enough for the country's champion driver, it might be good enough for somebody else, wouldn't you say?"

Joe blushed a deep red at having slighted the famous car, but he still didn't want it.

I lowered my voice. "You take the engine under the hood," I said. "That's not the one you get when you buy that from a dealer.

No *indeed*. That's Hudson's racing engine. And just between you and me, the Commodore and I put a few refinements of our own."

I put my hand on Joe's shoulder. "Were you figuring paying cash?"

"I don't know," he said, afraid to move. "I'm really just lookin' right now?"

"A fella could," I said, leaning on Joe, "go out and buy him a nice, new shiny car to race with. If he was looking for trouble, that is. I remember how we used to watch for the boys with the new cars."

"Take you, Joe," I said. "You buy a brand-new stock job to race with. What would happen? The other boys would look you over and see right off that you were newer than a wet colt. They'd know how you felt about that new car. Afraid you'd get it smashed up if you weren't careful. And they'd make life rough for you. My God, they'd really give it to you hard. They'd box you in, try to scrape your sides, and do everything else to scare you out of the traffic. You'd be inviting trouble. Asking for it."

I opened the door of the Hudson on the driver's side and half-pushed Joe into the driver's seat. "Try the safety belt on for size," I said. He buckled it and sat with his hands on the wheel, looking unhappy.

I appealed to Ronnie and Toad. "Looks good in it, doesn't he, boys?" Fred blinked, and Ronnie lowered his head. Joe looked about as much at home behind that wheel as a traveling salesman left to guard a harem.

"Now you take this car and make a track with it," I said. "The minute the other drivers took a look at it, they know that it's a car that can give as well as take. Some of 'em will recognize it as Commodore Tucker's old car. They won't know how you got it, but they'll know the car. And they'll figure that anybody pushing the Commodore's iron is a man to respect. They won't try any fancy tricks when you're in this wagon. You'll get a lot of room, and that means a shot at the purse. Because, son, I'm not telling you a lie. All you have to do is point this baby and give it enough gas, and you'll romp home up front. If you're man enough to handle it. Right, boys?"

"You ought to know, Ace," Ronnie said loyally. "I guess you've seen them all."

"You bet I have," I said. "And I'd hate to see this boy spend his money foolishly. Why, it would cost you five thousand dollars to put another alongside this one that has the same guts. She's beefed up, rigged for racing, and ready to make money for the right guy without another dime needed. I'm throwing in all the special race stuff I put on for the purchase price. Seven hundred dollars' worth that a man would have to buy if he wanted to win races with another car."

I looked at Joe. He wanted to argue a little, but he was afraid to.

"If you have any trouble," I said, "I'll check you out on it. Now, is the price right? I told Ronnie I'd let it go cheap to a friend of his. Twenty-five hundred."

"I don't know," Joe said, looking around with his pale eyes for some means of escape. "A Hudson this old don't bring half that around here. Even a cream puff."

"Man, I'm not selling you a used Hudson," I said. "I'm selling a racing car. Brand name doesn't mean a thing. Year doesn't mean a thing. This is a racing car. Put together to race. Are you buying fresh paint or an engine to race with?"

"I couldn't give you twenty-five hundred," Joe said, licking his lips. "I don't have that much."

"You should have told me," I said in a mad voice. I wouldn't have wasted my time. Hell—all that effort . . . How much do you have?"

"With what my car I got now is worth, I could raise about eighteen hundred. But I—"

"Joe," I said, "I'll tell you what I'm going to do for you. Maybe I'm wrong. Maybe you'll spread the word that Ace Jones is easy. But I want to start out right in Town and help everybody I can. You've just bought yourself a car for seventeen hundred dollars."

Joe's mouth fell open. "I did?"

"It doesn't make sense," I said. "These people heard you offer me eighteen. But I'm giving you back a hundred bucks to help pay your expenses to your first race. That way, I'll feel I had something to do with your success. Don't laugh at me, boys," I said to Ronnie and Toad. "The Commodore always liked to help new drivers up the hill, and I learned from him that no kindness is ever wasted."

I pried Joe's right hand loose from the wheel and shook it. "Seventeen hundred," I said. "And have that money back in the morning."

"I, I—" Joe almost bleated at me.

"Ten on the dot," I said firmly. "Drive it home now, boy. Start getting used to a real car."

Numbly, Joe turned on the key and started the car. It sounded old and tired and rough.

"Listen to that mill, Joe," I said over the sound of knock-kneed pistons. "You wouldn't find any new car that sounded like that. Be here at ten, now."

As Joe backed the car out of the garage, he turned and looked at me. There was a beaten, miserable expression on his face as he felt the rough motor under his foot, and the weary transmission under his shifting hand. He looked like he was going to break out in tears. I lifted my arm. "Take it slow," I yelled. "It's a bomb and you'll need time to learn her tricks."

Joe drove away. Toad looked at me and shook his head. Ronnie looked pained.

"You get a hundred bucks out of this, Ronnie," I said. "For play money. You ran the horse into the corral."

"I don't want—" Ronnie began.

"Because of you, kid, we're in business," I said softly. "You just helped get Sandy off a big, sharp hook. Take your cut. It ought to be more, but we need the rest for operating expenses."

"What do I get?" Toad grumbled. "I didn't call the police on you for what you done."

"I'll buy your dinner, you sour-faced old prune," I said. "I'm in a hurry because I want to talk to somebody down there. Mean talk. And believe me, Joe bought more car than he'll ever be able to handle."

Ronnie looked at us with his forehead wrinkled. He didn't understand yet about Toad and me, and our plans.

"What's going on?" Ronnie asked, walking outside with us. "What's wrong at the track? Who you got to see?"

I stopped walking and winked at Toad. "Well, Ronnie," I said seriously, "it's like this. There happens to be a guy around the track whose hide I want to nail to the wall. You see, boy. I feel so bad about being cheated out of my car by your friend Joe. I've just got to get some revenge before the day is out. Meet us at the track, kid. I'll need you."

Ronnie got in his car and drove off. Toad and I walked slowly up the street toward the cafe where we were going to eat. Toad laughed—or made the cackling sound that was as near a laugh as he could get. "I was wrong from the goddamn start." Toad chuckled. Hee-heeing with delight. "You're not a no-good bastard like old Bill after all."

"Blow your nose and talk plain," I said.

Toad snuffled and cackled. "You're worser without tryin' than Bill ever was gruntin' at it. God above, Ace, the times we're gonna have."

CHAPTER 6

TOAD AND I ATE DINNER AT THE COUNTER in the Town Cafe—
Toad called it the Town Cayf—and set out for the track on foot.

"Fill me in on the track lash-up," I said to Toad.

"It's simple, but it ain't sweet," Toad said. "It's a one-man deal.
Fella named Herpgruve is the sole owner, proprietor, promoter, and
puke head."

"Don't the owners and drivers have a piece of it? In a town like
this? Don't they have an Association?"

"Hell," Toad said. "You couldn't get any two guys here to agree
on which end of the horse the tail is hung on."

"What about Herpgruve? He run any cars?"

"He don't run nothin' . . . Toad grumbled. "He bought the track
a couple of years ago when there wasn't nothing doing on it. When
stock racin' started in the other towns, he opened the track. It's

all his. You run his way, or you don't run. You know how the boys are—they'd rather race than argue."

"What's his way?"

"About what you'd expect," Toad said. "He don't care about racing. He wants thrills. Lots of spins and crashes, even if he's got to buy 'em. Figures the crowd comes to see smash-ups."

"Fixed races?"

"Naw," Toad said. "Not that way. Everybody tries to win but he'll give some guy five bucks to spin some other driver off the track. Any time anybody gets spun out, the driver figures it was on purpose. If it's bad, he'll tear into the other guy right on the track. Makes for a lot of bad blood and mean driving."

"But it brings in money," I said.

"Every time," Toad said.

"Doesn't anybody ever balk?"

"Yeah," Toad said. "The good boys want to run clean. Bill tried to fight for some roles. He wanted to get away from fender bangin' and into hard racin'. Some of the guys were with him—while he lasted."

I looked at Toad. He didn't have to put any more into words. Bill had put up a fight. I knew the rest. Somehow, somebody would always be spinning him out, forcing him into the fence, hooking him, and dragging him out of a race. For five sure bucks. More than that, "somebody" might make all night just racing for the checkered flag. Hazards of racing. You couldn't prove it was done on purpose. You had to take it and fight back until you won. Until you proved you were too tough to take that kind of crap. If you didn't get the end of a fence rail through your guts first.

"Who did it?" I asked.

"A guy," Toad said.

"Paid for it?"

"I don't know," Toad said, "I didn't ask before I started in on his haid with a wrench, and he wasn't able to explain after."

Toad's lip curled back slightly in the furtive yellow-toothed bad-
ger grin. He snuffled out his cough-like chuckle and raised his head
a little. I saw his eyes. There were tears in the corners.

CHAPTER 7

As Toad and I neared the track, we were passed several times by drivers bringing their racers in. Some were towed, some rode on trailers, and a few were carried in trucks.

"Damn your long-legged soul," Toad gasped. "Slow down."

Seeing the racers go by had done it. Each one pulled me along a little faster. Just the sight of them going by—and knowing where they were going—made my throat dry, sent shivers through my middle, and pulled the canvas covers off my raw nerve endings. An old fire horse trying to gallop after the red trucks.

By the time we reached the track, customer traffic was heavy, the PA system was playing a loud record, and above it all, we could hear the rising and falling snarl of a gutty engine being revved. And I wanted to throw back my head and whinny.

A car came up from the rear. It sounded familiar. I turned to look, and it was my old car all right, with Joe at the wheel. He drove past slowly, trailing a steady wisp of blue smoke. As he went by, our eyes met, and I almost laughed at the forlorn expression that was still on his pale, chinless face.

But as I watched the stubby tail end of the Hudson disappear, and remembered what we had been through together, recalled the battles and the way the scars had been won, I wanted it again. Wanted it to be my own. But it was gone, ridden by a pimply stranger who hated it. Gone, and with it, a big chunk of my life. All that it had been—and I had been—was over for us both. I was glad the end had come, glad I was out of the safety belt for good. We had nothing further to share, the old Hudson and me. Only memories to forget. But the parting, though planned for, was not easy. It was like being divorced and seeing your ex-wife again suddenly, with a stranger, remembering all the good things she had given to you and now offered to another. Toad began to swear. "What's eatin' you?" I asked irritably.

"The ungrateful little punk," Toad grumbled. "It's six more blocks to the track. He knows we're goin' there. And after all we done for him, he wouldn't even stop and give us a ride."

The track was at the edge of town, near the shallow river I had crossed coming in. It didn't look like much. Not many small tracks do. There was a high unpainted board fence that encompassed track and bleachers. There were a couple of little gates on the south, where the crowd was funneled in, and a large gate to the west for the racing cars to use. It was at least an hour before sunset, and longer than that to race time, but the crowd was coming in. Their cars bumped along the parking field slowly, kicking up dust, directed by attendants wearing sun helmets and carrying red-tipped flashlights.

I stopped to look the place over, listening to the sound of an engine that was being revved, detecting a high rpm miss. How many times, and at how many tracks, had I heard that sound? How many times had I made it, sun-broiled, sweating, and angry with an engine that wouldn't sweeten up, and time running out? How many tracks reached after a nightlong drive? How many pits toiled in? How many last-minute adjustments to the music of warming engines on every side?

How much coffee gulped? How many hot dogs shoved down with a greasy hand? How much indigestion carried at top speed for twenty-five, fifty, two hundred laps through dust or mud, through fumes and heat-wave patterns, under the merciless sun or the glare of lights at night?

How many circles turned? How much life spun away riding a roaring merry-go-round that let you off right where you got on, sick, dizzy, and minus youth . . .

It never changed. The long lines of cars turning into the parking place, the noise, the talk, the laughter, the irritation as people got out of their cars and walked toward the ticket office, carrying blankets and cushions and light jackets.

The same people who were always there, everywhere.

The teenagers in jeans, the boys slouching, the girls stepping like trotters in their tight pants, wearing men's white shirts. The older folks, walking leisurely in groups. The women chatting as they picked their way around rough spots, the men in quiet thought, jingling their keys as they wondered how long it would take before the plank benches jarred aged prostates into backaching protest.

Even the families were the same, strolling, hurrying, with kids and without, holding hands or domestically chaste in public, they made their swarm at all the ticket offices everywhere. The same people. I knew them. They had been at every race; they would never miss one in the future. That girl with the dark hair and the white halter, the white-haired woman in slacks and a Mexican jacket, the new father who carried the baby while his wife carried the accessories, the group of fifteen-year-olds with their motorcycle caps and their hands in their pockets, trying to look bored, the young wife in a summer dress with two fussy children, trying to look interested.

I knew them all, almost by name. I had seen them at every race, in every part of the country. They had cheered my wins, booed them, screamed at my crashes, gasped with relief at my escapes, watched me a thousand times on a thousand tracks. Strange that now they could walk past me a pace away, look at my face, and pass on, as though they had never seen me before.

It was the same, and I didn't want any part of it. I goddamned myself for stopping in Town, for getting snagged by the uptilt of a widow's breasts, for getting involved with the garage. Didn't I know it would lead me to the track? Didn't I know?

Toad made a funny grunting sound. I looked at him. He had his hands in his pants pocket and was huddled down into himself as though he were out in a blizzard in his summer underwear. His mouth was hanging open, and he was listening. Listening to engines.

"Where can I find Herpgruve, Toad?"

Toad pointed toward a small wooden building near the ticket window. "In the office."

"We'll get us some pit passes," I said.

We went inside. Herpgruve was a red-faced man, with egg-like eyes. He muttered, "Hello, Toad."

"This here's Ace Jones," Toad said, blinking in the light. "He's takin' over Bill's garage. This here's Herpgruve, Ace."

Herpgruve looked at me, scowling. The hand he had started to stick out stayed put. "Seems to me I've seen you before," he said, narrowing his eyes.

"We've met," I said.

"I can't place you, offhand."

"On the highway," I said. "Just before noon."

His lips thickened around the cigar and his face went a shade darker. "You planning to run Bill's cars?"

"We don't know yet," I said. "Depends on what's in it for us."

"Same as anybody else," he said. "As much of the purse as you can win."

"We'll think about it," I said.

"Glad to have you out. Nothing like a full track to pull the crowd." He didn't sound very glad, and I didn't blame him.

"You don't mind if I look around a little," I said.

He pulled open a little drawer in the table. "I'll give you a couple of season passes. Good for the pits, of course."

"Thanks."

Toad and I waited silently while he filled out the passes. "We could use another good car or two," Herpgruve said, sliding the passes toward me. "Bill drew a lot of people. There's a place down here for a driver who ain't afraid to crowd on the turns." The eggs in his head popped out at me resentfully.

"Maybe you can help me find one," I said. "I'm just a mechanic. I never race, myself."

I went out with Toad right behind me. We walked over toward the pit gate and found a grassy spot where we could sit down and watch the cars coming in. Looking through the gate, I could see the track. It was a rough quarter or three-eighths or whatever the hell it was. Almost more of a circle than an oval, the chutes weren't too long. By the time a driver came off the corner onto the chute, he was practically in the approach to the next corner. I sat and chewed grass and watched the boys bring their cars in.

A convertible with three men in it bumped past, towing an orchid-and-white coupe with a crumpled right side where it had been rammed or hit the fence. A stock truck covered with country dust ground past, carrying a stubby little '34 Chevy. In the truck cab was a husky, farmery-looking boy who drove the truck and probably the racer. An older man sat next to him, and on the right, a young woman holding a baby. A black rod like Ronnie's pulled a black-and-red jalopy that had large patches of paint burned off and the deep gouges of a collision still puckering its body.

There were more. Red, yellow, black, multi-colored. All with numbers, some with names like *Bombshell, Speedy Eddie, Little Gem,*

Fencebuster. All but a few carried the names of some sponsor. The garage-sponsored cars were professionally lettered. The cars that were advertising grocery stores or other merchants were crudely lettered.

It was like sitting at an aid station behind the lines, watching the corpsmen bring in the wounded. But these wounded, these battered and crushed veterans, were streaming toward, not away, from the front. What happened to their bodies mattered little. They suffered only when their throaty, roaring guts were pierced, clogged, or blown apart, and their toed-out wheels could no longer turn in combat. The show here was not one of glitter and color. It was a nine-act performance of noise and violence, of crush and collision, of hurtling iron and smashed fences that pulled the crowd. It was the spin, the rollover, the locked horns at sixty-five miles an hour that attracted the slouching teenager, his girl, the young parents with the baby, the old folks with their pillows and piles.

"Here comes Barney Oldfield," I said to Toad.

Toad looked up and saw Loren Peale's car. "Haw!"

Peale was pulling his flashy charger behind a tattered Buick that was twelve or thirteen years old. Its black paint was checked and rusty, the windows were cracked and discolored, the fenders undulated flabbily with each turn of the old wheels. It growled in protest as its aged valves panted and the dying pistons wheezed for compression.

As Peale drove by, I saw Ossman sitting on the right side, pipe in mouth. There was a woman between two men, but all I could see of her was a flash of very light, fluffy blonde hair. The back seat was jammed with kids who peered out of the windows like little gophers peeking out of their holes.

"Twenty-seven," I said to Toad. "Is that good?"

"We've had better'n forty and less than a dozen," Toad said. "But twenty-seven ain't bad—if they'll all run."

More engines were starting. A dozen of them barked in a wild, exciting chorus. I felt my hands shaking. Even here, at this dinky track, stuck away under the crupper of civilization, where machine cripples sputtered for five laps and exploded—even here, it was the same.

Toad felt it too, the same way. His mouth twitched, and there was a rigid, glazed look in his eyes, like a tomcat frightened by a dog bark in the middle of mating.

The engines roared, belched, fired shots of protest, and settled into defiant, powerful snarls. A score of angry voices yowling in the pit. The exciting stink of gasoline fumes drifted through the gate and stung my nose. I wanted to jump to my feet and run into the pits. I wanted to be a part of it. I needed a car. Any car. I acted like the guy whose bride got locked in the hotel bathroom on his wedding night. To get what I needed, I was ready to ram through a wall with my head, willing to fight with feet and fists, tear with my teeth, and smash with any weapon that came into my hand.

The crowd was where it belonged, the high compression beasts were caterwauling in the pits, and the race would be on. And Ace Jones was sitting on his tail in the grass outside, looking on.

Half a dozen cars were on the track now, beginning their slow warm-up circling. They raised a swollen doughnut of dust, and the faint hot currents of moving air carried the dust into the stands.

"Where the hell's his water truck?" I growled.

"I tol' you," Toad said. "Herpgruve don't do nothing he don't have to. He lets the rain do the waterin', and the rollovers do the blade work."

"Isn't there anybody with guts enough to get a decent track to run on?"

"There was," Toad said.

"There'll be some changes made before we put rubber on that track," I said, "A guy like that oughtn't to be allowed to own a track."

"Why don't you buy it from him?" Toad snickered.

"Maybe I won't have to," I said. "Maybe he'll get generous and offer me a piece."

"What the hell do you want with a track?" Toad complained. "You're gonna have enough troubles keepin' the garage afloat without takin' on the track. I never saw anybody so greedy to git in trouble."

"I just hate to see a good track go to hell," I said. "That's all. Tracks have been where I made my living. I like 'em. I hate to see anybody mistreat 'em. If I could get my hands on this one, you'd see some changes made. Make something decent out of it."

I don't know what I was getting mad about. It wasn't any of my business. I was in Town for what I could carry away in a tote sack, not to reform any evil conditions. Maybe it was professional pride. Maybe I saw a way to pick a few extra bolls while I was in the field.

I got to my feet and brushed the loose grass from my clothes. "Let's poke around the pits a little," I said.

Toad stood up. "I was wonderin' if we was gonna watch from out here." We went through the pit gate to the track. When there was a break in the warm-up traffic, we walked across to the infield, where a couple dozen jalopies were being readied to run. The pits . . .

CHAPTER 8

SEEN FROM THE STANDS, THE RACING CARS are crowded together on the semi-dark infield in a kind of helter-skelter disorder, as though blown there by the wind. The figures of the drivers and the crews are small, indistinct, remote. There seems to be little activity, and most of the people seem to be standing around with their hands in their pockets or watching the races from the roofs of cars. At each race call, the dozen or so numbers running come noisily onto the track and take their places. The race is run, a victor and the vanquished, healthy and cripples, disappear into the gloom of the pits until called again. The drama is on the track, in the race. Seen from the stands.

Invaded, the pit area is a battleground with two score hostile armies bivouacked side by side. Motors whine, roar, or cough, hammers beat, men labor, sweating, swearing, smeared with dirt and grease, swarming on, around, and under their battered machines.

Carburetors are pulled and changed. Plugs are checked and rechecked. Radiators are babied or bullied. Wheels go on and off in endless succession. Tools and parts are scattered on the dark, oil-soaked ground to mingle with empty pop bottles, dented fuel and water cans, piles of wheels, wrenches, and lights. Jacks are borrowed, re-borrowed, called for, lost again, sworn for. Faces are tense, voices are curt, words are rough. An air of violence, hope, frustration, fear, and delight swirls over the sweating men and their belligerent machines.

Nearby, the ambulance waits, its crew leaning against it, sitting on it. The tow trucks wait, drivers ready for their call buy coffee at the concession stand set up for their use, and walk around drinking out of paper cups, puffing on cigarettes, and waiting for the signal to run. Toad and I bought coffee and found a place to watch from.

Two-thirds of the cars were on the track, taking their fast warm-up. They roared around and around through the dust looking for tonight's groove, testing acceleration against a tough competitor, listening to the engine. The boys were nervous. The fast warm-ups were like that. A dozen different challenges were made and accepted for half a lap, carried through a turn, and broken off. The throaty Ford and Merc engines roared in deep voices. The few Chevys and GMCs countered with singing, high-pitched whines as they wound up on the chutes. Exhausts fired through the roar and whine as drivers backed off for the turns.

When the cars were flagged off the track so that time trials could get underway, Toad and I wandered slowly among the cars, watching the furious work to make last-minute adjustments.

Here in the pits, there was a caste society. The poorer independent drivers worked with few tools and many hopes, roaming the area to borrow what they needed, making up with profanity for what they lacked. The garage-sponsored racers were the pampered ones. Coveralled crews of three or four mechanics hovered over them. The garage trucks stood alongside, loaded with boxes of tools and spare parts. The drivers, working for a split of any purse they won with the garage supplying the equipment, looked on. They worked too, said what they wanted, and were impatient to race. But with someone else footing the bill and supplied with the best engines and assistance, they could afford to be more relaxed; more casual.

We passed the three guys I had visited earlier, with the bent cam in their yellow racer. They looked as though they hadn't stopped to eat or rest since we'd seen them. They were haggard, red-eyed, and on edge. But they wanted to run. They grunted an acknowledgment of our presence.

They started the engine. It sounded smooth enough. I looked at Toad. He hadn't said anything about their getting a cam from us.

The boy who was going to drive got his goggles out of the car and rubbed them with a handkerchief. "We pulled the engine after you left," he said. "Couldn't tell if you were right or not, but we put in a stock cam just for the hell of it. That was it, all right."

"It'll run," I said, "but where?"

The boy shrugged, "As long as I run, I've got a chance at something. Can't win any money not running at all."

"Good luck," I said. Toad and I moved on. We picked a spot just inside the fourth corner to watch from. It was where the boys would be lead-footing it as they headed for the wire.

One by one, the cars came out and ran their trials. A warm-up lap, a timed lap, another warm-up lap, and a second timed lap. Best lap was posted.

Toad squatted by me and filled me in on the drivers and their cars. He didn't have to tell me which ones were the boys to beat. It was more than the time they made. It was the way they made it.

A stubby orange coupe named *The Flying Fugitive* wound up on the back chute and slammed into the turn. The driver backed off for a second as he broadsided, then tromped again. His controlled slide brought him out high, tires biting deep as his engine wound up again. When he went by, I saw him bending forward over the wheel, face intent, strong arms in complete control. He roared past the wire in under twenty seconds.

"That's Phil de Marco," Toad said.

"He's good," I said. "Too good. Who does he drive for?"

"Town Garage," Toad said.

We watched the next car run its trials. Toad didn't bother to identify the second-division cars. There was nothing to worry about running against the sick engines, the drivers who backed off too soon, fishtailed in the turns, and ran four or five seconds slower than the top boys.

A navy-blue coupe went around. Deceptively quiet, it seemed to be crawling. The driver, who was wearing white coveralls as well as a helmet, sat back, looking relaxed. But the way he stuck in the groove and cut his turns as neatly an old lady cutting a Thanksgiving pie accounted for his time. It was right there with de Marco's.

"Larry Jensen," Toad said. "Drives for Awin Tractor."

One of the few GMCs was taking its turn. It sang like an angry bee as it tore down the chutes and bounced through the turns.

"Bob Towner," Toad said, watching the black '34 coupe go by. "Runs a GMC 270. A good boy. Lots of guts."

Loren Peale went by, wearing goggles and a snowy helmet. He made good time on the chutes, but he went into the turn like an old lady driving an electric car up Pike's Peak. He ran over twenty-two seconds, but he hadn't got his car dirty.

The stock-cam boy wheeled his yellow coupe around, trying hard. But trying didn't give him any torque shooting off the corners. By the time his stock car caught up with him, he had a worse time than Peale.

I got restless watching other drivers and began wandering again. Toad followed. I stopped by a blue and yellow coupe that was getting a right front wheel changed. About ten guys were standing around watching one boy working. He worked fast, and he knew what he was doing. I jabbed Toad in the ribs and nodded at the boy.

"Chip Vann," Toad said. "Knows more about Fords than old Henry ever did."

Chip pulled the wheel and examined the spindle. What he saw caused a stream of profane comments. But there was a happy-go-lucky ring to his complaint, and after he had finished cursing the bent spindle, he looked up and grinned. He had a round face with a big cigar stuck in his mouth, a butch haircut, and a round, little boyish head.

"I knew that sucker wasn't handling right," he said, chewing on his cigar. He held out his hand. "Give me a spindle, somebody."

Nobody moved. Chip looked around and spotted the Town Garage truck near him. "Hey!" he yelled. "Give me a goddamn spindle for this wheel!"

One of the mechanics brought the part over. Chip took it and went to work again at a furious pace, muttering to himself a half-humorous complaint. When he had the wheel on again, he went around to the front of the car and checked the toe-out by lying on the ground and looking at the front wheels. Swearing and chuckling to himself, he made a further adjustment on the wheel. "There!" he said, throwing down his wrench.

The wrench landed near me. It looked familiar. I picked it up and looked for Bill's mark. Chip's voice cut into my search. "That's not one of your goddamn wrenches, Jones."

I raised my head. He was standing in front of me with the big cigar tilted in the air. He was short but stocky and wore an undershirt, a pair of jeans, and engineer boots. His arms were folded across his chest, and there was a reckless look in his eyes.

I finished examining the wrench and tossed it down. "You know me," I said.

"Word's got around," Chip said. "We seen you pussyfooting all over the pits, lookin' for your tools. Why the hell don't you just ask for 'em if you want 'em back?"

"I'm asking," I said. "If you find anything, bring it around tomorrow."

Chip looked curious. "You gonna run any cars?"

"I'm not the boss," I said. "But we will try to keep anybody running who needs us."

"I'll come around and see you, maybe," Chip said. "Now, who's got my hat? I got to run in the trophy dash, and I can't run without my hat."

He moved off, muttering.

"We could use that boy," I said to Toad. "Where does he stand?"

"Nobody knows," Toad said. "Not even him. That's his car. He runs it when he can, and when he can't, he drives for somebody else until he can fix up his own. He's a hard ridin', reckless son of a bitch, but he's got more guts than Armour has in its packin' house, and he can drive. But he won't give an inch, and he's always tanglin' with somebody out there."

We walked back to the turn, to watch the trophy dash, and met Ronnie. "I've been looking all over for you," he said. "What do you think of the set-up here, Ace?"

"We're looking over the competition," I said.

"What do you think?"

"I'll tell you when I see the boys run."

"Don't judge them by the trophy dash," Ronnie said. "The ten fastest cars run, but nobody wants to win. Winning only pays off with a trophy, and second place gets money. If you win two trophies, you can't run it anymore. So all the guys try to come in second."

I didn't answer. The ten cars were on the track, lining up in inverse order, with the fastest cars at the back. Five deep, two abreast. The starter worked down the line, checking with each driver. When he reached the end, he turned and came back down between the two rows of cars. A rolling thunder of exhausts boiled after him as he got to the rear and raised his hands in a ready signal. Above, leaning over the track in his little platform, the flagman had the green flag up, held stretched out in two hands. The engines were all revving now, the cars trembling, inching, as drivers played with the clutch to get the jump.

The flag dropped. Ten clutch pedals flew back, and ten right feet stood on ten gas pedals. Dust flew as wheels spun, and the cars moved.

By the time the cars were into the first turn, they were lost in the dust. When they came onto the back chute, they were still jammed together, fenders and bodies banging together, sparks flying as metal rubbed metal.

De Marco had taken the outside and had moved up to fourth place. Jensen and Towner were on the inside, caught behind slower cars. Chip Vann flew out of the dust and charged headlong into the traffic.

The field was still bunched as it roared into the west turn. Sliding wheels churned up dust thunderheads as the boys jockeyed around the turn. I heard the crunch of two cars hitting and saw one of the cars go into a slow spin. Halfway around in the spin, another car charged through the dust and smacked into it. The struck car headed toward the outside wall. The ramming car spun its tail toward infield.

There was another smash as the first car hit the wall in a glancing blow and stalled. The driver hit his starter button, the motor roared into life, and he was off after the pack, one fender dragging. The second car bounced off the track into the pits, narrowly missed a pile of spare wheels, and roared back onto the track to keep up the chase. The rest of the field, moving down the track at sixty-five miles an hour, was into the east turn. A squat black coupe with a streak of silver lightning painted on the side sprang into the lead of the fourth lap.

"Golly," Ronnie said. "What was he waiting for? They've been trying to spring him ever since the first lap!" The crowd cheered as the unknown broke into the clear, leading all the top drivers around the track. Toad snuffled.

Jensen and de Marco were making the race for second. It was funny, in a way. They'd go like hell to beat each other out, but when they did, they pulled up on the black coupe. Then they had to back off or pass him. Chip Vann held to fourth place, blocking Towner's efforts to get by.

On the ninth lap, Vann made his bid for second. De Marco and Jensen were playing tag, coming into the west turn, trying to stay behind the black car. Vann came up hard and brought the crowd to its feet by pouring on the coal and taking the two fast boys on the turn. He closed in on the black coupe.

"If he's not careful, he'll get first," Ronnie said. "What's he trying to do, anyway?"

Chip was riding the black car's tail, as though he was trying to get past. As they went past the stands and into the tenth lap, the black car hit the turn harder than he had been doing and almost spun out. But as he started to switch ends, Chip nudged him on the inside and straightened him out.

The air was filled with shooting exhausts as the trailing cars backed off to avoid taking over first spot.

Then the black car was off again, with Chip crowding and Jensen and de Marco close behind. The crowd screamed at what seemed to be a four-way fight for the trophy.

Even the driver of the black car must have believed the others were after him. As he came into the last corner, he held his foot down, his eye on the checkered flag that was being readied for him. Only, he held his foot down too long. As he threw his car into the turn, the churning rear wheels took over and slid him rear end first into the wall. Chip flashed by with an expression of horror on his face as he realized he had taken over first place. He leaned over his wheel and pretended to be trying to get every ounce of effort out of his car, but he was backing off as much as he dared without risking detection by the crowd. He took a quick look behind, to see where Jensen and de Marco were. To the crowd, it looked like the apprehensive glance of a man who scented victory. But the guys in the pits, those who stood and those who perched on their cars to watch the race, roared with laughter as Jensen and de Marco banged together and rubbed fire between their cars and came in squarely behind Chip. They almost pushed him over the line as they picked up second and third money.

The cars bounced back to their places in the pits while Chip went up to claim his trophy. It was presented on the judges' stand by the announcer at the PA system. The crowd applauded as Chip went up to the mike to get his trophy. The words of the interview were audible in the pits.

". . . and here he is, folks, the boy who gave you this thrilling race to win the trophy . . . Chip Vann. How's the track tonight, Chip?"

"A little rough in spots, but pretty fast."

"That was quite a race you had there, wasn't it?"

"Yes, it was."

"You beat out some mighty fine drivers to win this trophy, didn't you?"

"Guess I did."

"Is this your first trophy this season?"

"No. I wish it was."

"That's right. You've won two, and can't compete in the trophy dash until next season, right?"

"That's the way it is."

"Well, good luck in your other races."

The crowd applauded again as Chip threw the trophy into his car and drove back to the pits. When he stopped, he was swearing in his usual half-funny way. He climbed out through the top of the car and dropped to the ground. De Marco, black-haired and black-eyed, came over, grinning. "What happened to you, Chip?"

"My brakes wouldn't hold!" Chip shouted.

De Marco chuckled. "I thought we were going to have to push you across."

"What the hell happened to Peterson?" Chip said. "What'd he spin out for? I had second money all won."

"You spun him out," De Marco said.

"Hell, I did! I wanted to chase him in. I had second money all sewed up. Now I'm out of the goddamn race all summer." Chip looked at the trophy, a gold-colored replica of a car mounted on a tall base. "What the hell am I going to do with this?" he demanded. "I already got a shelf full."

De Marco laughed and lit a cigarette. In the light of the match, his face was dark and intense. His hands were shaking slightly, and there was a worried look around his eyes. That was bad. A driver like that was a devil on the track—when he drove, he drove hard, with everything he had. I knew. Too well, I knew how hard a guy drove when he got wound up for the race. My future didn't look too bright. No matter what I did to 72, Ronnie wouldn't stand a chance against drivers like De Marco and Jensen. They'd blow him off the track in two laps, unless I taught him everything I knew.

I was already stretching out the lessons I'd have to give Ronnie when I remembered something with a jolt. Ronnie wasn't going to be around. When he made his bid to drive or quit, I was going to hold the door open so he could walk out, and I'd have a clear field with Sandy. That was the plan of 2:00 p.m.

The eleven cars in the first heat bumped out of the pits to the track. Another race was in the making. The serious business of the night had begun. The sharp smell of "shoe polish," a mixture of nitromethane and methanol, cut through the gasoline fumes. Engines sputtered and roared again. Drivers sat tensely in their dark cabs, their cigarettes glowing.

What the hell . . . suppose Ronnie did have hot pants for Sandy . . . what was she to me? I wasn't going to get serious with her. Not with any woman, after what had happened with Thelma. Never again. All I had in mind was a little diversion for the couple of months I would be in Town. Then out.

It had happened once, but it wouldn't happen again. I'd never let a woman mean enough to me that she could make a fool out of me. Not again. Why ask for trouble over Ronnie? Keep him. Teach him to drive. Bring him down to the track and run 72. It wouldn't be the same as driving myself, but it was the next best thing. It was being at the track, in the pits, hearing them wind out, smelling their hearts burning, watching them go. It would help time pass, and it would help dull the pain, just to be around a track. Like sniffing the opium somebody else was smoking. Not good enough to make a dream, but better than nothing. Better than nothing.

And I didn't have to keep Ronnie. If 72 was hot, I might be able to steal one of the other drivers for as long as I stayed around. Somebody like Jensen or de Marco, who would run in front night after night. Always time to give Ronnie the deep six.

The sound was a surf of machine noise, and the first heat was off. This was for blood. Somebody would be on his head before the tenth lap. Miss this to play footsie with Sandy or any other woman?

"Hey," Ronnie shouted in my ear as the pack slid past. "Whose hide you nailing to that wall?"

"Huh?"

He started to repeat the question, but I shook him off. Three cars were aiming for the same groove on the west turn, and somebody wasn't going to make it.

CHAPTER 9

THE HEAT RACES DIDN'T COME UP WITH ANY SURPRISES. The best boys stayed on their feet and finished in the money. The boys who trailed in the fast heat weren't discouraged. They still had a shot at some money in the Australian pursuit, the consolation, and the semi-main or main.

Things went more to hell in the middle and slow heats. The times were slower, but the driving was wilder. There were a couple of spin-outs, one rollover that brought the crowd to its feet, and a couple of boys who tangled and dragged one another to a stop. But I watched, with a certain amount of satisfaction, the number of cars that couldn't make it with nobody bothering them. Cars that blew hoses, overheated, ran sick and slow, and died half-trying.

By the time the heat races were over, eight cars had been scratched for the night. The way things were going, the final events were going to be very thin, and the crowd wouldn't like that at all. A small field might give them a hard race, but they paid their money to see a dozen or fifteen cars trying to get around in the same groove at the same time, with the resultant crash, crush, spins, and rolls.

So far, it was the driver-owners who were pulling out—the independents who had one of everything and were through the first time something went wrong that couldn't be fixed with two hands and a minor spare part. That was good. That's where my business would come from.

Toad dragged along at my side, giving me a rundown on every car, able to recite from memory just how many parts had been bought from Bill, put on the books, and forgotten. Everybody in the pits but the garage-sponsored outfits was into us deep.

Some of the boys who were through for the night were getting ready to shove. They were loading their racers or hitching them to trailers, ready to go home. The men were dirtier, wearier, and angrier than when they had arrived. They had worked like hell to prepare for the races, and now they were out, without having made dime one, and there were bent wheels, blown gaskets, and busted radiators to fix or find before the next race night.

Ronnie stood next to me, chewing gum, his hands in his pockets. He had a look of youthful disdain on his face as he saw the cripples getting ready to crawl away. He was going to have Bill's garage behind him when he raced. And he'd have me and Toad to rebuild a wrecked car between the heat races and the main event.

"Ronnie," I said, "tell those guys not to go home. There's going to be a drivers' meeting at the pay shack after the races."

Ronnie looked toward the spot where the announcer sat at the mike. "They didn't announce—" he began.

"They don't know about it yet," I said.

"Do what I said, now."

"But Herpgruve didn't—he won't like anybody trying to run his business."

I gave Ronnie a slight push. "Do it," I said. "I'll handle the rest."

"Okay," he said reluctantly. He went off to spread the word.

"I suppose," Toad said, "that you'll be takin' over the mayor's office in the morning."

"Yeah," I said. "Be there early so I can swear you in as chief of police."

We climbed on a tow truck to watch the Australian Pursuit. It was run by the dozen fastest cars, and it was the only race that had a running start. Any car that was completely passed had to drop out. The race lasted until there was only one car left, with a limit of fourteen laps.

It was the same old story. Jensen, de Marco, Towner, and Vann. They hung back until some of the slower cars had been eliminated, then went after each other. It was a rough race. Drivers used every trick to keep from being passed. They blocked, crowded, shoved, and weaved. When it was over, three more cars were done for the night.

The crowd buzz that was going at the end of the pursuit didn't subside as the consolation was announced. If anything, it got louder. The announcement had gone out that nineteen cars would be on the track, and everybody was expecting blood. They would be lined up three abreast, and there would be no restart of the race unless the track was blocked. Ordinarily, a race wasn't on unless everybody made it around the first turn, but not the "consey."

The consey was the last chance the tailenders had to make gas money for the night, and something of their desperation was communicated to the crowd. And there were drivers who hoped to split a gas-money purse with their guts and find enough left over for hamburgers. Drivers who had to win something, and who would smash one another to bits trying to make two or three bucks. That's what made it such a good race for the crowd. There was no kick in watching somebody run an easy win way out in front. It was the tooth-and-nail stuff that made the night good and brought the people back again.

The announcer called the cars for the consey. The crowd sounded disgusted when there were only thirteen entries. There were cat-calls when a note came from the pits that four of the thirteen had called it quits and were scratched. A nine-car consey didn't promise enough excitement. Too much room for everybody.

The consey was slow getting started. One car quit on the track and had to be pushed by another to get running again. There was confusion about where the cars in the race should line up. The crowd was noisily impatient.

I saw Loren Peale in the line-up. He was in next to the last row, on the outside. His car stood out like Lana Turner in a leper colony. I watched him when the green flag dropped. He pulled sharply to the outside, and I expected him to pour it on and take the others before they reached the turn. But he was last into the turn, still riding high, eating everybody's dust. And he stayed there.

Around and around the track, trailing at a respectful distance, his car beautiful, his white helmet gleaming. Up front, the cars were cat-and-dogging it, grinding together, shoving, sliding back and forth, shooting fire, steaming, risking wreckage for a few bucks. Peale stayed where it was safe, speeding up when he dropped too far behind. Cars dropped out with engine trouble, one spun into the infield, and one hit the fence on the back chute and stalled in the middle of the track. If the race lasted long enough, Peale would win a dollar or two just by staying.

The losers in the consey were a beaten, furious bunch. They came back into the pits, finished forever with racing. "Forever" being until the next race night. And even as they came off the track, the call went out for cars in the semi-main, and some of the consey racers had to go out again, knowing they were licked, knowing they couldn't last fifteen laps if God was their copilot, navigator, and crew chief. But they were called, and they lit fresh cigarettes, swore, and turned their dirt-smeared faces toward the starting line.

I saw Ronnie moving from car to car in the pits, spreading my message.

"Come on," I said to Toad.

"Where?"

"I want you to hold a hide while I nail it to the wall."

We headed for the track. Drivers we passed were watching others get ready to run or working furiously to make needed adjustments on their cars. I heard a dozen voices cursing the night, the condition of the track, the dust, racing in general, and some balky engine in particular.

Walking through, I saw a dozen hostile faces look at me. There was no mistaking the hatred, no attempt to hide it. With all their other troubles, I was going to put the squeeze on to get back tools, parts, money. I was the last straw. I heard what they said about me as I passed, and I smiled to myself. Everything was right and ripe.

CHAPTER 10

HERPGRUVE WAS IN HIS COUNTING HOUSE, counting out his money. When I walked in with Toad, Herpgruve put the stacks of bills in a green metal box and rested his arm on top of it.

"Tired of watching them run?" he grunted at me. "Not much to watch," I said. "Most of the cars soured out long ago."

Crowd and engines roared together in the background as the semi-main got underway. There weren't many engines.

"We do the best we can," Herpgruve said. "Maybe now that you're in business, you can help some of the boys keep running. We've had as many as forty cars out here. That's what the crowd likes to see. Lots of traffic."

There was a long crowd "Oooooohhhhh," and the ambulance siren wailed. Then a burst of applause as the announcer's voice came cheerfully over the PA system. "He's all right, folks, all right.

He's getting out by himself. That was a nasty roll by Harve Kipton, but he's all right now."

"That's what they like," Herpgruve said, rolling his bug eyes. "Nothing like a couple of good rolls in the last event or two to send them out happy. That's what I try to give 'em. I tell my drivers I want aggressive racing. Nothing dirty, you understand, but aggressive."

"Yeah," I said. "That's fine. Only, I don't think you'll have more than four or five cars out there on your next night."

"Nonsense. Why those boys can fix up a wreck in hours. They— what do you mean, Jones?"

"Well," I said, laying on the Texas, "as Toad here can tell you, I've taken over the widow's garage."

"You already told me that."

"And I figure it's my duty to her," I said, "to get things cleared up as soon as possible."

Herpgruve showed a flash of apprehension. "What things, Jones? Don't talk in riddles."

"The boys out there owe her a lot of money," I said.

"That's their business."

"And mine," I said. "They're all running with our parts in their cars. Either I get paid for those parts before the next race date, or I'll have 'em back in the garage."

"Good God, man!" Herpgruve shouted. "I thought you knew more about racing than that! You know those poor guys out there are broke. Where are they going to raise the money? They've got all they can do to keep running now. You'll wreck racing in this town if you do that."

He was sweating.

"I can't help that," I said. "I've got my duty to my partner. The boys pay up, or they see my lawyer. I'll slap an attachment on ninety percent of the cars out there. How they get the money isn't my affair. I want the money or the parts.

"Man, be reasonable!"

"The widow was reasonable," I said. "Now she's about broke. I don't care if you never run another race here, Herpgruve. It's no money in my pocket. All I'm saying is that I'm collecting accounts long overdue before I lay a hand to a tool."

"Have you talked to the men?" Herpgruve asked. "Did they refuse to pay?"

"I'm going to talk to them," I said. "I passed the word around for all drivers to show here after the race. I'll lay it on the line then. But I wanted to talk to you first. You pay . . ."

"I don't owe your widow anything," Herpgruve yelped. "And I'm not paying anybody's bills but my own."

"That's all right," I said. "But it's going to hurt you if the boys can't pay. You won't have much of a crowd out if all they have to watch is two or three cars."

"What the hell do you want me to do, Jones?"

I got up and walked around, looking over the inside of the shack. "If I had some kind of financial interest in a place like this, I could make it hum," I said, looking at Toad. He blinked back.

"If you want to buy in, I'll listen to you," Herpgruve said. "You tell me how much money you've got to put down, and I'll tell you how much of a piece you'll get. I haven't wanted any partners here, but with your garage to help keep the boys on the track—"

"Money?" I said. "To put down? I guess you didn't hear what I was saying, Herpgruve. If I get nasty, you won't have any cars at all. If I play ball and let the boys run, you're in business. Seems to me I've already bought in. And deep."

Herpgruve's face turned red. "That's blackmail!" he thundered. "Blackmail. You can't come in here and—"

"I'm in," I said. "And I'm not kidding you about what I figure on doing. I'll close you down tighter than a midget's jockstrap unless I get paid. And I don't care whose money takes care of the bill."

Herpgruve looked at the green box. "How much do you figure the boys owe?"

"With what they charged, and what they borrowed and what they stole, plus labor and use of tools," I said, "going back to the time the track opened, I figure it must be about twenty-five or thirty thousand dollars."

"You're out of your head," Herpgruve gasped.

"It's on the books," I said. "Some of these people had expensive tastes. As long as they didn't intend to pay anyway, the best was none too good. And those pretty little wrecks you like to see on the track ruined a lot of parts that had to be replaced ten or fifteen times."

"You couldn't raise twenty-five hundred out of that bunch," Herpgruve said. "Not a chance."

"Then we'll have to repossess," I said regretfully. "And there goes your racetrack."

Herpgruve looked whipped. "I can't afford to close down," he said. "But I can't pay anybody the money you ask to stay open. What the hell can I do?"

"Make a deal," I said, taking a chair. Toad reached out and got my cigarettes from my jacket pocket. His face was pinched and expressionless, but there was a gleam in his eyes.

"What kind of deal?" Herpgruve demanded.

"A fair one," I said. "I'll let you stay open for half the net take."

"*Half?*"

"Don't get any heart attacks," I said. "You won't lose so much."

"*Half!*"

"Herp," I said, "you're running this place like it had sticky valves. You listen to me, and we'll more than double the crowd out there. Your half of the net will be more than you're making now. And you're getting off the hook easy," I said. "If the widow lost the garage to the mortgage people, they wouldn't worry about the track. They'd crack down and get what money they could. I'm giving you a choice, and a chance to make more money."

Herpgruve's head settled down toward his shoulders, forcing rings of red fat to stand out at the back of his neck.

"All right, I'll take your squeeze play. But under these terms. First, I want my man to go over your books and check every account."

"Done," I said.

"Second, I want your share of the money to be deducted from those debts. When the books are clear, you're out as my partner."

"What else?" I said. "I figured on those two."

"I'm just warning you," he said. "I'm going to look for the hole in your blackmail deal. And when I find it, I'll make you squeal like a cat with his tail caught in the door."

"Fair enough," I said. "With a nice honest start like this, we ought to get along just fine."

He leaned back. "I'll have my lawyer draw up an agreement tomorrow. That is, if he can't find me a way out."

"No lawyers," I said. "No contracts. I'm not going to be anything to you on paper."

"Why not?"

"We want to run a car or two," I said. "They'll run good, too. But I don't want the other people to think we're running in front because I own a piece of the track. You send your man down to look over the books and figure how much I've got coming. You can make your checks out to the garage. When you're all paid up, we're through."

"It'll take years."

"I'm in no hurry."

There was a rumble of activity outside. The crowd was coming out. Long lines of cars crept past the shack toward the highway. In a couple of minutes, the drivers would be coming in. Herpgruve looked at me. "What do you want me to tell the drivers?"

"My name," I said. "I'll do the rest."

The flagman and his helper came in and put their bundles away. Herpgruve opened the green box and paid them off. The scorer came in next with the payoff sheet, which he dropped on the table in front of Herpgruve. Gravel crunched outside as drivers and owners drove up to the pay shack from the pits. Herpgruve went to the door and looked out. "Everybody here?" he asked. No one answered. I joined him. Most of the boys were squatting on their heels just outside the door. Their women and kids sat patiently in the cars, waiting.

"I want you people to meet somebody," Herpgruve said.

"The hell with that," somebody called out. "Let's get paid so we can get out of here."

Herpgruve held up one hand. "You'll get your dollar and a quarter, Mike. Don't worry." The other boys laughed. Light flashed on metal as several of them drank beer out of cans.

"I want you all to meet Ace Jones," Herpgruve said.

"Maybe you've heard that he's taken over Bill Richard's garage. He wants to say something."

Herpgruve stepped back, and I took his place in the doorway. The dark, dirty faces that ringed around me were sullen and hostile. They didn't want any part of me. I heard somebody say, "I don't want to hear no speeches." A beer can rattled on the gravel as it was thrown away.

I leaned against the jamb, looking at them. A voice called across the circle, "Get your hankies out, men, he's going to cry for his tools."

"If you think I'm going to ask you to return the stuff you borrowed from Bill, you're thinking wrong," I said. "Anybody here who wants to hang on to a wrench or a screwdriver he's got stuck away in his pocket can do it."

"Thanks," a driver drawled.

"However," I said, "from what I saw tonight, most of you boys aren't doing too good a job on the little gems you drag down here. Maybe you like to sour out on the first lap. I don't know. If you do, that's your business. If you want to run, that's my business."

There was a little stir of interest in the crowd.

"I'm a racing man," I said. "I figure on picking up where Bill left off and running a garage for men who want to run a good race. I can't do it without tools. So, it's up to you. The more stuff I get back, the better I'll be able to take care of you. I aim to keep a good stock of parts, and if you come around, I'll do my best to keep you running."

They were quiet. I knew what they were thinking.

"Most of you," I said, "are on the books for a lot of money. I know you can't dig up what you owe, and I'm not going to be tough about it. We'll let past debts ride for a while. And as for any work you might want from Toad and me, I think we can get together on how it can be paid for. The main thing that all of us want is a good field of cars out here. The more people we pull, the better the purse will be, and the more you boys make, the easier it will be for us to do business together."

"All right, all right," another guy yelled. "Now let's get paid."

"You hold your britches until you hear the news," I said into the semi-darkness. "It won't make you sad. Beginning next race night, there's going to be a water truck out here to wet down the track. Courtesy of Ace and Sandy's garage, formerly known as Bill's." That remark was greeted by a chorus of pleased profanity. I held up my hand for attention. "That's not all," I said. "I'll also see that the track is disked and rolled—if Mr. Herpgruve will allow me to move in on his territory like that. And I'll pay for that, too." There was a few yips of approval. "There's more," I said. "As soon as I can swing it, I'll have a truck at the track with spare parts and a welding unit. Use of the unit at the track will be free. Any help we give you at the track is free. All you'll have to pay for are the parts."

They were really pleased now. I waited a few minutes while they talked back and forth, and then they quieted and looked toward me. "What the hell?" I demanded. "Are you expecting more? I've said my piece." I turned and went inside the shack.

I sat on a box in a corner while Herpgruve paid off the winners. The folding money went to the top three boys. By the time the independents stepped up to collect for fourth or fifth place in the consolation, Herpgruve was looking for change. Fifth place paid a buck and a half. That was the kind of money the guy had spent five or ten dollars and a couple of days' time to collect. And he was happy to get it. Happy as the guy who hits the quarter machine for three dollars after pouring in fifteen. A win is a win, when the thrill is pulling the handle and watching the symbols spin.

When they were paid off, the drivers nodded to me before they left. A couple came over and introduced themselves. Gaunt, weary characters who needed the most work and were nervous about getting in any deeper. Even the top drivers, like de Marco and Jensen, stopped to say hello as they put away their winning bundles. In a way, they were the most pleased of all. They knew that a racing car was only the beginning. It was the driver that made the big difference, and these boys could drive. The more competition they had, the better the racing, the bigger the purse, and the bigger their winnings. They knew what I knew—that the white corpuscles of racing's blood were the score of second-division Christians who were eaten up every race night by the roaring lions that always ran in front. It was on the battered bodies and broken bones of the also-rans that the winners found their fat meat. It was so much easier to look good when there was a bunch of guys whose function in life was to have you make them look bad.

No wonder they were friendly. When it was over, and the drivers were gone, Herpgruve looked at me with a bitter smile. "Great guy, that Ace Jones," he said. "Gonna water the track and sandpaper out the bumps and give everybody a full-house Merc so everybody can win first place. Hooray for Ace Jones!" He slammed the green box closed.

"By the way," I said, "I'll bill you privately for the cost of the water truck and the roller."

"Bill me?"

"Sure," I said. "You don't think I'm going to pay for it, do you? That's the track's job."

"Cute, aren't you?" Herpgruve sneered. "Playing big-hearted missionary with all those free services. Now I find out all that stuff comes out of my pocket, and the guys have me figured as the louse."

"That's the way it goes, Pard," I said. "Be seeing you."

I walked out. Toad shuffled out after me.

I looked around for Ronnie's car. "What happened to Ronnie?" I asked Toad. "I wanted a ride home."

Ronnie answered my question with a hail that came from the shadows. We turned that way. When we got closer, I saw he was leaning against my old Hudson, talking to Joe.

"Let's go," I said to Ronnie. "I'm beat."

Ronnie scuffed a boot in the gravel. "Joe wanted to talk to you a minute, Ace."

"Tomorrow," I said. "We've got a date for ten in the morning. Joe knows the time and the price. There's isn't anything else to talk about until then."

Joe started to say something, but I was already walking away. "Come on!" I ordered Ronnie without looking at him. I got into his car with Toad crowding in after me. Ronnie lingered at Joe's window. "Come on, Ronnie!" I yelled.

Toad coughed and reached for my cigarettes. "I seen you," he said.

"Seen me what?"

"Driving them cars tonight." He made a bubbling noise in his throat. "You had your hands closed and you was steering in every race. Leanin' on the turns, twitching your feet."

"Habit," I said. "Got that from being around so many tracks."

"I been around a lot of tracks too, in my time," Toad said.

"Meaning what?"

"I ain't fooled."

"Shut up. Ronnie!" Ronnie trotted to the car and got in behind the wheel. "You guys want to eat first? We can go where all the guys go after the races."

"The garage," I said. "We're not hungry."

"I'd kinda like a—" Toad began.

"The garage," I repeated. Ronnie started off in his usual style, spinning his wheels in the gravel. I poked him in the ribs. "Get rid of that habit."

"What?"

"Spinning your wheels. Any knucklehead can sit and spin his wheels. If you want to win any races, you've got to learn how to get off in a hurry. From now on, you practice seeing how fast you can get going without spinning."

"All right, Ace. If you say so. By the way, what Joe wanted to tell you—"

"He'll tell me tomorrow," I said.

"Right." Ronnie concentrated on his driving. He didn't like being stepped on, but he was going to learn how to take it. If he was going to drive for me, he had to obey orders without question. Like a bootcamp marine.

We stopped in front of the garage. Toad and I climbed out. "Go home and go to bed," I said to Ronnie. "I want you here at eight in the morning—awake."

"Okay, Ace." He put his car in gear and started to take off slowly. Suddenly, he tromped, it sending a shower of gravel over me and Toad.

It had to be on purpose. Show me he wasn't too easily tamed. I swore, and Toad snickered.

We went into the garage and turned on a light. I sat down in the office swivel chair and put my feet on the desk. Toad sat on the desk and dug his nose—finger into his right ear.

"It's been a busy day," I said.

"Too busy," Toad mumbled.

"What do you mean, you old artfay?" I demanded. "All you've done has been rob me of cigarettes."

"You know what's going to happen to you, don't you?" Toad said with a tone of sadistic pleasure in his voice.

"What?"

"What happened to the octopus that was makin' love to the electric fan. Had the time of his life until somebody plugged the damn thing in."

I dropped my feet to the floor. "There's one tentacle that's got work to do," I said.

Toad rubbed his eyes. "Where are you goin' to sleep?"

"Sleep!" I peeled off my jacket and tossed it on the desk. "Man, you and I are about to start working. If the kid's going to be driving in two weeks, he'll need a car. We can't do anything with Sandy around, so you and I are going to roll old Seventy-Two inside and start the reconstruction."

"Hell, Ace," Toad complained. "It's after midnight. This ain't no time to start foolin' that old bolt. I'm an old man, and I need my rest."

Whining like a withered child, Toad followed me outside and put a shoulder to 72. It didn't roll easy, but between us, we managed to get it inside, under the lights.

I walked around it slowly. The red-and-yellow body slanted down toward a point behind the front wheels. That was good. A racing car needed that ramp. The right front wheel was set out wide and toed-out, the left front still carried a smaller tire. The rear wheels had been put on by somebody who had carried away the good ones. The wheels looked bent, the tires shot.

There wasn't much left to 72 besides the block and the heads. The plugs had been removed; the carburetor, generator, distributor, and coil were taken.

I stared thoughtfully at 72. With the right work, that Ford mill would be able to put out 170 horsepower. Others were doing it, and we'd have to be right up there with them. But there would be more if we wanted to win. We'd have to play with rear axle ratios to find the right one for this track and hunt for the little refinements that added up to an extra ounce of punch when needed. There were a lot of things we could do—if we had the equipment—and the right driver.

We got underneath the car and began looking at it from the ground up, checking the shocks, the steering linkage, the condition of the frame. All things that decided how well a car would corner and track. Lying under the car, we talked and planned and figured. By the time we wheeled 72 back to its outside spot, the sky was light.

I threw my sleeping bag on the desk in the office and lay down on top of it. Toad hunched himself into a corner with his head on his knees, his back braced. I started to think about what I was doing, and why. But I was asleep before the questions were asked, let alone answered.

CHAPTER 11

IT WAS PLEASANT TO BE AWAKENED BY THE SOUND of a woman's voice. For a moment, I lay on the desk and enjoyed it. But when I opened my eyes and saw the look on Sandy's face, the enjoyment ended. It was a look of doubt and distrust. When I stood up and looked into the small mirror she had on the wall, I could see why.

I was dirty, unshaven, red-eyed, crumpled. Not exactly the kind of man anyone would want to look at and say, "This is my new associate, Mr. Jones."

I turned toward Sandy, rubbing my face to hide it. "I'm sorry we overslept," I said. "We were up late, planning."

Sandy nodded, not very reassured. She had dressed up little for our first full day together. A flowered print dress, nylons, white summer shoes. Her hair looked golden in the morning light; her brown eyes were soft and clear. She looked beautiful and clean. Even Ronnie, who had come in with her, had washed and combed his hair and looked civilized. Only Toad and I were like leftover ashtrays,, unemptied from last night's party.

"I'll clean up a little now," I said. I wanted to smile, but was afraid the brown taste would show. "Anyway, you've seen how your new partner looks when he gets up in the morning. So you're one up on me."

She didn't smile. "I'll take over while you're gone," she said. "I know how tired you must be. Ronnie told me you worked late."

I gave him a quick look. He was rocking on his booted heels, young, big, with the freshness of youth. There was a peculiar expression on his face as he looked at me. He was noticing the beard stubble flecked with gray, the hollows in my cheeks, my wrinkled thinness. I didn't look quite so grand and all-knowing this morning, and he was showing it.

"I told her what you said to the drivers," Ronnie said. "About providing a water truck and all that."

"We'll get a bite and be back," I said to Sandy, stifling a yawn. I turned to Ronnie, who was about to sit down. "You can start out by washing down the garage, Ronnie. I want it done by the time I get back."

He hesitated, then let himself down in the chair. "I'll get to it," he said, tilting the chair back on two legs and looking me in the eye.

"Take your time," I said. "Just so long as it's done by the time I get back."

"Uh-huh." He looked disinterested.

"Throw me your keys," I said.

"My . . . keys?"

"Your car keys. You don't think I'm going to lug my suitcase around on foot, do you?"

Reluctantly, he gave me the keys. I got my suitcase and took off in Ronnie's car with Toad sitting sleepily beside me. "That cub needs to learn his manners," I said.

"Be careful how you start teachin'," Toad said. "That kid's got a punch like a mule's kick."

"What's wrong with him?" I said. "He acts more like a high school boy than a kid two weeks away from being a man."

"He's been sat on too much," Toad said. "You know how it is when the big brother's a daredevil. Little brother ain't allowed to go up and down stairs by hisself. And when Bill went, Sandy gave him more of the same."

"It's about time he got out on his own," I said.

"He will," Toad snickered. "Only don't be too surprised if your neck looks like the first step to him."

We drove to the Town Cafe. I went to the washroom and cleaned up, shaved, and changed into a clean T-shirt and khaki pants. It wasn't any substitute for a bath. I made up my mind to find a room in a hurry.

Toad was eating breakfast when I came out. He held his fork like a hammer and shoveled in the hot cakes.

"What do you think about running a three fifty-four rear end on Seventy-Two?" I asked Toad.

"Town Garage runs a five thirty-eight."

"That's too much as long as the track is in bad shape," I said.

"He winds up awful fast."

"What's better?" I said. "Winding up to five thousand rpm with your wheels spinning, or getting a bite at three thousand?"

"You're the boss," Toad said. "But running a three fifty-four rear end on a quarter-mile track—there'll be a lot of second-gear driving."

"So be it."

"It's hard on the car."

"We're a garage. It's always hard on cars to run in front."

"Where's all the money coming from?"

"Why—" I stopped. I was going to say from the sale of my car, the bite on Herpgruve, and the business we'd get. But that wasn't the way I'd planned it. My idea in getting things rolling was to get my hands on all the cash I could scrape together in a couple of months and then blow. Not to make any investments. "We'll figure a way," I said to Toad. "Let's get back to work."

He grinned at his plate, enjoying a private joke.

When we got back to the garage, Ronnie was wearing a pair of rubber boots and a rubber apron and sullenly hosing down the deck. Sandy was in the office, her brown-gold head over the account books. When she looked up, she smiled. My clean face gave her confidence, and it gave me an idea.

"We're open," she said. "All we need is business."

"We'll get it," I said. "Toad, call Ronnie in here."

Ronnie came into the office with his lower lip stuck out. "You want me, Ace?"

"Yeah. Now look. Most of the cars that come in here will be dirty. When we give 'em back, they'll be clean. Ronnie, any car that has to stay in here for a while is washed before we give it back. Actually, we'll lose money on the deal at first, but—"

"I don't like the idea," Ronnie said. "If people want their cars washed, they'll ask for the job—and pay for it. I won't be doin' nothing but washing cars around here. That's no job for me."

"Listen," I said. "We need to get people coming in for work and going out satisfied. You know as well as I do that a clean car always seems to run better than a dirty one. It's a psychological trick, maybe, but it's true. We'll have customers thinking their cars are running like new, just because we tinkered inside a little and washed off the dust."

"Couldn't we ask them if they wanted a wash job?" Sandy suggested.

"No," I said. "That would make it look like we were trying to sell them something they didn't want. As far as they're concerned, it's a courtesy wash at our expense."

"You wouldn't pad the bill, Ace!" She really meant it. It was hard not to laugh.

"Of course not," I said. "We'll be reasonable. But the extra effort on our part will mean a bigger volume. Americans like to get something for nothing. We're just giving them what they want."

"And I get the dirty end of the stick," Ronnie complained. "I have to wash the cars. Why can't we hire a wash boy?"

"On account of we've got one," I snapped. "Remember what I told you, son. You don't have to stay if you don't like it here."

Sandy looked upset. "Please, Ronnie," she said. "We need you."

"I'll do it for you, Sand," Ronnie said. "But I don't like getting all the dirty details around here." Ronnie went back to his job. Toad snickered when he was gone.

"Ronnie's awfully sensitive," Sandy said.

"He'll get over it," I promised. "Once things start humming."

That didn't take long. Our first customer was a farmer driving a three-hole Buick. He walked into the office, looked us over, and said, "Marchfield told me to come here."

"Who?" I asked.

"Marchfield. Neighbor of mine. You fixed his car yesterday."

"Sure. I remember. What can I do for you?"

"She don't handle right," the farmer complained. "Too much play in the steering wheel, for one thing."

"That's easy enough checked," I said. "Maybe all we'll have to do is take up the sector a notch. Run it in, and we'll see."

He drove in, and I went over his steering system. Then I rolled out from under the car on the spider and stood up. "You must drive a lot over rough roads," I said.

"I do," the farmer said.

"You don't crawl along."

"I get where I'm going."

"You don't feel the holes with soft shocks these days," I said, "but those front wheels hit a bump with a two-ton punch. They take a beating. I can make your car handle better for a while for a couple of dollars. You'd be all right as long as you took it easy on the back roads. Twenty miles an hour or so."

"What's wrong?" the farmer asked.

"Your knee-action units are shot," I said. "Even if I patched a few weak spots, you could lose all control of your car any time at all. Hit a bump and—no steering."

"What would it cost me to have the job done right?" the farmer asked.

"If you turn in your old units, I could get a rebuilt set for about fifty dollars. Your labor costs wouldn't be high. We work fast."

"Ummmm," the farmer said, frowning.

"I could," I said, "put in a new king bolt set. That wouldn't cost much, and it would help your steering. But it wouldn't help those dead shocks. That's what would kill you."

The farmer scratched his head. "I guess you'd better do it right," he said. "If Marchfield said you was all right, I guess I can trust you." The farmer grinned painfully. "I thought maybe I'd come out for fifty cents myself."

"If I could do it for that, I would," I said. "Believe me."

"When can I get the car?"

"About five tonight," I said. "We'll go after the new parts and get right at it. And satisfaction is guaranteed here, too. We'll take it out for a run together before you pay the bill."

Sandy looked radiant when I told her the news. "Imagine," she said. "Starting off with a good-sized job like that. Who would have thought it?"

"Word gets around," I said. "We'll have all the business we can handle."

I had Sandy make out a bill for the parts, then went to see Toad, who was waiting by the Buick.

"Get under the car and make noise," I said. "The steering-gear housing is loose on the frame. See if you can get a wrench and tighten it for about five hours' worth of labor."

"What if Sandy catches on?"

"Well . . . take the front wheels off and repack 'em. That will look like something."

"If that farmer ever finds out—"

"He won't," I said. "Don't worry about it." In a way, I felt almost good about what we were doing. At least it proved that Ace Jones wasn't going soft, that he still had his eye on a quick killing and fast takeoff. And besides, I was helping Sandy, and she needed the money more than that hayseed.

Toad fished for one of my cigarettes and went to work. I went back into the office and sat on Sandy's desk. "You got your clean clothes dirty looking at that car," she said. "You ought to have coveralls."

"I'll get some," I said.

"You haven't forgotten, have you?"

"What?"

"About tonight."

"Tonight? Oh . . . you mean the . . ."

"Victory dinner," I said. "Am I still invited?"

"Of course. Seven o'clock all right?"

"That's when I get the hungriest."

I looked into the brown eyes. "You know," I said softly, looking away, "yesterday I was a wandering, footloose mechanic without anything I could call my own. Just a hobo on wheels. Drifting. And now I've got something I've always wanted. A place that's part mine in a way, something to work for, a place to live. I feel as though I've come home."

I said it and she believed it. That I figured. But I couldn't understand why I almost believed it too.

"Ace," she said, "I'm awfully glad your water pump broke and you came here to have it fixed."

I took her hand. God, but it felt good. I'd almost forgotten what it was like. "I'm glad too," I said. We kept holding hands, looking at one another and smiling.

"I'm through, Jones!"

I turned. Ronnie was standing in the doorway looking as though he'd like to kill me. I smiled at him and held on to Sandy's hand. "Through?"

"Through washing the floor. Anything else?" He stared at our hand-holding, his face getting red.

"Yeah," I said. "Wash that Buick. And clean it on the inside, too."

He didn't move for a minute. He stood big and angry in the doorway, his dark eyes burning. Then he turned and stalked away, stamping with his rubber boots.

I looked at Sandy. "I guess Ronnie didn't like seeing us shake hands."

"I know," she said, withdrawing her hand slowly. "He thinks it's his duty to protect me now that Bill is gone. It's silly. I'm much older than he is."

"You are very pretty," I said. "And you don't look any older than girls Ronnie's age. There's something about you that's more mature, but as far as your features go, and your figure—"

"I have some work to do," Sandy said abruptly, turning toward the typewriter. She sounded very impersonal and businesslike. I took my cue from her. I talked the same way.

"We might have some of our tools brought back today," I said. "Would you give receipts for everything we take in?"

"Certainly."

"I'll see how Toad's doing with that Buick, then."

She turned her head and looked over her shoulder. And she gave me the *softest* damn look as she said, "All right Ace." Then she smiled and turned back to her work.

I was checking the few supplies we had on hand when Joe drove up with my old Hudson. I went out to see him. I wanted to talk to him away from Sandy.

"Morning," I said. "How do you like driving a car with racing shocks. Ever drive a car that cornered like this one?"

"I ain't gone around many corners," Joe said, plaintively. He rolled his sad eyes back in his head, trying to look up at me.

"You bring the money like you promised?"

"Well, in a way I did. But I wanted to talk some more about buyin' the car or not."

"Talk!" I said roughly. "Damn it, Joe, if you weren't a friend of Ronnie's, I'd haul you out of that car and whip the ass off you. You talked me out of the car yesterday, so I had to turn away other people who wanted to see it, and now you're trying to back out of the whole deal. You made a contract, boy. I've got witnesses. If I take this to a lawyer, you'll wind up without the car or the money. Now pay for your purchase like a good boy before we have any trouble."

Joe sat with his head bowed, his lips quivering. "But I don't want your car!"

"You've got it," I said in a low voice. "Now, do you hand over the money, or do I come and get it?"

I looked at Joe's pinched, unhappy face, and I wanted to kick myself with spurs. I was brought up to pick fights with people my own weight and reach, not to twist kids' arms until they dropped their pennies. But I needed the money, and Joe would part with it.

Joe reached into his pocket for an envelope. "Didn't Ronnie tell you I didn't want—"

"Ronnie doesn't tell me anything," I said. "I tell him." I took the envelope from Joe's fingers. I looked inside and counted quickly. It was all there.

"Fine, Joe," I said. "I'll take care of the transfer details. And believe you me, boy, you'll never regret buying this car. Now get the hell out of here and don't come back."

"Yes, sir," Joe whispered. I turned my back on him and went inside, where Ronnie was washing the Buick.

"Son," I said to Ronnie. "I want a word with you."

He turned around. He was still mad about seeing me hold hands with Sandy.

"Son," I said, "what the hell do you mean trying to mess up my deal with Joe?"

"Well, Joe thought it wasn't a good deal, and I thought—"

"It was my deal, son," I said, moving in close. "And from now on, we'd better understand each other. When I make deals, you keep your snotty young nose out of them. Understand?"

"Joe's my friend—"

"You don't have any friends," I said coldly. I talked low, so Sandy couldn't hear. "You want to be a driver, don't you? You want to drive for me, don't you?"

"I guess so." He wasn't backing down, and he was getting madder.

"Then you've got to learn to be tough," I said. "You won't have any friends on that dirt circle, son. Every guy out then will be out to get you. The only way you'll make it is to take my orders and learn to fight back. If you're soft, forget about driving. This is no kindergarten we're running. Damn it, where do you think the money's coming from to put you on the track? From Joe?"

"Well," Ronnie glared at Toad, who was taking it all in with a sly grin. "I still don't like it."

"From now on," I said, "you'll like what I tell you to like. You like my deal with Joe. Understand? And you like my being here and being Sandy's partner."

There was fire in his eyes when I said that. I decided to let him have the whole works at once. He had to know who the boss was going to be.

"You quit butting in when I'm busy with Sandy," I said. "We've got business that's no concern of yours."

He struggled for words. "You . . . be careful. . . . You better keep your hands off my brother's wife."

"Grow up, kid," I snapped. "Your brother's turned his last lap in that bucket. And who the new chauffeur is, is none of your goddamn business."

It felt as though a brick had come flying out of the wall and hit me. Ronnie had swung fast and hard, and I got it square on the jaw. I was carried back off balance and landed on my tail with a thud, then fell over backward, my ears ringing.

I saw Ronnie making a dive for me and rolled out of the way. By that time, Toad was tangled in Ronnie's legs, and the kid was slowed down. I stood up, and when he saw I wasn't coming after him, he stopped fighting Toad and looked at me with killer's eyes, his body trembling.

I stared back at him. "Finish washing that Buick," I said evenly. "And when that's done, I'll have a new job for you."

I turned and walked out the back door of the garage and sat down on an old, rusted block. My jaw ached, and my head still spun a little. It had been one hell of a punch.

Toad peered out of the garage, then shuffled over to my side. He was grinning his wrinkled little prune-grin of delight as he rolled a cigarette. "Told you," Toad said, "punch like a mule's kick."

"The little punk," I said. "If I didn't need a driver . . . he's in love with her, that kid. . . . She's out of his class. . . . Damn him, and her, and everything."

"He sure made you fly," Toad said. "Whyn't you hit him back? I was lookin' for a good fight."

"I'm a mechanic, not a hero," I said, feeling my jaw.

Toad giggled. "I tol' you he could hit."

"It shows he has guts," I said. "He won't push easy on the track, and once he learns to handle a car, he'll pull purses for us."

We went back inside the garage. Ronnie was washing the car, but when he saw me coming, he dropped the hose and set himself, ready to pick up the fight where we'd left off. I walked toward him, my face grim. He closed his hands into fists.

That's the trouble with the young. They only have room for one emotion at a time. Whatever they feel, they feel all over and at once.

I reached into my pocket and got Joe's envelope. I took out a hundred-dollar bill and held it out. When Ronnie didn't reach for it, I stuck it in his pocket. "Your part of the deal," I said. "Thanks for your help."

I'd taken a couple of steps away from him when he came to life. "Ace. Wait."

I turned. His face was crimson with embarrassment. "I'm sorry I got mad, Ace."

I stared at him coldly. "That's something else you can forget," I said. "Being sorry for anything you do. It makes you soft. Now do a good job on that Buick, kid. It'll bring business."

CHAPTER 12

THE DRIVERS STARTED COMING BY FOR A SMOKE, to return a tool or
three, and to talk racing. I held court out back in the shed where the
old junk parts were piled, sitting on an old Ford block.

In the light of day, away from the track, out from under tension,
the race boys were human beings again. Most of them were in their
early twenties, nice-looking boys with good tans and muscles. But
you could tell by the way they walked and talked, and looked at a
car, that the mark of the machine was upon them.

They moved among the parts and around the cars with something of the same air as an old wrangler moving quietly and know-
ingly among horses. They belonged. They understood the wild
spirit that was imprisoned in the metal they touched. To them, a
carburetor was a living thing, with a personality unto itself, and no
more like a distributor, for instance, than a Shetland pony was like
an unbroken stallion that shared the same corral. Each part of the

machine was different and had to be handled and humored differently if it was expected to work.

And so, I sat with my tail on the warm iron seat, and the boys came by and stirred my blood with the big ladles of their talk. This was part of racing too, this sitting in the sun, swapping lies that were truths to the extent that the wish made is the deed done.

"We had a stuck valve and an hour to race time and forty miles to go. So, we loaded the old bolt onto the truck, and while Tom drove, I worked on the engine. I couldn't get the valve unstuck, so we doped her up and ran anyway. Would have won first in my heat if I hadn't blowed a hose on the sixth lap. . ."

"I had the Main at Parrtown sewed up. Could have sat there and stroked to a win. But no. I had to see if I could lap just one car. Tried too hard and spun out, and didn't win dime one. Jist couldn't stand the thought of winnin', I suppose . . ."

And so on. And on. Not much talk of big wins. We all knew who won the big ones. De Marco, Jensen, Towner . . . Mostly about almost wins, and troubles. And the frustrating, heartbreaking, backbreaking, expensive labor of putting the old bolts back together after every contest, with the hope each time that now it would run in front. Now it would win. Even if it never did.

Loren Peale showed up, dapper and nervous, accompanied by the blond, pipe-smoking Ossman. When these two came, I was having a lazy, exciting talk with Tom Rawlins, the boy who had the cam trouble, and a pug-nosed redheaded kid by the name of Red Merwin, who had won the consey the night before.

"I heard what you said last night, Ace," Peale said, finding a clean place to sit down. "It sounded mighty good. About not being tough on past accounts, I mean." He laughed guiltily. "I guess that means me, too, doesn't it? Along with the rest of the boys?"

"Depends," I said. "The arrangement I'm making with these boys, they'll give me their trade and pay off with a percentage of what they win."

Peale touched his mustache as though to make sure it still grew under his nose. "That's good enough for us, ain't it, Duke?" Ossman nodded gravely, vacantly

"It might not be good enough for me," I said. The other drivers were looking at the ground. They liked a good dogfight, but they didn't want to see a hound grovel while being whipped.

"I don't understand," Peale smiled nervously, seeming puzzled.

"Hell, man," I said, "I saw you run last night. You couldn't win enough in a season to pay for a set of used plugs."

"Well, look, Jones. Ain't I as good as the other boys?"

"You might be, but you're not now," I said. "Not after the way you ran last night. I'm running a garage, not a hobby shop." I was chopping him away from the group he wanted to stick to. He looked at the others for help, but they were looking elsewhere. A desperate, stricken look came into his eyes.

I thought he was going to cry.

"Why not me?" he finally asked. "Why? I got a right to run, don't I?"

"I've got just so much time," I said. "I can't waste any. As long as you're going to run ass-end Charley with that geek wagon of yours, I've got no time for you. When I see you in there fighting, like the rest of the boys, I'll give you the same deal."

"Others run out of the money, too!"

"They go down fighting," I said.

He sucked his upper lip between his teeth and licked his mustache. He was thinking about the beautiful coupe, and what would happen to it if he really scrambled for money. He didn't want it hurt, but he wanted to be on the track. He wanted any secrets I might have carried in from California. He wanted to come in like the others and swap lies and be one of the crowd. But he didn't want to pay the price.

I didn't like the little runt, and I liked seeing him squirm. I knew he wouldn't fight back.

"I'll try to do better, Ace," he said, making marks in the dirt with a stick. "You've got me all wrong. I can prove that. You just caught me on a night when I wasn't arcing. I've run in front, and in heavy traffic too, ain't I, Duke?"

Ossman nodded. He was thinking about something else.

Peale said, "I can't run again without some work bein' done. I'll raise the money somehow. I'll show you I ought to get the same deal as the others."

I wished Ronnie was around. I'd told him that Peale would be our first customer. Cash in hand. He'd find the money somewhere, somehow.

"Okay, Loren," I said in a friendly voice. "When you show me, I'll make you the deal."

"You were pretty rough on him," Tom Rawlins said. "The poor geek's got a lot of pride. You walked all over that."

"The hell with him," I said. "If he can't keep up, the hell with him. This is no nursery."

The others drifted off, leaving me with Toad.

"What have you got against Peale?" Toad asked, scratching his little pot belly.

"Nothing," I said. "I just don't like him. He's a phony. And if he wants to play with my toys, it'll cost him."

"He's got track fever too," Toad said. "In his own way."

"I know," I said. "That's why he'll find the money to stay in the game. When a guy gets the fever, he's a handcrafted sucker. You're doing him a favor to take his money away before he loses it."

"Mr. Jones . . . ?"

The guy in the back door of the garage was wearing a nylon cord summer suit and carrying a briefcase. At first, I thought he was Herpgruve's lawyer, but the big friendly smile on his face tipped me off to the truth. He was a salesman.

"Yeah?"

He came forward, his hand out. "I'm Jack Makin, of Western

Supply. Mrs. Richards said you were out here. I had the account when Bill was alive."

"Word gets around fast," I said to Toad.

"Yes, it does," Makin said, spreading a handkerchief to protect the seat of his pants. "And I'm certainly glad to see this place active again. A fine woman, Mrs. Richards. She deserves the best."

"Which is what you're selling," I added.

"I can see you're no stranger to Western Supply," he said smoothly. "Nothing but the best. I understand you're going after the racing trade. You'll need some equipment for that. Not to mention the hot rod kids who'll look you up if you can take care of them."

"We'll do what we can," I said.

"That won't be too much," Makin said. "I looked around inside. Pretty empty. Bill used to have a beautiful setup here, but practically everything had to come back when he was killed. I took it for granted you'd want to have as good a setup as Bill had. In fact, you can have more than that, and for less money."

I wanted to get rid of him, but I wanted to see what he had. I knew what the other garages would have, and if I wanted the speed trade, I'd need good equipment.

"I've jotted down a few essentials I think you ought to get right away," Makin continued. "Nothing fancy, but the basic tools." He opened his briefcase and took out a catalogue. He flipped the pages, and my mouth watered. What I could do with that stuff . . .

"This welding unit is a must," Makin said, marking down the item on a pad. "You're dead if you can't weld."

"That's for sure," I said.

He held the catalogue over where I could see it. "Did you ever see a nicer, cylinder-boring bar? It's a beauty. We'll have to sell you one when you're ready to take on that kind of work."

I looked at Toad. Damn it, we needed the boring bar. Otherwise, we'd have to send our blocks somewhere else and hope we got the right sizes.

"Nobody in Town with a bar like that," Makin said. "The first garage that takes it will make running expenses just on that one item alone. Town Garage might buy one, they said."

"How much for your outfit?" I asked.

"Balancing scale," Makin murmured. "This one's as accurate as a Swiss watch. Balances to one-tenth of a gram. I don't have to tell you how important it is for a racing engine to be balanced, do I, Jones?"

"Balance alone will boost an engine," I said. "I've seen an engine that was balanced to six grams rebalanced down to half a gram. Nothing else done. Picked up five miles an hour in top speed, and it ran like silk."

"Your balanced engine will last twice as long, too," Makin said. "That's a money saver." He made another notation in his book.

"What I really need," I said, "Is a valve refacing machine. What's your price on that?"

"We make the best one in the country," Makin said. "I can just see your place, Jones. You'll be getting business from all over the state. There isn't a good garage or speed shop within two hundred miles that can do a complete job for the boys. You'll have them waiting in line—if you can do the job."

I could see it. With the stuff he was showing me, I could produce beautiful racing engines. Without that stuff, all I could do was patch.

". . . even a dynamometer," Makin was saying. "That costs as much as a Cadillac, but no speed shop can really function without one. You're working in the dark unless you can check your efforts on the dynamometer."

He was right. So right.

"A soldier can't go into battle unarmed," Makin said. "That would be suicide. So would trying to run a speed shop without the tools. The only way to start is with a complete setup."

"Money," I said. "You've been showing me eight or nine thousand dollars' worth of stuff. We're busted."

"Well . . ." Makin started putting his stuff away. "I thought you were prepared to equip this place. I'll call back some other time."

"Wait a minute," I said. "You don't have to have cash for all that stuff, do you?"

"No."

"Ten percent down enough?"

"We might work out a deal," he said. "Say, ten percent down and the rest in three years. That kind of contract will cost you six percent, but . . ."

"But hell," I said. "You carry people on better terms than that."

"Only some people," Makin said, smiling. "I can take a chance with old, established customers. I know they'll make the grade. But this place went broke once, and you're a stranger to me. I can't take too great a risk. If you prove you have a going concern here, you won't have a thing to worry about. Of course, you don't need everything we discussed . . ."

"I do, and more," I said angrily. "Either you run a garage, or you don't. Come back later, will you, Makin? I need to talk this over with Mrs. Richards."

"I'll be back at three," he said pleasantly. "I'm sure you're going to have a great place here, Jones." I sat and swore after he left. Toad giggled. "Got me over a barrel," I said angrily. "We can't do a thing without some of that stuff, and we're nailed to the wall if we take on a big debt—what with everything else."

"If you're gonna run against the other garages," Toad said, "you got to get in the heavy traffic."

"You'd think they'd give us a decent break," I said.

Toad chuckled. "How does it feel to wear half of Loren Peale's mustache, Ace?"

"This is different," I snapped. "We haven't got the money to pay out for tools now."

"But you'll git it," Toad said, blinking. "You'll git it. Just like he'll get his. Somewhere."

The Hudson money was still in my pocket. The first of the easy money I was going to take out of Town. But damn it, I couldn't get people to the garage if all I had was an honest face and two bare hands. I could walk away from the balance of the debt when I left Town, but there wasn't any way around the big down payment. I had to risk that.

I sighed, thinking of the equipment I wanted to buy. With the setup I had in mind, I'd be able to do anything. They'd come to me from hundreds of miles away.

Well, if things boomed, I didn't have to run off at the end of the racing season. I might hang around through the winter, too, building my stack. I could always leave.

I walked inside the garage and looked around, mentally noting where I wanted to place the new stuff, and seeing the place jammed with cars that needed the thousand and one refinements that made them run fast. There'd be work, and talk, and the wonderful voices of engines. A good place. A snug place. Where I could do everything around a track but drive. And I wouldn't miss driving too much if I kept busy.

As long as I could be around some part of racing, I wouldn't be too restless, too isolated. Maybe, in time, I'd lose that awful urge to get behind the wheel. Maybe the tension would ease and the frenzy be forgotten. That was the only thing that could spoil my setup. If I got on the track and lead-footed myself to another freeze-out or oblivion.

I sighed and puffed on my cigarette. Ronnie was doing a beautiful job on the Buick's white sidewalls. Toad was sorting out returned tools. Sandy passed the office door and saw me. She smiled and waved.

A strange feeling sifted into my blood. At first, I didn't recognize it, and then it scared me. Contentment.

I felt the money in my pocket. I'd pay. I'd get the stuff. The mechanic in me wouldn't let me start business half-cocked. I wanted everything, and the best, if I had to patch my pants with old rubber tubes to keep out the chill night air. Another Loren Peale. I knew it. That's why I hated him.

CHAPTER 13

I LAID DOWN FIFTEEN HUNDRED BUCKS to Makin and ordered like a starving man who had just inherited a restaurant. "Here we go," I said to Sandy. "Keep your fingers crossed."

"They've been crossed," she said with a wry grin, "ever since we shook hands." Again, that strange, searching look that started out hungry and ended afraid, that made me want her and feel uneasy in the wanting.

It wasn't too bad, I figured. The deal I made with Herpgruve would bring in some good money during the racing season, and we could use that to pay on the equipment. The business we did would pay other expenses and profit. And the money we made racing would be the dessert. The only thing, I didn't quite see where I was going to build up my little fortune, but that didn't bother me either. When I had a chance to sit down and think, I'd find a way.

I borrowed Ronnie's car and found myself a room in Town. When I got back to the garage, the farmer came back for his car. When he saw it, he looked mad. "By God," he said, "I didn't order no wash job. It's costing enough—"

"That's on the house," I said.

"You washed it for free?"

"I hate to see a dirty car leave the place. Now let's take a spin before you pay. I want to be sure you're satisfied." He drove. "Handles like a dream again," he said. "And it's really clean. No complaints, mister."

He paid cash and left happy. "You're not a mechanic, Ace," Sandy said, looking at the bills in her hand. "You're a magician." She put things away neatly. "I'll see you at seven. We're having steaks."

"Roger." I patted her arm lightly as she went by, and she smiled. She was happy, and she was in my care. Maybe she had just shut her eyes and jumped, because I seemed to be holding a net. But I caught the feeling. It was like having a small, strange child confidently reaching up to take your hand while crossing the street.

When she was gone, we pushed 72 into the garage, with Ronnie helping, and started pulling the engine.

"It won't be long now," Ronnie said, grinning. "I'll blow those guys off the track."

"You guys are so smart," Toad said. "What's Sandy gonna think when she sees the engine out. She'll know something's going on."

"Had it figured," I said. "We'll lay in one of the junk engines out back and keep this hidden. By the time Ronnie's twenty-one, we'll be ready to roll."

"I hope I'm around when some of them cards fall out of your sleeve," Toad said. "You got too many tricks workin' at once."

"Shut up and get me some creep-in oil," I said. "These damn bolts are rusted on."

I'd been wondering, too, what was going to happen when Sandy found out I'd been playing the sneaky game behind her back. I was going to have to slow down and figure out some kind of yarn that I could tell her to her face, but I didn't have time to stop right then. The time would come when I'd have to talk to her, but it wasn't yet. And maybe later something would come up and make it easier. I'd figure something. I'd find some story she'd believe. I'd better.

"When can we go out to the track and practice?" Ronnie asked.

"When we get there," I said. "But I want you to learn something before you ever turn a wheel: Never feel that you have to win."

"I'm racin' because I want to win."

"I know," I said. "But never feel you have to. What I mean is, it's better to be somewhere in the money than to kill yourself trying for first. You look at drivers like de Marco and Jensen. They know when they've got a chance to win and when they ought to sit back and take a sure second or third. I want you to be like them."

"If you say so," Ronnie grumbled.

"They're fat," I said. "They run four or five times a week, and most of the time they're in the money. That adds up. The guys who need the money spin themselves off the track trying to move up one position when it can't be done because they're desperate for every buck. You won't be like that. You're going to get the driver's forty percent of what you win, and the garage will take sixty and foot all the bills. You won't need to win radiator money, gas money, or eating money. So, you'll win all kinds of money. It's the desperate guys who'll crack up. You'll be able to run fast, and hard, but you won't be missing any meals if you're beat, and you'll always have a car under you if you don't win a dime."

"I want to drive hard," Ronnie said. "I'm not scared."

"You'll drive hard," I said. "But not foolish. I don't care how many times we have to rebuild this crate because of hard driving. But you lose out doing something foolish, and I'll boot your tail right out in front of everybody."

Toad leaned over the engine as though he wanted to smell it. "Let's git the chain hoist," he grumbled. "I think we can pull her now."

"Our stuff will start coming the first of the week," I said. "Old seventy-two will be our best ad, if Ronnie, here, does his job."

We pulled the engine and lifted the dummy into its place. We examined the chunk of rusty iron that was to carry our colors.

"What do you figure on doing?" Ronnie asked.

"Increase the bore to three and three-eighths inches," I said, "and lengthen the stroke to four inches. We'll put in a track-grind cam, dual-point distributor, hot coil, big valves, and heavy-duty springs."

"That's the way most of the guys are running," Ronnie said. "I thought I'd get something special."

"You'll get what you can handle," I said. "We're putting in a Lincoln-Zephyr twenty-six-tooth transmission kit. That'll make you a bomb in first or second."

"How about high gear? Or do you want me to run in second?"

"Depends on the track, the night . . . We'll try a three-fifty-four rear end for when you run in high. If it doesn't work, we can always go four-eleven or five-something. We'll have to see. The track will tell where we're right and wrong." We looked at the block and talked about what it would need. I didn't want to modify any more than I had to in order to win. The hotter you make an engine, the trickier it is to keep it running. The point you look for is that place where reliability and performance meet, wearing their best behavior. Toad yawned and coughed. "I'm hungry. Anybody want to eat?"

I looked at my watch. "Oh, God damn!" I said. "It's half past seven. Sandy was expecting me at seven. The damn steaks will be burnt to a crisp."

Ronnie looked at me with a heavy expression settling on his young face. "You had a date with my brother's wife?"

"We're celebrating the partnership with steaks," I said. "Or we were going to . . . Maybe I'd better call and tell her I can't. Didn't know time was getting away like that. Damn racing engines anyway."

I looked down at myself. Dirty. Smeared with grease and rust and dirt. T-shirt a mess, pants worse. Filthy, sweaty, dirty.

"She's seen dirty mechanics come in late before," Toad said. I turned to Ronnie. "Give me your keys. I'll figure an excuse on the way over."

"I need the car tonight."

"Son," I said, "you are Mr. Toad's assistant tonight. That drive shaft has to be straightened, and the spider gear in the differential welded so you can have a real professional locked rear end. Give me the keys, boy."

He handed them over. "You coming back?"

"Yeah," I said, looking him in the eye. "When I'm through. Now do what Toad says. It's all being done for you, and I want you to know what you've got under you."

He lowered his head and turned away angrily. He didn't want me to see Sandy at her house, but he'd held his fire. Maybe he was learning to take orders. Let him be mad. And let him take it out on the track, the way I used to. Only I'd be around to see that he didn't make my mistakes.

Before I left the garage, I ducked into the office and called Sandy. "It's Ace," I said contritely when she answered. "I'm awfully sorry, Sandy. But we had an emergency repair come in just as I was getting ready to leave."

I waited. She didn't answer.

"I thought it would only take a minute," I said. "But we had a little trouble. I wouldn't have stayed, but this is our first day, and I hated to turn anybody away . . ."

I stopped again and waited for her to say something. She did. "Are you going to talk all night or are you coming over?"

"You aren't mad, Sandy?"

"Of course I am," she said, without sounding angry. "But you might as well come over."

"Sandy, I'll have some good news for you when I show up."

"I'll try to have a decent dinner for you."

"Be over in a couple of minutes. Bye."

"Goodbye." The phone clicked as she put it on the hook. She hadn't sounded mad, but very cool and distant.

I drove to my room, washed quickly, and put on a fresh under-shirt under my jacket. My last clean one. On the way to Sandy's, I figured out how to break the good news.

The good news was that we were getting half of Herpgruve's net take at the track. She'd want to know why he was suddenly so generous, and I wanted to have a good story for her. Something that would make me look good. I'd spin her some kind of yarn about how I'd shamed the man into coming across. She might not like the idea of the way I'd forced him to give. Any story that would make me out as her guardian angel would do. Funny. Herpy getting her husband killed and paying for it now. That was life.

By the time I reached Sandy's house, I had a story figured. A sort of modern version of St. George and the dragon, with me on the horse. I turned in at Sandy's drive and braked just behind a familiar-looking green Olds hardtop.

Herpgruve's car.

CHAPTER 14

HERPGRUVE WAS DEEP IN AN EASY CHAIR, his feet resting on a hassock and crossed at the ankles. He looked at home. We exchanged grunts, and I turned to Sandy. She was wearing an apron over her dress. I was prepared to find her angry, but she was self-possessed and gracious.

"I suppose dinner's ruined," I said. "Steak dried, salad wilted. I'm really sorry, Sandy—"

"Nothing's ruined," she said. "I learned from living with Bill that the time to start broiling the steak was when he came in the door. You mechanics are all alike."

"That makes me feel better," I said. I looked at Herpgruve filling the easy chair, sucking on his cigar. I was afraid Sandy would ask what the good news was while he was around, and that would queer my story. I wondered what in hell he was doing there anyway.

"I dropped by the garage to see you, Jones," Herpgruve said. "They told me you were coming here, so I drove over."

I sat down on the couch and picked at a platter of hors d'oeuvres that were on the cocktail table. Herpgruve had already been at them.

"You didn't have to," I said.

Sandy came in from the kitchen carrying a tray with a bottle of Scotch, one of bourbon, a bowl of ice cubes, and glasses.

"Well . . . Sandy," Herpgruve said. He sounded surprised. "I didn't know you drank."

I looked at his lapel, but didn't see his pin for perfect attendance at Sunday school. I couldn't figure him. He actually looked shocked.

"More of Bill's estate," Sandy said. "They haven't been touched since he—I don't know what you take, Ace, but I took it for granted it would be on the rocks. Bill always—"

"Bourbon," I said. "And you're right about the rocks. Herpgruve?"

"Scotch. Just a drop." I poured the drinks. Herpgruve and I presented glasses. "To the success of Ace and Sandy's Garage," he said. We drank on it. It was my turn. "To the continued prosperity of Town Raceways."

Sandy looked at us, smiling. "Can I tell Ace now?" she asked Herpgruve. "I can't keep a secret."

"If you want to," Herpgruve said, settling back in his chair, glass in hand and face red.

Sandy sat beside me on the couch. Her eyes were shining. "Ace, before you tell me your good news, I'll tell mine."

"Yeah?" I said cautiously.

You can't imagine what Herbert is going to do for us."

I looked at Herbert. He was staring at the ceiling, his lips smiling around his cigar.

"What?" I asked, wondering how much he had told her. "Well, you know how much the drivers owe the garage. And you know how hard it would be to get any of that money."

I forced a smile. "I know . . ."

"Well, Herbert is going to assume their debt to us!"

"That's mighty generous of you, Mr. Herpgruve," I said.

"It's my way of helping a friend," Herpgruve said. "An old . . . and . . . dear . . . friend."

"Herbert and I have known each other since we were in kindergarten," Sandy said. "He's always been a very good friend to me . . . and Bill."

"Two of my favorite people," Herpgruve said. "Although I guess it's no secret that you've always been my very favorite person, Sandy."

I broke in. "That's a pretty big debt, Mr. Herpgruve. Not that I don't appreciate what you're doing. But it's quite an obligation . . . How do you figure on handling it?"

"When Bill Richards was alive," Herpgruve said, his voice thick with sentiment, "he did more for racing than any other man in the state. Not only was he a fine driver, he was a fine man. He helped others, and by helping them, he helped me maintain the track. I figure l owe him something."

Herpgruve stood up and took a folded paper from his pocket. "Sandy," he continued, "I've wanted to do something like this ever since Bill died. But when it looked like you were losing the garage, I knew you'd think I was trying to give you charity, and you'd be too proud to accept—even from me."

Sandy bowed her head, her lips tight. I silently cursed Herpgruve clear back to the monkeys. The clever bastard.

"And now, Sandy, that you have a good partner, and the garage is a going concern again, I'm making my offer. As I said, if you and Mr. Jones are willing, I'll assume the drivers' debts and pay you a percentage of the track profits until that debt is wiped out."

Sandy lifted her head as though to speak, but Herpgruve motioned her to keep silent. "Wait, Sandy. Believe me, I'm not acting unselfishly. The better your garage operates, the better races well have, and I'll not suffer financially or any other way."

Herpgruve moved toward the door. "I'll leave you two alone now," he said gruffly. "You can talk it over and decide what you want to do. I've held up your dinner long enough."

Sandy went to the door with him. I heard her saying, "Herbert, you *are* a good friend. I don't know how to thank you . . . This means so much to us."

They were silent for a moment. I poured a couple of fingers of bourbon into my glass, listening for the sound of lips on the porch.

"Is our date still on for tomorrow night?" Herpgruve's voice was loud enough for me to hear him. Sandy may have nodded her agreement, because the next sound was Herpgruve's contented voice saying, "Fine. I'll pick you up at eight. Night."

"Good night, Herbert. And thanks."

Sandy came bouncing back, excited and happy. "Isn't he wonderful to do that? Herbert's like that. He always was unselfish and thoughtful. He asked me to marry him once, but when I married Bill instead, Herbert sent us the most expensive wedding present of all. And now this."

She gave me the paper Herpgruve had taken from his pocket. A nice little document, all legal. In it, he assumed the debt, and Sandy agreed to let it be paid off by taking 25 percent of the net profits of the track. And also agreed not to take any action against the delinquent drivers as long as the agreement was in force. Herpgruve had signed, and there was a place for Sandy to sign. A place for me, too, as a witness.

"I thought ten percent would be enough," Sandy said. "But Herbert insisted on twenty-five. That's the way he is."

"Did he tell you how much twenty-five percent would average?"

"I didn't ask," Sandy said. "It didn't seem the thing to do. Being critical of a gift. I didn't say anything this afternoon, but I was worried when you ordered so much equipment from Western Supply. I didn't know how you could ever pay for it. And now Herbert has come to our rescue.

And seeing her there, her eyes shining because of another man, I knew a piece of the truth. This house, this room, this woman were what I had been searching for. She wasn't like the others, like Thelma. This was a different breed. This was the ever-loving wife type.

Damn Herbert!

"What was yours?" Sandy asked. "I've been so excited by Herbert's offer. I didn't give you a chance to tell me."

"Tell you?"

"The good news you mentioned over the phone."

I was too disgusted to think up a good lie. "It was just a couple of phone calls from people who wanted their cars fixed. I thought it sounded pretty big—before Herbert showed up."

I looked at my watch. "It's pretty late, Sandy. Maybe we'd better forget dinner. Tomorrow night—"

"There'll be another emergency," Sandy said firmly. "Come on in the kitchen and help me. We can talk while I work."

She took hold of my hand and towed me into the kitchen, taking me over easily, confidently. On her home ground, she was in complete control. But the familiarity of her gesture surprised me. It went with some of the warm looks she'd given me, but it didn't go with the freeze-ups that followed them. I knew I was stimulated physically by her. I wondered if I had the same effect on her. Whether I did or not, one thing was sure, and it made me sore.

She was a collector, just like the rest of them. She had Herbert on one string, and she wanted me on another. I followed her into the kitchen, thinking dirty thoughts about her. The more she attracted me, the more I fought against the feeling. Falling in love made a sucker out of a guy. It made him soft. And when you were soft, you could be hurt. Don't be fooled by the apron, the soft eyes, and the clean look. There was a way to do it. Go after her. Take her, and prove to yourself she's no good. Then you won't fall in love. You won't go soft.

She was at the counter, her back toward me. She was humming while she worked. I watched her thighs and hips move as she shifted her weight from one foot to the other. I put down my glass and walked across the kitchen, not stopping until I was pressing against her back. I put my arms around her, one hand on her belly, the other cupping a breast.

She didn't move. She'd known it was coming, the bitch. She said calmly, "I wouldn't do that to a person with a knife in her hand."

"Wouldn't you?" I pressed her against the counter.

She rested her hands on the counter and waited, like somebody waiting for a bus, as though unaware of my hands. As though I was still across the room. The lack of reaction made me feel like a fool. I relaxed my grip and eased off the pressure of my body. I didn't know what to do. "You're holding up the french fries, Ace."

Domestic. A domestic who wrote grocery lists in bed and broke off a kiss to complain about the price of onions. Who made you self-conscious and ashamed. This was as bad as the other. Worse to fall in love with.

I let go of her and moved away, going after my drink again. Damned if I understood her. Damned if I did. Or myself. She wasn't a pushover. In a way, I was glad, but I knew it could ruin my big ideas about being nobody's man but my own.

CHAPTER 15

AFTER THE WAY I'D LAID HANDS ON SANDY in the kitchen, dinner was an awkward meal. My palms wouldn't forget the feel of her, and I was afraid she'd see what I felt if she looked in my eyes. So, I sat behind my steak like an adolescent, with my head down, trying to remember to keep my elbows off the table and to chew with my mouth closed.

The noise of the knife and fork was like thunder. I sneaked a look at Sandy. She was sitting very properly, her eyes downcast, eating daintily. Once we both reached at the same time for the salt. Our fingers bumped, and we both blushed and made a big to-do about giving it to the other first.

I began to feel better with the coffee when I could smoke. I tried to keep the talk professional.

"You should have asked Herpgruve for fifty percent," I said.

"That wouldn't be fair," she said. "I couldn't do that."

"I could. If it wasn't for your place, his track would have folded. We're bringing him back to life."

"I don't know," Sandy said. "I think it was very dangerous of him to offer twenty-five percent. He didn't have to."

"Why do you think he made the offer?"

"To help us. It isn't the first time—"

"Come down to earth," I said. "He offered twenty-five because he knew we could have got fifty. That's what he ought to give. That's what I'd have made him give. But he came sneaking around here with that miserable offer of twenty-five, and you grabbed it."

"You didn't say anything when I did."

"You had me outnumbered," I said. "The way you were falling all over yourself to thank him. I didn't have a chance. The cheap slug. He's just trying to make himself look like a big shot for your benefit."

Sandy had been looking irritated, but suddenly she was sure about what was eating me, and it brought a little teasing smile to her lips and a devilish glint to her eyes. "I suppose you could be right," she said. "But isn't that a natural way for a man to act with the girl he wants to marry?"

"If he's such a great guy," I said, "why don't you marry him? What are you waiting for?"

"I might," she said coolly, enjoying herself. "I could do worse than marry Herbert. He'd be kind, and thoughtful, and generous, and he'd be home at night. On time for meals . . ."

"That's not love," I said.

"That's a strange word coming from you. I thought you didn't believe in love. You told me people were no good. If that's true, how could they love?"

I looked at her steadily. "Love isn't something you have to be good to get," I said. "It isn't something you make up your mind about. It makes up your mind for you. Sometimes in a hurry."

She wouldn't meet my look. She stared at her coffee cup and played with the spoon. "I married for love once. Where did it get me? I didn't have a husband or a home. The broad shoulders I liked were always on the garage floor, under a car."

"A husband has to work," I said. "And that's the garage business."

"That's the *racing* business," Sandy said. "That's why I hated it. That's why I would never go to the tracks to see Bill race. It would have been like going along to hold his coat while he made love to another woman."

"Racing takes up your time," I said. "You can't run if your car isn't racing."

"A rival is a rival," Sandy said, coloring slightly. "It doesn't matter why your husband prefers someone—or something—else over you. He does. You're jealous. And jealous women do terrible things."

"Jealous men, too," I said.

And there we sat, each with a sharp tooth from the past gnawing at us. Silent, uneasy, and guilty.

"I wasn't happy," Sandy said abruptly. "I loved Bill, but I wasn't happy. It was worse than being married to a doctor. At least a doctor has a worthwhile reason for giving up his personal life. But to be neglected for a car! If I didn't feel well, Bill was annoyed. But let somebody's filthy engine cough once, and he'd stay up all night to make it well again. Cars always came first in our lives. And Bill was willing to sacrifice everything to them. The garage, me, even himself."

"Why'd you marry a guy like that?" I asked.

"I loved him."

"But if you knew what he was like—"

"It was different before we were married. Then it seemed daring, and dangerous. Life in Town wasn't very exciting. It's a very dull place to grow up in. Bill seemed to be what every girl is looking for. Romantic, reckless . . . It seemed wonderful from the outside looking in."

"So you picked him over Herbert," I said, smiling. "That was the first time," she said, looking at my shoulder.

"I didn't know any better. So, I wasn't happy with Bill, even though I loved him. Maybe I could be happy with Herbert, even though I don't."

"If Bill made you unhappy, how come you kept the garage open? Why didn't you get rid of it? Hating it the way you did—and do, I guess."

Maybe I was wrong, but the way I saw it, Sandy was letting me know where I stood. That I was the kind of guy she fell in love with, but this time she was afraid. Once bitten . . . It was almost funny. Two of us with the same fear.

"I—have a reason for keeping the garage," Sandy said. There was a faraway look in her eyes, and a downward curve of pain at the corners of her mouth. Like she was fighting something that had her whipped.

I thought I had it figured anyway. A mixture of morbid romantic feelings and guilt. Probably sorry because she'd been mean to Bill, and trying to make it up to him by keeping his name alive. Guilty because she hadn't been happy. Ashamed of hating him. Feeling it strongly now, because I looked like another Bill, maybe, and she didn't want to add another sin.

"Well . . ." Sandy said, shaking off the dark mood. "Now you know all about me. What about you? I'll get you some hot coffee, and then you tell me all about yourself."

"Not much to tell," I said. "I'm just another track hound. Or was."

She filled my cup, standing close to me. I wanted to lean my head against her hip. Just lean—and talk.

"You really want to know?"

"I'd like to. Since we are partners. And—I know from the way Bill felt, and what I've seen of you, that you live for racing too. How could you quit? Bill said he wanted to, but he couldn't. How could you?"

"I had to."

"Oh?"

"I might as well tell you. It isn't a very pretty story."

"If you want to."

"I want to," I said. "I used to be a pretty good driver: made all the big tracks. Won my share of the purses. It was—you know—it was my life. That was all I wanted. To be a good driver, and learn, and move up to bigger and bigger races. I was really on my way, too. I'd have had one of the favorite cars in the Mexican Road Race this fall if it hadn't been for—her."

"A girl," Sandy said, half to herself.

"I married her. She wasn't like you. She couldn't cook or anything. I guess I didn't care when I married her. I didn't care what she could do outside of the bed."

Sandy's color deepened.

"It's that kind of a story," I said. "Maybe you'd rather not hear it."

"I've been married," Sandy said. "You won't shock me, if that's what you're worried about."

I rubbed my chin nervously. "Her name was Thelma," I said. "She was good in bed. Too good."

Sandy's eyelashes flickered slightly at that, but she was looking to one side of me. Giving me a chance. And I told her. Told her about Thelma, the tall, full-busted girl with the big blue eyes, a big, soft mouth, and blonde hair so light it looked almost white. She went in for tanned shoulders and strapless dresses. She got her tan in bed too, from a lamp.

I'd met her at a track, of course. She'd come down to the pits after a race with some friends, to look at the winner's car. It happened that I won that night. I'd given her the only look I had left in my eyes, and she liked it. She asked a few silly questions, and I gave her a few silly answers. But all I saw was that tall, willowy body rippling under the soft material of her dress. The big blue eyes and the big, soft, red mouth.

Flashy, and I liked it. Walk with her and you heard neck bones creak ten thousand to a mile. Everybody looked at her. Everybody wanted her. God knows how, but I got her.

We lived in bed. Love affected her the way crackerjacks are supposed to. The more she got, the more she wanted. And I thought I was lucky. I used to hear some of the other guys bitch about their wives being cold, and I'd smile and feel sorry for them. The one I had couldn't do enough for me enough times.

I was happy. I raced a lot and won a lot. And what I won, I took home and gave to Thelma. I wanted her to spend the money on herself, and she did. And we lived such a crazy damn life, always on the jump, that we were happy if all we had was a room with a bed and enough to buy hamburgers once in a while.

Yeah. Life was good. I even thought it was funny when I had to back off on the passion. What with the long and crazy hours, the strain of racing, and the lack of food, there were times when she called my number and I was stalled in the pits.

It wouldn't have been so bad, maybe, but I was riding high, and I had to brag about my blonde mill. Kid the boys who were having a hard time with the old lady and purring in public because mine was always revved and ready to go. I thought they were hard losers when they tried to talk about something else. I didn't know they were trying to make it easy for me.

I found out the night I was supposed to be running on an out-of-town track. Thelma was staying home. She didn't like to make the short jumps that meant being on the road and the track all night. I wasn't due back until morning, but a couple of miles out of town, a guy ran into me. It wasn't a bad smash, but too bad to run on the track. I turned around and drove home.

I walked in and found out why Thelma didn't mind if I wasn't always in shape to wrestle. She wasn't missing any. She liked it. That's what I'd told the boys. One of them (at least) could swear in court that I wasn't a liar.

Things went to hell after that. I said I forgave her, and nobody was an angel, and anybody could make one mistake, and we stayed together. But it didn't work. Whenever I saw the guy on the track I chose him. I smashed him up again and again, at the cost of running out of the money. I got so I was afraid to leave town if Thelma wasn't with me. I made her go along, and she was miserable. My driving got worse, my cars got worse, and I got wilder. Home life was just as bad.

I got that far, and I had to quit. I didn't know how long I'd been talking. Both Sandy and I had built a mound of cigarette butts in the ashtrays in front of us. The coffee was gone. The leftover food on the plates had turned cold, and the beef juice had hardened to lumps of fat. We didn't care. Not now. Now Sandy had been inside me like no other human on earth had ever been. I'd taken her further than I'd even gone by myself.

But it wasn't the end.

"Did you leave her?" Sandy asked.

I shook my head. "She finally ran off with some other guy. I divorced her and tried to forget her, but she'd made too big a fool out of me. That was the part I couldn't take. I got to thinking all the guys at the tracks were laughing at me behind my back, and I hated them.

"And when I was in a race, I'd still look for Thelma. And when she wasn't there, it would be more than I could take. I didn't drive to win anymore. I drove to smash people. I didn't care who. I didn't care what happened to me. Pretty soon, the other guys wouldn't race if I was on the track. I got ruled off the tracks. So, I got in my car and headed east, without knowing where I was going or what I was going to do when I got there. And here I am."

I didn't add the last thought in my mind. Here I am in Town, with a homey, brown-haired girl feeding me a steak dinner, and wanting to fall in love with her—and afraid to—because I was afraid it would all happen again, and I couldn't take it twice.

"So, you see why I won't race," I said, trying to make a humorous thing of it. "There's no place to go except around."

Sandy gave me the look I wanted. Tender, understanding, as though she would like to put her arms around me and comfort me.

And that's what I wanted. How I wanted it! She stood up, and I thought she was coming to me, but she picked up a couple of plates and asked, in what seemed to me a weary voice, if I would help her dry the dishes.

We didn't speak, except in the line of duty. But I knew what I felt about her, and what I had to do about it. I had to prove that this nice girl was no good, so I wouldn't fall in love and have her make a fool of me, too. I had to prove that everything, everybody was rotten and mean. That way I'd never be tempted to trust anybody, or like anybody, and I wouldn't get taken again. Nobody would ever be able to laugh at me behind my back again because I was a sucker.

But as Sandy moved about me, and the comfort began to seep into my bones, I wanted to hope. I'd made a pass at her, and she'd been cold. Like the wives the drivers had complained about. That was good. If she was cold, she wouldn't be easy. She wouldn't need too much. We could be friends, live together on steaks and bourbon, make love once in a while, and be happy, and build racing engines.

Comfort, quiet, ease. A home to live in. A place to hang your hat. The same place every night. A place in the world. With someone you could trust, because she could leave sex alone. Someone safe. Never make a fool out of you. No flash here. No teasing hip swing and strapless dress. No baby-blue eyes and hungry red mouth. Just a normal, attractive, pleasant American girl, who would let her man schedule the sex.

Safe . . . Safe . . .

The dishes were done, and we seemed to turn to one another at the same time with the same feeling of accomplishment. I was going to say, something like "Glad that's over," and I think Sandy was too. But instead we moved together, as though we had rehearsed the scene a hundred times, and my arms were around her, and our lips were together.

When finally I lifted my head to look tenderly into her face, I was jolted by her expression. It wasn't love, or tenderness, or passion, but a wild, lost look. There was fear in her wide eyes, and she breathed quickly and unevenly, like a frantic, trapped animal. Her body trembled against mine, but I held her fast.

"Please, Ace . . ."

"Sandy . . ."

"No, Ace . . . *No.*"

"Oh, Sandy . . ."

My lips were against hers again, and she kissed and struggled and whimpered hungrily and fearfully, and when I relaxed my arms, she was shedding the tears I had tried for too soon the day before.

"Sandy . . . Don't cry . . ."

She was talking to herself in broken, gasping phrases. "Not again . . . I can't . . . can't . . ."

"It won't be the same, Sandy."

"It will be. I know. I know."

She broke away suddenly, trying to regain control of herself. Trying to be prim. "We're being childish, Ace. Let's go in the living room and sit down and act like grown people. This is . . . silly."

I crossed to her and took her in my arms again. I could feel her body go rigid to hold me off.

"Sandy . . ."

"Leave me alone!"

She broke free again and ran from me. I followed her. She went into her bedroom and tried to close the door, but I held it open with my foot and went in after her. She retreated to the side of the bed. I went to her, shaking like a leaf.

She watched me come with stricken eyes. "Go away," she said, her voice breaking. "Please . . . please go away."

I put my arms around her again and tried to kiss her. She turned her face away. Her body felt like a board. I put my right arm around her neck and forced her to turn her face toward me, and held her head locked inside my elbow. Slowly, I bent to kiss her closed eyes, and the tears that flowed from them. There was a look of pain and weariness on her face as I moved my lips to hers. They were tight, unresponsive. Her body had turned to stone.

We swayed against the bed, and she fought to keep her feet. We went down sideways, and I held her as tight as I could, still kissing her stiff lips.

Her lips relaxed. She gave a long, shuddering sigh, and then her mouth was hungry against mine. I strained toward her, over her. Her leg nearest me moved toward me, the other spread away, and her body moved up to meet mine, and her arms pulled me down to her.

"Sandy . . . I love you." I put my lips against her ear. "I love you . . ."

She answered in the voice of a woman. "Are you going to talk all night . . ."

— — —

I lay on the bed and smoked in the semidarkness. Sandy next to me, on her back, her hair dark on the pillow. Her eyes were closed, but her face was relaxed. There was a faint smile on her lips. I looked at her and traced the outline of her white body with my hand. She sighed softly and moved her body toward me. I pulled back my hand.

"Ace, honey . . ." Her voice was silky, sleepy.

"Yeah?"

"I was just thinking. It's kind of strange, isn't it?"

"What is, Sandy?"

Her voice was almost childlike in the darkness. "You were looking for something and I was waiting for something . . . you were looking for me and I was waiting for you. All the time. Don't you think so?"

"It could be."

"We've both been very lonely. I didn't think you had been— until you told me about . . . her. Now we won't be lonely anymore, will we?"

"Never again."

"I'm afraid, though. Afraid I'll be . . . neglected again."

"We have to try to forget our ghosts," I said. "I'm not Bill, and you're not Thelma. We can't let them ruin our lives. We're us."

Sandy sighed and turned her head away. Then she made a sound that sounded like a giggle. "Ace . . ."

"Yeah, honey?"

"Isn't it nice we don't have to get up and do the dishes?"

Somehow, that chilled me. It made me wonder if she had planned it this way all along. If I'd been trapped. Suddenly, I wanted to get out of the bed. I was scared.

I looked at her lying naked and unashamed beside me. Two days. That's all it had taken. Two days. I could have done it in one if I'd tried. This was the wife type I'd figured to be hard to get. The kind who didn't demand too much, who waited. Two days!

I looked at the sprawled legs, the firm belly, and the round breasts. Who else knew what she looked like at this moment? Ronnie? Herpgruve? I sucked on the cigarette and felt sick to think of Herpgruve knowing. But it figured. It figured. It had been a year since Bill had been killed, and she hadn't been without a man for a year. She *couldn't* have been. Not a woman who had feelings as strong as hers.

One woman had been a flashy teaser, and one was a clear-eyed, modest widow who blushed. But they were the same. The same.

I ground out the cigarette. Why hadn't she fought me off? Why hadn't she made me leave? Why did she have to give in?

I jumped when the phone rang. I reached for it, but Sandy took it from me, lying across me as she talked. She put her hand over the mouthpiece. "It's Toad," she said. "He wants you."

I took the phone. "Yeah?"

"Joe's here with your Hudson," Toad said. He shouted in the phone as though trying to chase it away.

"Kick him out."

"Cain't," Toad said. "He's gonna race tomorrow."

"What? He can't do that. That mill will blow up on him if he tries to run it. He's crazy. Why didn't he tell me he was going to do that? I wouldn't have let him drive away with the engine the way it is."

"He's gonna run," Toad said. "Want to come down and see what you can do for him?"

Sandy was still lying across me. She started rocking her body gently.

"Damn it, Toad—!"

"I know, Ace. What should I tell him?"

"We can't let him run this way."

"I know that, Ace."

"I'll be down."

Sandy's body was still. I hung up and lay back.

"What is it, Ace?"

"Some guy's broken down. We're the only place in town with a light. Toad wants me to come down now."

"Are you going?"

"I . . . said I would."

"You couldn't let the man wait, like the other garages do."

"We need the business," I said.

"I suppose so."

She rolled off me. I got out of bed and stood up.

"Ace . . ."

I looked at her. Her eyes were bright. She reached out and put her hands against my hip bones. "Can't you wait a little while?"

I stared at her. That was the way Thelma had looked. The same wet glow in the eyes, the same hungry mouth, the same demanding hands and body.

I pulled away. "I have to go, Sandy. It's important."

"Important." Her voice sounded suddenly dull. "Important. I'm not important."

"Don't be greedy, Sandy. I'll be back again."

"Don't be greedy," she said in a hard, angry voice. "Why shouldn't I be greedy? Why not? Do you know how long I've waited? Even before Bill died, it was like living alone . . . Why shouldn't I be greedy? I've been starved!"

"God, Sandy," I said shakily. "What do you think I am? I'm no kid anymore. I'm not Ronnie."

"*What?*" She didn't shout it. It came out low, like a whispered scream.

"I'm not fifteen years younger," I said.

"I heard what you said," she answered in that same low, shuddering voice.

"I didn't mean anything." I was annoyed with her. I was trying to figure out what we could do to get Joe in shape to run on a track.

"I know what you meant. You said you wanted to marry me, and you could say a thing like that."

"You're human," I said. "What do you want me to think? How do I know you made it any harder for the others than you did for me? You seem to like Herbert so much. How do I know . . ."

She didn't say anything. She rolled over on her stomach and cried into the pillow.

When I was dressed, I lit another cigarette. I was beginning to be sorry for what I had said. And seeing her still uncovered, still beautiful, I was sorry I had promised Toad I would come down. But damn it, you couldn't let a man go into a race with a lousy engine!

I went out without saying goodbye. I closed the bedroom door and turned off the lights in the house before I left. For all I knew, Herpgruve might come back, and if he saw a light, he'd come in. And the way Sandy was feeling, it would be easier for Herpgruve than it had been for me. If it hadn't already been.

I got in Ronnie's car and tore out of the neighborhood, flooring the car between every shift. So, I'd proved it. I'd proved that Sandy was another Thelma. That she could be had. And wrecked my own dream doing it. God damn her anyway! Why did she have to give in so easy? Why did she have to like love?

CHAPTER 16

THE NEXT MORNING, SANDY AND I were formal enough to satisfy Ronnie, if he noticed. I gave her a good morning and a smile, but there was no emotion in her response. She acknowledged that I was alive and had spoken, and that was all.

I didn't have time to worry about it right then, because we were getting busy. We were getting town trade, and that would be good. I scheduled the work, got Toad busy, and had Ronnie start his car-washing routine. Evidently, word about that had spread, and it was paying off.

Herb Herpgruve was in early. Toad and I were looking over a car in for a tune-up job when Herpgruve came in. I tried to look at him through Sandy's eyes. He wasn't attractive, but he was younger than I had first thought, not quite as fat, and he dressed well. He had the solid citizen look. I had seen pretty girls with uglier husbands.

Herpgruve acted more cheerful than he should have. There was nothing for him to cheer about because we were going to get 25 percent of his net—even if it was better for him than paying out fifty. Maybe he looked happy because I showed that I was miserable.

"Morning, Jones . . . Toad. Sandy sign that paper?"

"Yeah. She's got it."

He rocked back on his heels. "I brought your share of the loot over."

"Give it to Sandy," I said. "It's her department."

"Thought you might like to see the check, Jones." He grinned.

"Let's see it."

He took it from his pocket and handed it to me. "You'll have to take it and like it. You can't shut down on my cars now."

I looked at the check. Twenty-seven dollars!

"Come on, give," I said. "You're holding out."

He shook his head, his face red with triumph. "You can look at the books. After expenses and what I have to set aside to pay the bank—what did you expect, Jones? This isn't Indianapolis."

What had I expected? I didn't know. A couple of hundred, probably. From the size of the crowd. I'd been counting on that money to pay Western Supply. But at this rate, I'd go bust faster than Bill had. I was hooked. My own money gone, and now this—twenty-seven dollars.

"You were pretty cute in my office," Herpgruve said. "Only I was cuter. I knew what was coming."

I looked at Toad. He couldn't have told. I hadn't told him what I planned.

"Not Toad," Herpgruve said. "Bill. Bill was all set to pull the same deal. I could see it coming a mile away when you walked in my office."

"Okay," I said. "So, you knock me out of business. You might get Sandy that way, but it won't help you at the track if the boys can't run."

"They'll run," Herpgruve said, his smile becoming broader. "And you'll help them. You said you could build up business at the track, Jones. I want to see how. I'm doing all right on my cut from the track, but yours is pretty thin. If you want to keep your head above water, you'll have to fill the stands for me. But that's your problem, not mine. It's up to you to build attendance. I'll watch you and collect seventy-five percent of the net for my trouble."

"And if I flop, and we go busted here, you'll stand by to catch Sandy," I said. "Very neat. You couldn't persuade her to quit and marry you, so you'll get at her through me."

"She'll see how unreliable you are before long," Herpgruve said. "When things go to hell under you the same way they did with Bill, she'll have had enough of your kind."

"Don't be too sure they'll go to hell," I said grimly.

Herpgruve laughed. He really was amused. "They've already started to go, Jones," he said genially. "You're just another guy with track fever. You won't last. You'll never make a buck without spending two to get it. Just like the others."

There wasn't a damn thing I could say to him. He was whipping me, and I had to take it.

"You thought you were pretty cute," he said. "Thought you'd sail into a hick town and take the citizens for a ride. But we're not all rubes. Some of us could see you coming from a long way off. See you later . . . partner."

Herpgruve chuckled and went into the office. I started after him. Toad giggled. I grabbed him. "Damn you, Toad," I said, "why didn't you tell me Herpgruve and Sandy were old friends?"

Toad looked at me with a faint, ironical grin on his gray lips. "You're the only stranger in this town," he said. "What made you think none of the others had met?"

"So, I can't even trust you," I said bitterly. Toad reached for one of my cigarettes. He made it an insolent gesture. "You come here," Toad said, putting the cigarette behind his ear, "and you got a knife in everybody's back before your hoss has stopped sweatin'. You got about eighteen different schemes goin' at once to screw forty-seven people. How do I know I ain't one of them?"

"You know better than that, you miserable old shite-poke," I said.

"Don't call me no names," Toad said. "I don't know nothing about you at all, Mr. Jones. Only that you can tell an awful lot of lies to anybody who'll stop and listen, and your intentions is about as honorable as a rattlesnake's. I don't care what kind of a mess you get in with Herpgruve or any of the drivers. But I was a friend to Bill, and am to Ronnie and Sandy, and I don't like to see strangers come in and make them sad. Or do 'em harm. That makes me mad, and when I git mad, somebody gits hurt."

I sat down on an old box and lit a cigarette. What a mess to get in, and two days doing it. I felt alone. More alone than I had ever been. Toad had been the last straw.

"I ain't hurting any of your friends," I said roughly. "You know that."

"I know the phone's in the bedroom," Toad said. "And you was right there to take it from her."

I looked up at him. He was angry. "I asked her to marry me."

"Uh-huh. Before or after?"

I didn't have an answer. There was no way to explain something I didn't understand myself. Why I had to degrade Sandy so I could hate her—when I wanted to love her—if anyone was hurt, it was me.

Herpgruve burst out of the office and headed toward us. His fat face was beet red, his body puffed with indignation. "Jones," he yelled. "I want to talk to you!" His voice shook. I looked around for a wrench. Toad stood where he was. Ronnie turned off his hose and drifted toward us, wondering what was up.

Herpgruve stopped in front of me. He was trembling; his eyes bulged. "What the hell did you do to Sandy?" he demanded hoarsely.

"What the hell are you talking about?" He pointed toward the office.

"She's in there crying. I want to know why!"

"Ask her," I said. "She's crying."

I thought he was going to swing, but the tremor passed. "Sandy's my friend, Jones," he said in his gravelly voice. "I've known Sandy a long time. I don't like to see her cry. What did you do to make her cry?"

"Well, for crying in the tank," I said. "What the hell's going on here? Every time I turn around, somebody's jumping me about Sandy. She's a grown woman. If she's got any beefs, she'll bring 'em to me herself." I spoke to Toad. "Who's the mayor of this place—King Arthur? I never saw so many guys who made a business of aiding maidens in distress."

Herpgruve stood where he was, big legs spread. He still wanted to tear into me, but he didn't know how to start. "I'm warning you, Jones," he said. "If any hurt comes to Sandy, I'll . . ."

"You'll what?"

He lowered his head. "I'll get you, Jones. So help me, if it's the last thing on earth I do, I'll get you."

"Thanks for the warning," I said. "It's more than Bill had."

"What!"

I'd forgotten about Ronnie. He stumbled forward in rubber boots, a wild look on his face. Herpgruve stepped back.

"Nothing," I snapped. "Bill got his in a hurry. You know that. There's nothing for you to get excited about."

Ronnie looked from me to Herpgruve and back to me again. "What's this about Sandy? Why's she crying?"

"Another county heard from," I said in disgust.

"Why's she crying?" Ronnie repeated.

"Ask her!" I shouted. "I don't know why women cry. They cry because they're sad or happy or bored or—because they're women."

Herpgruve gave me a last sullen look. "Remember what I said, Jones. I like that kid. You be careful around her." He turned and walked away, and there was dignity in his fat-rumped waddle. Herbert Herpgruve, protector of innocent womanhood. God! This *was* a small town.

I turned to Ronnie. "Come on, kid, get the cars washed!"

"What was Herpgruve talking about?"

"None of your business," I said. "Now get busy." I lowered my voice. "We've got a lot of work to do on seventy-two tonight. I want you on that track as fast as we can get you there."

"Okay, Ace. Okay." He clumped back to his work and picked up the hose. The water ran noisily. That took care of him, I thought. But he looked at me over his shoulder, and in that look there was suspicion and dark anger. That damn kid. He could kill you if you didn't watch out. If he ever found out what had happened . . .

I went back to work with Toad helping me. "Looks like I'm gonna need a bodyguard around here, with everybody making threats."

Toad leaned on the fender of the car we were working on. "When you and Sandy gettin' married?"

"What?"

"You said you asked her."

"I did."

"What'd she say?"

"Nothing."

"When you gonna ask again?"

"That's my business."

"You ain't gonna ask."

"Maybe I changed my mind."

Toad stared at the engine. "Mebbe that's a good thing," he said.

"Why?"

"You wouldn't do her no favor by marryin' her. You make up for one bad night by handin' her a thousand more. You're trouble. With the preacher or without one."

"What do you want me to do, Dad?" I asked sarcastically.

"Pick up your marbles and git the hell out of here while they's still time. Before she's hurt too bad. Let her marry Herbert and git something outa life. You ain't got nothing to give her but trouble."

"Yeah," I said slowly. "Maybe you're right, Toad. Maybe I just ought to walk out and hit the road. Nobody'd be sorry see me go. Not even you."

"Damn right I wouldn't," Toad said. "I'd be right with you."

"What?"

"We don't belong here, Ace," Toad said, his face twitching. "I don't want to be nursemaid to Ronnie. I want to be mechanic to a driver. You and me's the same, Ace. We don't belong in no nest. We belong to the tracks. The big tracks. I don't know what made you quit drivin', but we could lick it. And git back to the big time. You and me."

I looked toward the office, where Sandy was inside crying.

"She don't mean nothing to you, Ace," Toad coaxed. "You and me don't travel good with a lot of baggage."

"It's too late, Toad," I said. "I'm washed up. Out. I got too hairy. I get on the track, and I get crazy."

"You could lick it if you wanted to," Toad said. "Others has."

"I'm afraid to try. I might kill somebody."

"We could find out," Toad said.

"Yeah?"

"We could run two cars here."

"I don't want to murder children."

"We could go and be mechanics, if you won't drive. That'd be better'n hangin' around here."

"I can't go," I said. "I blew my wad on the down payment to Western Supply. The only thing I can do is stick it out here and try to make it back. We're doing business. It's a good spot."

"Can't go or won't go?" Toad grunted.

"I don't know."

He gestured toward the office. "What about her?"

"I don't know about that, either."

"But you ain't leavin'?"

"Not yet."

Toad picked up a wrench and started unbolting the carburetor. I watched him for a few moments, then drifted away. I went outside and began looking over the junk to see what could be salvaged. For the first time in two days, I felt like a stranger in Town.

I didn't want to be a stranger and alone. Not anymore. Not without a place to go, or people to go to. It made me think, this feeling of fear I got when I felt myself being shut out.

Bill had been dead a year. Was there any reason why Sandy shouldn't have gone to bed with others if she felt like it? A man wouldn't think twice about it. Why did it have to be different with a woman? Why didn't it matter to me if she had been in bed with Bill, but it shook me up when I thought she'd been with others? What difference did it make what she did before she met me? What had I done in the past year, if she should care to know?

Herpgruve wanted to marry her. It couldn't have been with him. Not after seeing them together; there wasn't that invisible bond that exists between a man and a woman who have slept together, even when they are trying to ignore each other. Ronnie? If so, what difference? Bill's brother. Why worse than Bill?

I'd been a damn fool. There were no two ways about it. I loved the girl. I knew it. Now she was inside, bawling because I'd hurt her. There was only one smart thing to do. Forget the past. Go in and make things right with her, and try to figure out a future . . . If only she hadn't been so easy!

I went into the garage and into the office. Sandy wasn't crying, but she had been. There was a stark, pinched look on her face. I hadn't meant to do that to her.

"Sandy . . ."

"What is it?" Her voice was impersonal and a little shaky.

"I'm sorry."

"Sorry? For what?"

I couldn't say it. Couldn't put it into words. I looked at her tired eyes. "Sorry for the tears, Sandy."

"It's not your fault," she said hollowly.

"Yes, it is," I said. "I should have known . . . Well, I shouldn't have . . ."

She picked up a letter on her desk. "You? You had nothing to do with it. It was Bill."

I thought she was losing her reason. "Sandy . . ."

"The insurance money," she said, handing me the letter. "I should have known. Other people buy policies with established companies. But that wasn't good enough for Bill. He had to find some company down in Texas no one ever heard of before. They won't pay."

"The mortgage," I said. "This was to pay on it."

She gestured helplessly. "Now what do I do?"

"We'll get it," I said. "We're getting all the business we can handle. We'll make out."

She looked me full in the face. "I don't know if I want to," she said wearily. "I don't care anymore."

CHAPTER 17

I CARED. I LOVED HER. I wanted to marry her and settle down and have a good garage and a home and maybe some kids, and a couple of square feet of the earth that I could call mine. No matter what her past had been, or mine, I loved her.

She didn't look at me as she sorted the work tickets. But I looked at her, loving the soft curve of her cheek, the warm tones of her skin, and the shadows under her eyes.

I went around the desk and placed my hands on her shoulders. She stiffened. "Sandy," I said. "Will you marry me?"

She winced, as though I had hit her. She answered without emotion. "I think we went through that routine once, Ace. And then another one."

"Sandy . . . Listen . . . I'm sorry. I know I acted like a heel, but I'm sorry. I love you. I want to marry you."

"So you can come home every night and accuse me of having . . . been intimate with other men?"

"I'm sorry," I said. "I just got scared when you were so . . . warm. Afraid it would happen again the way it did with Thelma."

Sandy shook off my hands and got to her feet, turning to face me. She was angry. "I like the people you compare me with!"

"I told you so you'd understand."

"I understand."

"Well, then . . ."

"That doesn't mean I want to live with it."

"I'm just trying to tell you the truth about myself," I said. "I want a wife I can be, well, one I can be sure of." I turned red when I said that. Weak, miserable thing for a man to say.

"Are you sure of me now?"

"I want to marry you."

"Does that mean you're sure of me?"

There was something strange about her. Something abandoned, and reckless. I felt she was baiting me, and I didn't know what to do about it. If I hadn't known better, I'd have thought she'd been drinking.

I gave in. "Yes. I am. I really am."

She laughed strangely. "Don't be."

I froze. "Why not?

"You're a racing man," she said, leaning against the wall with her back. "You ought to know there's no such animal as a sure thing forever and ever. Not even a husband. Or wife."

"You'd try," I said, trying to figure her out. "The . . . other one didn't even try."

"How do you know I'd try?" She had the knife in. Now she had to twist.

"Damn it, you wouldn't marry me if you weren't going to try to make a go of it!"

"Who said I was going to marry you?"

"I said so!"

She shook her head. Suddenly she was subdued, seeming without hope. "I'm not going to marry you."

"You love me, don't you?" She went over to the desk and picked up the letter from the insurance company and read it again.

"Don't you?" I demanded.

"Yes," she said calmly.

"Then why in the hell can't you marry me? You loved Bill, and you married him. Why not me? I don't get it."

"What if you're unsure of me?" she asked. "Am I supposed to hold back the love I feel because it might frighten you? What kind of marriage would that be? And to what kind of man?"

"Don't be afraid of that," I said. "Believe me."

"Maybe I'm afraid of something else."

"What else could there be, if you love me?"

She looked at the letter again, a strange, hopeless smile on her face. "I'm afraid . . . you might treat me the way Bill did," she said. "You might neglect me, the way he did. The way you were last night. Cars come first with you, too."

"They won't, ever again."

"They might," she parried. "It might be like it was with Bill all over again. I'm afraid."

I went to her and put my arms around her. "I won't be afraid, and you won't be afraid," I said firmly. "Got that?"

She shook her head. "But you don't know what I'd do if I got mad at you."

"I'd take that chance," I said. I gave her a little squeeze. "I'm not afraid of you," I said, trying to cheer her up. "I'm bigger than you are.

"But Ace . . ."

"Never mind the talk," I said. "Forget your fears and give me a kiss, and we'll figure out a wedding day. Come on."

She lifted her head obediently, and I kissed her. It felt as though she was trying to respond, but her heart wasn't in it. I was wondering if I'd done the right thing asking her to marry me when the door slammed behind me. I lifted my head and turned around. It was Ronnie.

I had a recent and still-painful reminder of how hard Ronnie could hit, and in view of my forthcoming marriage, I thought it my duty to Sandy to protect her future groom. I stepped behind her.

For a moment, there was a look of hurt anger on Ronnie's face, but he didn't make a hostile move. He wanted to tear me apart, but he needed me—at the moment.

"I want to speak to you and Sand," Ronnie said, wrinkling his forehead. It made him look angry.

"Can't it wait?" Her voice was under control, but tight.

"No," he said. "I guess it can't. I might as well get it over with now, Sand."

"Get *what* over with?"

"Soon's I'm twenty-one, I'm gonna drive at the track."

I thought Sandy would try to put him in his place with a few crisp words. Instead, she shook her head and said, "Please don't, Ronnie."

"I have to," he said. "Otherwise, everybody'll think I'm yellow on account of what happened to Bill. I just thought I'd tell you."

"You can't. Ronnie—you promised me you wouldn't."

"I changed my mind."

"Who'd give you a car?"

Ronnie shot a quick look at me. "I want you to."

"*Me!*"

"I want to drive Bill's old Tudor," Ronnie said. Sandy put her hand to her head and stared at the stubborn boy by the door. "Let me talk it over with Ace," she said slowly.

"Okay," Ronnie said, smiling, and went out. "I can't let him do it," Sandy said. "I can't."

"Don't," I said. "*If* you don't want to."

"You did this," Sandy said slowly. "I know what you're doing. Getting Bill's old car fixed up again, behind my back. It had to happen. It had to."

"Slow down, honey," I said. "You know jalopies are out of my line, and Toad has been teaching me how to work on them. We're using the Tudor for a classroom."

"I don't believe you," she said. "I can't."

"I'm not going to drive it," I said. "And if you want my advice about Ronnie, I say let him quit. No one around here will give him a car, and he wouldn't be pestering us to drive Bill's. I can get another kid to wash cars. Maybe one who's a good mechanic too. Like Chip Vann."

"Who?" Sandy asked sharply. "Chip Vann," I said.

"Why him?"

"Why not?"

"I don't want him around," Sandy said nervously. "I just don't want him around."

"Why not?"

"Don't you know?" She looked at me suspiciously.

"Know what?" I was getting tired of all the mysteries. Sandy didn't answer my question. "It had to come," she said dully. "I knew it would. Ronnie in Bill's car." She shuddered.

"Look," I said, "if you feel that way about it, let's not give him the car." I was thinking about how much it would cost to keep Ronnie on the track, and how few purses there would be. I needed somebody like Chip Vann in my car. What the hell did she have against Chip? "*If* anything happens to Ronnie, you'll blame me."

"I won't blame you," Sandy said. "It's my fault. *If* Bill were alive, he wouldn't let Ronnie drive. But he isn't alive. Ronnie *will* drive. And if he's killed, it will be my fault too."

"Be reasonable," I said. "How can you blame yourself for Bill's death? You couldn't make him quit."

"*No,*" she said quietly. "I couldn't make him quit. So, I had him killed."

— — —

Now it made sense. Now the sudden mood changes, the near hysteria, the helplessness, and the misgivings all made sense. And her fear of marrying me.

She was sitting in the chair by the desk. I sat on the desk, waiting for her to say something. Her hands were folded in her lap, and her head sagged. She looked as though she were waiting for the police, or the executioner. I wanted to ask her about it, but I was afraid to talk. The wrong word now, and everything would go to hell. I still couldn't believe her. It seemed unreal—until I looked at her. She looked old, beaten, helpless.

So, I didn't say anything. I leaned over and kissed the top of her head. That made her cry, and after the tears had broken her loose, the trembling words came out. She clutched my hand while she talked, sometimes pinching the skin so hard I almost yelled.

"I didn't want to hurt him," she said. "I didn't want him hurt. I only wanted him to stop racing, so I'd have a husband again. I didn't *know*."

"Didn't know what, hon?" I asked quietly.

"That anyone could get killed," she said in a tight voice. "I hated racing because I never saw Bill. I wouldn't even go to see him race. But late at night, when he did come home, all he could talk about was how much it cost to keep his car running. Cars were always getting wrecked, and no one ever got hurt. That's where I got the idea."

I could see it coming.

"Bill was complaining about how deep in debt we were. And he began saying he was going to quit racing. He'd lie in bed and swear about the damage that had been done, and how foolish he was to race, and how he was getting sick and tired of racing. He was always threatening to quit because he couldn't afford to race. I made the mistake of believing him.

"I thought if he was disgusted enough, he would quit. The way he was always saying, 'If I get piled up again, I'm through!' I couldn't forget it. It seemed to me the only way to make him quit was to see that he had to quit. So, I paid a driver to wreck Bill. I didn't want *Bill* to be hurt. I just wanted the car to be hurt, so Bill would quit. The way he said he would and nobody had ever been hurt on the track before. . . . Oh . . . God . . ."

Sandy put her head on her arms and sobbed.

"We all make mistakes," I said.

"Mine killed him."

I took a deep breath. "I guess that's racing, too. That too."

"As if anything could have made him quit," she said forlornly. "That's why I'm afraid of you, Ace. I couldn't go through it again. I had to tell you. I didn't want to, but I had to. I was afraid not to."

"You don't have to worry with me, Sandy," I said. "I turned my last lap on the track. See? It's all right."

"You still want to marry me?" she asked in a thin voice. "I ought to be in jail for what I did."

"I'm still going to marry you," I said. "And you don't belong in jail. If you do, I do. I've spun a lot of guys off the track on purpose. If I'd killed anybody in a race, it would have been an accident. That's what yours was."

"I hope I can see it that way—someday."

"You will," I said.

"You see how it makes me feel about Ronnie, don't you? I have to look after him. It's my duty, after what happened. That's why I never wanted him to drive."

"We'll tell him no," I said. I still wanted Chip.

"We have to give him a car," Sandy said. "He'll drive anyway, and I'd feel better if he stayed with us and drove for people who . . . loved him . . . and would look after him." She managed a little smile. "We'll have to be his Mom and Dad from now on, Ace. He's our first baby."

"I like mine smaller," I said.

Sandy squeezed my hand again. "We have to watch over him," she said. "And protect him."

"If it makes you feel better, I'll watch over him. I guess you are right about keeping the boy close to us."

"Will you tell him?"

"I'll tell him."

"If he ever found out what I did to his brother—You see why I have to take care of Ronnie?"

"I see. I'll take care of everything."

She brought my hand to her face. "I love you, Ace."

"You, too."

I went out into the main section of the garage. Ronnie dropped the water hose when he saw me and ran over, his face eager and anxious. "What's the word, Ace?"

It would be expensive, and we'd win but few dimes. And we needed the purses. Needed them bad. Purses Ronnie would never win. But I put my hand on his shoulder, and I really felt what Sandy had said. That this was my big, rough, tough baby, who wanted to go out and play wrinkle-fender with the big boys.

"The word," I said, "is that you'll be driving old seventy-two for the garage."

"Thanks, Ace. Thanks a million!"

"That's all right," I said. "That's all right . . . son."

CHAPTER 18

SEVENTY-TWO WASN'T READY TO ROLL, and I had to teach Ronnie his new trade. It couldn't be done with talk.

There's no substitute for getting behind the wheel in competition, but we did our best. The first thing was to get Ronnie used to the track. Then I'd arrange some two-car practice races for him. Chip Vann helped us by bringing his coupe to the track early on race night and letting me use it to teach Ronnie what had to be done.

The first time we went out, Ronnie was so nervous his hands shook when he took the goggles and helmet from Chip and put them on. But that was all right. Drivers who shake before a race are usually rock steady when the flag drops.

"I've given you a lot of advice, kid," I said to Ronnie. "Now I'm going to show you. I'll take you around a couple of times, and then I'll ride with you."

"Okay, Ace. Anything you say."

I climbed into the bucket seat and Ronnie perched next to me, hanging on to the rollover bar, his feet braced on the frame. I started the engine. It was loud, rough, and gutty. Ronnie took a fresh grip on the pipes he clung to for support. I revved the engine until the noise was deafening inside the car. Then I eased off. "Ready, kid?"

"Ready." His face was tight.

"Here we go."

I drove slowly onto the track, getting the feel of the car. It was rough at low speeds. The sign of a hot cam. It would sing when the revs climbed.

I drove down the middle of the track at a moderate speed into the first corner, around to the second, down the back chute, into the third corner, the fourth, and down the front chute, past the judges' stand. It gave me the feel of the track, the degree of bank on the corners, and a hint as to where I would find the groove.

I took about six slow laps with Ronnie hanging on by me. I kept looking at him to see how he was taking it. His face looked tense and excited, but eager. He sniffed in acrid exhaust fumes and stared through the glassless shield opening as we bumped and rattled around and around the track.

"Like it?" I yelled. Ronnie grinned and nodded.

"Ready for a couple of fast laps?" The grin came in a little at the corners, but he nodded. I brought the coupe to a stop in front of the judges' stand. "We'll do this like a race," I said. "And here's the way I want you to start. You hold up your hand and drop it for the flag."

His hand went up. I dropped the coupe into low, shoved in the clutch, and stepped on the gas until I was hitting about fifteen hundred rpm. Then I eased out on the clutch until another fraction of an inch would make us move.

"Feel that?" I said to Ronnie.

"Yeah."

"Drop the flag."

His hand went down. I eased the clutch out quickly, smoothly, feeding more gas, trying to sense the bite the wheels were getting. We shot ahead with only a little wheelspin, and I floored the coupe. Seconds later, I backed just a little on the gas and slam-shifted into second. I was in high before we were into the first corner, with my foot down, and we were picking up speed as we went around with Ronnie barely hanging on. I had my foot all the way down on the back chute. I wanted to go deep, but it was better to teach Ronnie to back off a little soon at first. He didn't know that. He knew we were heading for the turn at close to seventy miles an hour, and it was like being on roller skates at that speed. I saw his knuckles turn white as he gripped his supports, and his body stiffened.

I went into the turn high, backed off, and kicked the wheel to the left, hitting the gas pedal as I did. The rear end of the coupe slewed around to the right, and turning my wheels in the direction of the skid, I poured on the coal. My wheels were pointed at the outside fence, but we had a locked rear end, with both wheels getting equal power all the time, and I brought it around the turn in a big loud squeal, backing off the gas pedal when the rear end tended to spin around, and gunning the car to keep the rear end going just enough.

We came out high on the turn, leaping and bucking under the power I was feeding. We streaked down the front chute close to the outside, and went into the east turn as fast as I thought we could take it. Again, I threw the rear end into a skid, controlling it with the gas pedal, and we went around hard, tires howling, and came out riding on the right-hand door handles.

I took Ronnie around like that for a dozen laps, pouring on the coal. I found the groove and we picked up speed. I was able to go around the turns faster, with less slide. When I slowed down again and the wind stopped beating at my face, I looked at Ronnie. His face was grim and white.

"Like to try that with a dozen other cars crowding you?" I asked.

He looked at me. "I was thinking about that."

"And?"

"I'd like to try it."

"Good kid," I said. "Now I want you to get behind the wheel and do what I did. Keep high on the track and go into the turns high. Like I did. You come down as you go around, and then you drift high as you come out. That's where you'll find your groove most of the time. It's the way to get around. Of course, you can't always do it when there are other cars out there. But it's what you try to do."

"I thought the pole was the place," Ronnie said. "The inside."

"Look what happens on the inside."

I took him around again, fast, on the pole. Trying to take the corners too close, I had to back off too much to keep from spinning. I lost speed and drifted to the outside.

"You see, kid," I said. "You take the pole, and you'll drift high, trying to get around. The guy who comes around high will be able to cut inside you on the corner and take you."

"I see," Ronnie said. "Can I try now?"

"Go ahead."

We stopped on the front chute and changed places. He adjusted his goggles and fastened his safety belt. I got beside him, crouching on the frame, with one hand gripping the back of the metal seat. "Easy at first," I said. "I'll speed you up when it's time."

He took off a little jerkily, his foot too heavy for the engine he was pushing. But he dropped into high and began to circle as I had showed him. The kid was a good road driver, and it didn't take him long to get the feel of the track.

He grinned at me as we cut a turn. "I like this!"

"You're only doing thirty or thirty-five. Let's see some action!"

He bent forward and put his foot in it. The little coupe jumped forward and headed for the east turn with a blistering roar. Ronnie cut off where I had showed him to, nosing into the turn. He hit his gas pedal again, too hard, jerking the steering wheel to the left, then turning his front wheels in the direction of the skid. The power in the rear end came too hard, and in spite of Ronnie's turning into the skid, the rear wheels churned and slewed around. He pulled his foot off the gas and wrestled the wheel as we made a complete spin on the track and stalled.

"Jeez!" Ronnie said, his face crimson.

I laughed. "It takes practice, son. It takes time to get the feel of a locked rear end. But you'll get it. Just take it a little easy at first. Let's try again."

And we tried again, taking the turns slower, then building up as Ronnie got the feel of the car and the track. Pretty soon, he was broad sliding the turns at a better-than-fair speed and shooting off the corners without too much lag. He turned into the pits when Chip flagged us down.

"Save me some rubber for the race," Chip complained cheerfully, the cigar wobbling in his mouth. "I can't run on the rims."

"What do you think of our boy?" I asked.

"He's a real chauffeur," Chip said. "I'm gonna have trouble with that boy."

"You'll be better'n Bill," Toad said, putting his hand on Ronnie's shoulder. "Better'n Bill."

Ronnie frowned at his engineer boots. "I only hope someday I can be as good."

"You got everything he had so far," Toad said. "The only thing we got to see now is how you stack up in the gut department."

"I'll be there," Ronnie said.

Toad spat. "We'll see."

Chip Vann turned his round face toward me. "Where'd you learn to drive, Ace? I thought you never did."

"I've run 'em around the track getting them sweet, that's all," I said. "But I've done it a lot."

"I'd say so," Chip answered. He wasn't unfriendly, but there was a hint of suspicion in his manner, as though he were afraid of some trick.

"How about letting Ronnie turn a few laps every race night until he's ready to run?" I asked Chip.

"Sure. If you'll buy the gas."

"I'll buy."

"When do you figure he'n be out?"

"As soon as we get seventy-two in shape."

"Bill's old car, huh?"

"It'll look like it on the outside."

"Don't make it too hot for the kid to handle."

Ronnie and Toad weren't listening. I dropped my voice a little anyway. "If it is, I'll find somebody who can handle it. That baby's going to run in front."

"Give me a shot at it sometime."

"I will," I said. "Maybe more than one."

"What about Ronnie?"

"We have to run in front. That's what about Ronnie."

Chip put a match to his cigar and looked at me over the flame. He wanted to drive 72 if he could, but he knew the terms. Run in front or get the old heave-ho. I could see what he thought of me for planning to get rid of Ronnie before the kid even had a chance to drive. But I didn't care. I had to have a winner. "You know where to find me if you need me," Chip said. He walked away. Business was over, and he didn't care for my company.

The time trials started, and I watched them go around. Jensen in his blue streak, de Marco slamming his orange coupe through the turns, Towner pushing his little Chevy. The V-8s thundered, the GMCs sang.

I watched and listened. I told myself I didn't have the wheel itch anymore, and I almost believed it. I had hung my crash hat for good, but I didn't have to leave racing, didn't have to be afraid of the track. I didn't want to drive anymore. I didn't hate anybody anymore. I felt like a puppy with a tongue a foot long, trying to be friends with all the world at once.

I watched the drivers around me. All young and rugged with a lot of fire. The track was for them, not for me. I'd had my kicks, my spills and thrills. Now I wanted my profession, three squares a day, a bed, and a wife. From now on it won be Ace Jones, solid citizen. I'd work hard to pay all my debt, and to help Herpgruve build up the track. Maybe join Lions and the Kiwanis or be a Scout leader.

Happy, happy, happy. The past was dead. Long live the future!

I saw Ronnie standing near the track, watching how the others drove. I decided I liked that big, stubborn kid. I'd look after him. Maybe get him steered away from racing. Try to help him avoid the mistakes I'd made. Ace Jones, babysitter.

"*Toad!* Come here a minute." Toad shuffled over, his head cocked to one side.

"I've got news for you, Toad."

"We leaving, Ace? We going back to the big time?" There was a pleading note in his voice, like a child asking for a big, expensive toy.

"Staying," I said. "Staying for good. I'm gonna marry Sandy, Toad."

"Can't we go, Ace? You and me? You don't want to git married." He moved closer to me, jabbing me in the ribs.

"You don't have to marry her, Ace." He grinned and winked. "You know *that*, boy. Whyn't you take what you need fer a while, and you and me can git when we've got some money. We could have some times, Ace. Some real times!"

"We're staying," I said. "Staying, marrying, and making something out of that garage. I'm in Town for good, Toad. I want to stay."

Toad reached into my pocket for a cigarette. A coupe roared into the turn behind us, half-spun, straightened, and rocked toward the wire. Another car rumbled out of the infield and started its preliminary lap.

"Well," Toad said, his face expressionless. "If that's the way you want it, that's the way you're gonna git it."

I looked past Toad at a shiny car on the track. It was streaking down the front chute, wound up tight. It went deep into the turn before the driver backed off, skidded, and roared as he came out under full power, bucking violently over bumps in the track.

"For Pete's sake," I said. "What's eating Peale? He's driving like he meant it." I listened for his time. It was good enough to get him a spot in the trophy dash, the fast heat, the pursuit, and the main.

I looked for a high spot to sit and watch. If even Peale had a burr under his saddle, there might be some real racing coming up.

CHAPTER 19

"JONES!" I LOOKED DOWN FROM WHERE I WAS SITTING on one of the racers. Peale stood below me, goggles around his neck, his white crash hat on his head. He looked excited and a little wild.

"Yeah?"

"You catch my time?" His voice was high and a little shaky. The little dude was trembling.

"I caught it."

"You watch me tonight. You think I can't run. I'll show you I can. I'll prove you ought to give me the same deal you give the other guys."

"Do your best," I said. "I'll cheer for you."

"If I win anything tonight and give it to you against my back account, is my credit good? Is that a deal?"

I grinned at his anxious face. "It's a deal."

"You watch me."

Peale was among the cars that rolled out for the trophy dash. He drove out hard, revving his engine impatiently. He was going to show me, right from the start.

Toad climbed up beside me. "What's eatin' Peale tonight?"

"He wants to prove he can run in front."

"He's in all the big ones tonight," Toad said as the cars took their positions and began revving up. "He could make some money."

The green flag dropped. Peale, whose car was in the third row on the outside, made a good start. He pulled to the outside and put his foot in it as the cars headed into the first turn. He went around high and fast, passing two cars that were caught in the traffic jam at the pole. On the back chute, he was running third by less than half a length and holding strong. The field roared into the west turn with the three leaders bunched. Peale was in the middle. Tires howled as the drivers squared into the turn and slid around in formation, churning a great cloud of dust. Coming out of the turn, there was the usual clash of metal and shower of sparks as the cars hit each other. There were dull bumps and the grinding sound of metal against metal as Peale was caught in the squeeze and bounced from one car to another.

Peale's lips writhed in agony as the jagged right fender of the pole car tore along the side of his coupe, leaving dents and scraping the glossy paint. Peale backed off and got hit again by the car on the outside. Then both cars passed him as he went down the front chute with his tail end whipping from side to side. By the time he reached the next turn, he was riding the rim again as of old, and the field went by. Before the race was over, he had been lapped by the two leaders.

There was a time when I would have hopped down and gone to meet him as he came into the pits, ready to feed back his brave words. But I was mellow now, comfortable and contemptuous of the little man. I even found myself hoping he'd smash up so bad he'd have to quit racing. Maybe then he could feed and clothe his kids. Planning some of my own, I was beginning to worry about others.

Peale was out again for the fast heat, running against Jensen, de Marco, Towner, and Chip Vann among others. They ran with the fastest cars at the rear, and that gave Peale the pole. I figured he'd keep it about three seconds.

Everybody was surprised when Peale jumped into the lead on the first corner and held it all the way around. His car could move, and he was out in front for three laps while the fast boys were working their way through the traffic. On the fourth lap, he had the fast boys bunched behind him, ready to eat him up. I saw Peale twisting his head back to see how close the others were and caught the desperation of his attempt to stay in front. It was the first time in his life he'd ever been there, and he wanted to stay.

Jensen tried the first pass. Peale was a little high on the west turn, and Jensen started to cut across on the inside. Peale saw the attempt and tried to fight off the pass. He nosed down toward the pole, hoping to shut Jensen off and force him back.

But the fast boys didn't stay in front on speed alone. Jensen kept his foot in it and went into a tight turn, sliding against Peale to stop his drift. The impact sent Peale high, just as de Marco's orange coupe came howling around on the outside. Caught between the two, Peale lost control, and de Marco slammed into him, hitting him behind the right front wheel. Peale's red and silver coupe spun to the left, broadside on the track. The crowd let out a scream as it saw what had to happen.

Towner and Vann, half blinded by dust and fighting each other, were fender to fender as they came around the turn just behind the leaders. Peale spun in front of them, and they both hit him before they had a chance to back off or turn.

There was a deep *crrruump* as Peale was hit. For a second, his car was carried sideways, on its feet. Then it went down in the dust, and there were a series of thudding shocks as he rolled over and over, bouncing in the air as he turned, smashing in the top of his car, crumpling the wheels, crushing the radiator, tearing hoses, and ripping wires.

The red flags were out on the track, and the ambulance tore across the infield, siren wailing and red lights flashing. No one noticed Towner hung up on the fence, or Vann stalled in the infield. All eyes were on Peale's smashed coupe, now resting upside down on the track.

I was off and running with the rest of them, trying to get a look inside, where Peale's head was hanging upside down. Before any of us got to him, he was moving his head and working to unfasten his safety belt. By the time we reached him, he had crawled out of the car and was standing by it, helmet in hand, looking at the wreckage with a stunned expression in his eyes.

There was a cut on his face and a nasty purple bruise with a split in it on his left elbow. But he shook off the ambulance people and stared at his battered car, all the while rubbing the back of his neck.

About fifteen of us laid hands on the car and righted it. The wrecker backed up and hooked on. One of the policemen got out his matches and prepared to burn the gasoline spilled on the track.

Something was missing from the scene, and I didn't know what it was. Peale was sitting on the running board of the ambulance now, feeling the pain. A bunch of guys stood around him, listening to his story of how it happened. Then I saw what was missing— Ossman. I looked around for him. He was standing to one side, watching the wrecker take the coupe. His hands were in his pocket and his pipe was in mouth, and his blue eyes were as vacant as ever. He could have been watching it on a movie screen.

Back in the pits, everybody got busy. Usually, a guy takes care of his own troubles, but Peale's fight had won him a few friends. And the pits being what they are, two guys with wrenches can get more work done in twenty minutes than a garage will do on a passenger car in a week.

The bent wheels came off, and others went on. The radiator was pulled and another one borrowed from a real sick car. The cracked distributor was replaced, the wiring put back together, and the carburetor adjusted. Thirty minutes after smash-up, Peale's engine was running, and he was ready to race in the main event when it came up. He stood beside his battered coupe, his eyes big; he told everyone over and over again what had happened and kept asking when they were going to run the main. His hands were shaking, and his teeth showed too much, but he was ready to run. I had to give him credit for that.

Just before the main, Peale was allowed to take a few laps to test his car. The crowd cheered like mad when he came out on the track and started around. The engine sounded fine, but he began to have trouble right away. He almost spun out on the turns and was all over the track on the chutes. He came back into the pits disgusted. The car was jacked up, and new trouble was discovered. Both legs of the transmission were broken. He was out for the night.

The others drifted away, now that he was done. He leaned against his coupe and smoothed his mustache with one hand, thinking. He saw me. There was nothing hangdog in his look now. "You satisfied?" he called out. "Do I get the same deal as the others?"

"Same deal," I said, amused at the dude.

"I showed you," he said. He turned to look at his car and almost wept. "Look at it now . . . It'll never look like anything now. . . . Damn you, Jones . . . but I showed you."

CHAPTER 20

AFTER THE RACES, THE CROWD POURED across the track to the pits to look at the cars and get autographs from the tired, dirty drivers. For the first time, there was a crowd around Peale's car, curiously examining the battered body and twisted doors.

The families came across. Wives of the drivers and their kids. A few of them looked happy, but most of the women knew that repairs would cost more than the money won, and they'd have to raid the sugar bowl or the sock or the grocery money before the little gem could run again. And run it would.

The kids climbed into their dads' cars and shimmied the wheels, putting on helmets and goggles and making noises. The losers alibied to their wives in low voices, and the wives sounded off in louder tones to the other wives.

I glanced toward Peale's car and my heart jumped. For a moment, I thought I was seeing Thelma again. But the blonde hair belonged to Peale's wife. I stared at her. She had the same kind of hungry, sexy look that Thelma had had. Only the Peale woman wasn't as fancy. Not now, after the kids, the poverty. Not now, holding one small child in her arms, with a couple of others clinging to her worn dress, and a gaunt look cutting into her baby-doll face.

Not now, but once she'd been a local Thelma, swinging her hips and making the most of her big blue eyes. She was the girl who had married the smooth dancer. This was where the ballroom romances led to. But, hell. Was it any worse what had happened to me? At least Peale still had his woman and their kids.

I moved in closer. She was still young, and the thin summer dress, pulled tight against her by her kids, showed a woman's figure. Good full breasts, a broad belly, strong legs, not too heavy.

I looked into the smeared, pale face of one of Peale's kids. A little blue-eyed towhead, who hung on to its mother and stared tiredly at the people. Tiredly . . . or vacantly? That familiar stare. Peale's wife did have blue eyes and blonde hair, and yet . . . why did I wait for the kid to pull out a pipe and stick it in his mouth?

I felt sick and sorry. Poor, miserable Peale. Even this. He'd been lapped again.

I raised my eyes and caught Peale looking at me. He knew what I was looking at and what I was thinking. I wanted to tell him I knew what it was like, and I was sorry, but I couldn't. I couldn't do anything for the little dude who mirrored every miserable thing that had ever happened to me. I did what I could. I grinned at him. He looked away. I knew he would. There are some things a man can't get mad about in public. Some things that make him want to turn his head to the wall and wish himself dead, like the old men of the African tribes.

A shrill voice rose above the crowd murmur. "He hit you on purpose. I saw him!"

It was Mrs. Peale, shouting at Loren. He looked embarrassed and muttered something to her.

"I won't keep my goddamn mouth closed!" she yelled. Turning toward Towner's car, where Bob and his wife stood talking to several people, "Bob Towner rammed you on purpose!"

Towner ignored the remark, but his wife didn't. She was a lean, rangy brunette, wearing a leather jacket and a scarf over her head. She flicked away the cigarette she was smoking. "The hell he did!" she bawled at Loren's wife.

Mrs. Peale took a firm grip on the baby in her arm and stepped forward, shaking off the kids who clung to her skirt. "The hell he didn't!" she yelled.

"Damn it, Irma, shut up!" Peale rasped. He turned his back to her, leaning on the window of his car. "It wasn't his fault. It happens in races. It can't be helped."

"He could have missed you!" Irma Peale shouted. "The son of a bitch didn't want to see you win any money! They're all in it together—him and Jensen and de Marco and Vann. I know!"

Towner's wife lifted her head and *looked like* a horse getting ready to whinny. "Buuuulll!" she cried in derision.

"I'll bull you!" Irma slapped her kids free and made for Mrs. Towner, *still* carrying her little one. Mrs. Towner went to meet her, fists doubled and chin stuck out. "You try something, you *blonde slut!*"

Irma swung with her free hand and caught Mrs. Towner on the chin with a hard left. The tall girl went down on the seat of her denims, swearing a blue streak.

"My God, Lois!" Towner yelled in laughter. "Don't ever lead with your chin!"

Lois bounced up and made for Irma, her hands outstretched. She missed Irma's hair and grabbed the top of her dress.

"Don't you touch my baby!" Irma bawled, her face a mask of fury.

"The hell with your baby!" Lois screeched. She pulled at Irma's dress, and it ripped at the shoulder. Swinging her baby away from

Lois, Irma pounded the tall girl with her left arm. Lois came in again, flailing, and connected with Irma's eye. She took a hard punch to the breast and yelled in pain.

Irma screeched in triumph, but Lois wasn't through. She began to circle around Irma, her long fingers curved into talons. Irma turned with her, one eye swelling, her blonde hair in wild disarray. The baby on her arm was bawling at the top of its lungs, and her other little kids were in howling tears.

Narrowing her eyes, Lois darted forward and grabbed Irma's brassiere strap and pulled. The cloth gave, and a full, snow-white breast popped into the open. Irma ignored it, turning to face Lois as the tall girl circled, her free breast swaying.

Lois came in again, but Irma was waiting for her. She closed with the tall girl and brought her knee up hard. Lois grabbed her groin and fell to the ground. Irma stood over her. Her uncovered breast heaved with her labored breathing.

"Start with me, you pig!" Irma spat at the prostrate girl. "I'll show you."

She turned her attention to the crying baby again. "Shut up, you!" she cried, suddenly aware of the audience around her. She stood indecisive for a moment, then swung the baby around and gave him her breast. The baby was quiet.

Suddenly, the scene was over. The baby sucked contentedly, and the men respectfully turned back to their cars, not wishing to stare.

Toad and Ronnie found me. Toad was chuckling, but Ronnie looked sick. Towner was bawling out his wife, and Peale was doing the same to his.

". . . only trying to stand up for your rights," I heard Peale's wife say.

"You helped me a lot showin' your tit to everybody in the county. Didn't you?" He laughed sarcastically.

I looked around for Ossman. He was on the far side of Peale's car, looking away from the spot where the fight had taken place.

His pipe was in his mouth, and he seemed to be staring into space with his usual detached, vacant look. But we walked past him, and I saw his face in the light, and it was different. His mouth was puckered tight around the pipe, and his eyes were half closed. He was crying.

We weren't out of the pits before someone ran up behind us and tapped me on the shoulder. "Can I see you in private a minute, Jones?"

It was Peale, with his long hair sliding down over his ears, dirt on his mustache, and a desperate, despairing look in his eyes. I stepped to one side with him.

"I'm all wracked up," Peale said, searching my face for sympathy. "Radiator shot, coil gone, battery smashed. And God knows what all."

"It happens," I said.

"How'm I gonna get running again? I need parts . . . I tried. I was gonna give you everything I won. Please, can't you let me—? Just once more, if you'll give me a break . . ."

He saw me looking at his left wrist. At the fancy watch that had more dials and hands than a gas meter. He grabbed the watch with his right hand, covering it. "Hell, Jones, have a heart."

"I need a watch," I said. "I broke mine."

"Aw, no!"

"You don't have any money," I said. "You're not going to have any. And I'm not running the Salvation Army garage. The watch to get you running again. And you're getting a break."

"Oh, God," he moaned. "I can't do it. Not this watch. Anything else I got. *Anything!*"

"What else do you have worth seventy-five bucks?"

"The watch cost me a hundred and a half!"

"That was new."

"I'll give you everything I win. I'll drive hard from now on. You'll see. I got nothing to lose anymore. I'll run in front, Jones. Honest, I will."

"You don't have the time for me. I don't have the time for you." Peale didn't smile. He slipped the catch on his watch, and pulled it off his wrist, and handed it to me. He didn't look while I took it from him and put it on.

"What's this little giz in the center for?" I asked Peale.

"It measures the speed of sound or something," he answered dully. "I don't know. It's yours now. You find out."

"See you tomorrow," I said. "I'll fix you up real good."

He stared at the white band of skin on his left wrist. "The only thing I ever had that was worth a damn," he said. "It ain't right." He lifted his head and looked at me bitterly. "You take care of my watch, Jones. I'm gonna win it back. So, you better take care of my watch."

"Sure," I said. "I'll wind it every night right after I say my prayers."

CHAPTER 21

"Ace Jones out there?"

Herpgruve stood in the doorway of the pay shack. I was leaning against a truck outside, drinking a can of beer and bulling with a couple of the guys. I was feeling mellow. Now that I'd decided I belonged in Town, I liked the people better. I began to see them as human beings, and nice ones, instead of dirty faces hanging over an engine. I went into the shack. Most of the drivers were inside. They were quiet as I entered.

"What's up, Herpgruve?"

Herpgruve sat down behind his little table. "Well, the boys have been wondering how soon they're gonna get that water truck you promised."

"As soon as I can get to it," I said, turning my back on Herpgruve. "What the hell, boys, I've only been here days, and the garage has taken every minute. You know that."

Their faces were blank. Damn them, they'd been glad enough when I promised the water. "You said you was gonna disc and roll too," one driver said. "When we gettin' that?"

"You'll get it," I said, getting a little sore about being needled by a bunch of yokels. "You've been racing on this track for a long time. Why get on my tail because I haven't got it fixed in a week?"

"You promised. Nobody else did."

I looked at Herpgruve. He was sucking placidly on his cigar. Me and my promises! I didn't have the time or the money to carry them out now, but I was on the spot. The drivers wanted the promises kept, and the harder I worked, the more Herpgruve would benefit without moving a muscle.

"I'll get something done by next race night," I said. "Good enough for you?"

"If it's done," another driver said. A second-division boy.

"Don't you give me any guff," I said. I should have kept quiet, but I was mad. Mad because they didn't seem to understand that I was trying to be a good guy. "You guys wouldn't know what to do on a *good* track."

"We can't help being small-town boys, Jones," Herpgruve said. 'We're counting on you to show us how things are done in the big time. Aren't we, boys?"

They laughed, but they were mad.

"I'll show you," I said. "I'll show you how to put some torque in those dogs you guys are pushing. Just be goddamn sure you don't try to trade 'taters and beans for cams."

"We're not all farmers," Herpgruve said. "And even if we were, that's no crime. Is it, boys?"

I sat down on the table. How the hell had I got into this hassle? With my new friends and neighbors. My new buddies. I tried to get back on the right road.

"Look, fellas," I said. "Give me a chance. I gave you guys a chance. I let you off the hook easy on the money you owe the garage, didn't I?"

Things had been happening so fast, I guess I still thought I had Herpgruve tied hand and foot. I'd forgotten what he had on paper. He didn't forget.

"That's another thing, boys," Herpgruve said. "I've got a little surprise for you. You boys have raced for me three years now. We've had our differences, but you're my boys, and I want to see you all running out there."

Herpgruve fished the agreement out of his pocket and held it up.

"What I've done, boys, is take the liberty to take over the debt you have to Sandy Richards." The drivers were silent, puzzled. Herpgruve grimaced, as though he hurt. "You boys know that you owe her over twenty thousand dollars, altogether."

Herpgruve waited until the clamor died down. "I have an agreement here in writing. I'm going to give Sandy a percentage of any track profits until that debt is paid in full. Sandy says that as far as she's concerned, you'll all be brand new customers with good credit."

The drivers whooped and yelled like a bunch of kids. Herpgruve held up his hand for quiet. His voice was low and full of emotion. "All you men knew Bill Richards. He was as fine a man as ever put hand to a wheel. He helped make the entire racing program possible. There isn't a man here who wasn't helped a lot by Bill. He gave everything to the game. Even his life. I guess it's not too much for me to give a share of my profit to help his widow. Especially since she's going to carry on in the work."

They cheered Herpgruve again, and there was talk of giving Sandy a cut of the purse. But Herpgruve thanked the boys for their generosity and assured them that he'd take care of all the debt. It was his way of saying thanks for the loyal way they'd driven for him over the years.

Then it was over, and Herpgruve was the hero, and I was the guy with the top hat, cloak, and black mustache. The guys went out, and most of them stopped to say a word to me. Let them off the hook easy, huh? What was I trying to pull?

There wasn't a thing I could say without making myself look worse. My idea of settling down in this "friendly" little town was taking a beating. It didn't seem to be in the cards. I was a misfit. I didn't belong anywhere, trying anything normal. Maybe Toad was right. Maybe I ought to forget Sandy and Town, head back to the big time, and try to belong there.

De Marco, the black-haired driver for Town Garage, who didn't need me for anything, sat down next to me. "You think we're small time here?"

"Damn right," I said. He smiled. He had a soft voice when he talked. "You're big time, huh?"

"I've been around it."

"Why don't you pick up some of the easy money on the track if we're so bad?"

"I'm not a driver. But I'll have a car out there before too long."

"You don't drive?" His lips curled into a faintly derisive expression. "Who'll drive for you? What big-time guy?"

"Ronnie," a voice said. I looked up. Chip Vann was standing near us, listening.

"Ronnie Richards?" De Marco laughed in my face and walked away. I looked at him crossing the room. I wished I could be on the track with him. He wouldn't laugh when our little race was over. God, how I wanted to drive. To get out there and show them all what real competition was like. But I had my reasons for not driving. And not the least was pride. After all, I was Ace Jones, and I'd won some pretty big races on some of the best tracks against the nation's best drivers. Come down to racing jalopies on a cow path in a country town, against farmer boys and gas-station boys? Not me!

I waited until I was alone with Herpgruve. He was pleased, stuffed to the neck with sweet revenge.

"Attendance wasn't too good tonight," he said, chuckling. "You won't be getting more than a few dimes. I thought you were going to build the gate."

I choked back what I wanted to say. I hadn't given up yet. I still wanted to stay in Town and marry and provide for Sandy. Even if it meant working with—or for—Herpgruve.

"I've been thinking about what to do, Herb," I said. "Want to hear about it?"

"Of course, Ace." He was mocking my attempt at showing friendship.

"First of all, let's advertise the new, fast, dustless track we're going to have. Make it sound like the boys will be able to go like jets. If we take a big enough ad, we ought to get the news story I want to plant."

"About what?"

"About our standing offer of a fifteen-dollar bonus to any out-of-town driver who can beat our local boys in the main event. That ought to bring in fans from the other towns, and more of our people too. Get the town-against-town rivalry started. It works in other sports."

"What else?"

"We need more noise. The louder the cars sound, the faster they seem to be going. I want to set up a couple of mikes along the front chute to pick up the engine noises. The people will think the cars are running up their backs."

"Sound ideas," Herpgruve said, smiling to himself. "Very sound. I'll put them into effect as soon as you're gone from Town."

"I guess you haven't heard the news," I said. "I'm not leaving. Sandy and I are getting married. You'd better get used to the idea of having me for a partner."

"I heard the news," he said calmly. "But the ceremony has been set for September, Sandy said. You won't last that long." He seemed so damn sure of himself. He got a little knife out of his pocket and began cleaning his nails.

"Sandy doesn't trust you all the way, Jones. She's waiting until September to make sure you don't turn out to be another Bill. That gives me the summer to make sure that you do."

"Thanks for the warning," I said. "But I won't go the way Bill did. He was a driver. I'm not."

Herpgruve looked at the ceiling, his thick lips pouting thoughtfully. "I don't know anything about you. But I do know that you'll have that garage in a hole so deep before summer's over that nobody can hear you hollering at the bottom." He closed the knife with a quick, angry movement of his hand. "You can kid yourself, Jones, but you can't kid me. You're hanging on now by a thin red hair. You'll be done in a month."

"Suppose you do get rid of me," I said. "That doesn't mean Sandy falls into your lap. She waited for a year after Bill died to find another guy like him. You get rid of me, and she'll wait for another like me."

He shook his big head slowly, confidently. "Not another like you, Jones. Two race-fever boys are her quota. And even if she doesn't want me, she won't be saddled with you."

"That's thoughtful of you."

"Yes, it is," he said slowly. "I saw what Sandy went through with Bill. I like her too much to see her go through all that again, with you. She thinks she loves you and won't look at the facts. But I don't love you, Jones, and I know the kind of life she'd have with you. I can see what's coming. Or what would be coming if you stayed. That's why you're not staying."

I got up. "And you've got it all figured out. Just how you'll get rid of me."

"All figured out," he said. "But I won't have to do anything to get rid of you. I'll just help you do the job yourself."

"All right," I said. "But let me tell you something. Ronnie Richards is going to drive for me out here. Don't try to get me through the kid. If your boys start shouldering the kid into the fence, I'm coming after you."

Herpgruve's voice was cold and hard. "Run your boy if you want to, Jones, but run him the same as the others. He takes his chances, or he doesn't race. Or do you want me to call a drivers' meeting and tell them that Ronnie's supposed to get special treatment? Ask them to back off and let him go by. Is that what you want? I'll tell the boys."

He had me. He was right. There wasn't anything I could say back. I spat on the floor and walked out, leaving him chuckling at his little table.

Toad and Ronnie were waiting for me. They could see I was mad about something, and fell in behind me, keeping silent. I'd gone about ten steps when Loren Peale came out of the shadows to block my path. He was carrying a can of beer. From the way he swayed in front of me, it must have been his ninth or tenth. He came up close and looked up at me. "Jones?"

"What do *you* want?"

"You made me do it," he said tearfully. "You tol' me I had to earn the money to pay you. But Herpgruve paid for me, too, Jones. He paid for me, too."

"Thank him," I snapped. "Not me."

"You made me do it," Peale repeated, beginning to rock on his feet. "You made me smash my car. I did it for you. And I din't have to. I din't have to!"

"I told you to bring the goddamn thing around, and I'll help you put it together again," I said angrily. "Isn't that good enough for you?"

"My beau'ful car," Peale mourned. "All smashed . . . smashed . . ." He caught hold of my jacket and thrust his face close to my chest. "I'll kill you for that, Jones. Kill you. 'Cause I din't have to do it. You made me. I kill people fer things like that."

I pushed him away. "If you had any brains, you'd get rid of that junker and get a job," I said harshly. "You've got no business on the track anyway. Get a job and see that your wife and kids have a home to live in an something to eat!"

"I . . . don't . . ." he began in a thick, sullen tone.

"I don't care whose kids they are either," I said. "They need food. I don't want your car or your money. Stay the hell away from me!"

I was mad at Herpgruve but taking it out on Peale.

I pushed past Loren, angry at him, angry at myself for sounding off. I'd taken about three steps when something hit me in the back, hurting. I swung around. Peale stood swaying and panting, his fists clenched. The beer can he had thrown lay on the ground at my feet.

"You little bastard!" I started for him, feeling a scream of rage building up in my chest. This, from Peale!

I ran into a stone wall. Ronnie was in front of me, his hands gripping my arms, pushing me back. His face was white, but he hung on.

"Don't hit him, Ace." Ronnie pleaded. "He's drunk."

Ronnie's voice was soft, but his grip was like iron. I didn't want to wrestle him like a mad kid. I stopped pushing. "All right," I said to Ronnie, trying to get back some of my dignity. "You're right. I just got sore."

I turned around and walked away, with Toad and Ronnie following. Seeing us retreat, Peale raised his voice in a series of vile and violent threats. I was ashamed of myself for making that crack about his wife and kids. He wouldn't forget that. No man could.

We got in Ronnie's car and drove to the garage. None of us said a word on the way in. When we reached the garage, there was someone waiting for us—pasty-faced Joe.

"Mr. Jones—" He came forward, blinking his eyes and coughing.

"Yeah," I said tiredly. "What do you want?"

"I raced the Hudson this afternoon like I said I was gonna."

That saddened me. The thought of my car in these hands.

"How much did you win?"

"That's the sad thing," Joe said, laughing self-consciously. "I didn't win a cent."

"With that car? I don't believe it."

"The car was good enough, Mr. Jones. But I got wrecked, I did. On the tenth lap. And I was doing real good. I figure if I can get running again, I can be in next week's race up north."

"Running again? You can't run now?"

"Can't turn a wheel," Joe sighed. "I figured since you knew the car and all, I'd better bring it back to you to look at."

"Where's the car?"

"I had it towed around back."

We all went around to have a look. Ronnie went inside and turned on the yard light. The Hudson had been rammed and rolled. It would have to be hammered into shape again, and the frame and running gear gone over and repaired. There was the usual smashed radiator, broken fan, and other internal damage.

"What do you think?" Joe asked anxiously.

"It's a mess," I said.

"I'm sorry. I was doing right well until that tenth lap. I guess there wasn't room for everybody to get around that turn at the same time. I'm sorry, Mr. Jones."

"So am I," I said.

"When's the next race?" Ronnie asked Joe.

"Next week. I figure the only way I can get back my money is to win it back, like Mr. Jones said. So, I brought it back here. I can't pay right now for the work, but if I win next week . . ."

"All right, Joe," I said. "We'll take you in."

"That's swell, Mr. Jones. I'll give you every cent I win."

As the fellow says, if it didn't hurt so bad, it would have been funny.

Toad came to me for a cigarette. He needed a haircut. His white hair was sprouting over his ears. And he looked tired and gray, his face pinched like a morning glory closing slowly at the end of day.

"We gonna work on the Hudson tonight?" Toad asked. "It's midnight."

"Not tonight," I said. "Tonight we've got our work cut out for us on seventy-two."

"You'll get at it soon, won't you, Mr. Jones?" Joe asked anxiously.

"In the morning," I said.

"We've got that ring job to start in the morning," Toad said. "And that farmer's comin' in with the bad starter, and we promised that Buick he'd be out by noon. And Peale's comin' by to git the work done you promised. And Rawlins is ready for the new cam. We got to pull the engine for that—"

"Ronnie can start tearing the Hudson down while you and I get rid of those other jobs," I said. "Joe, you come in and help . . ."

"I gotta wash those other cars," Ronnie said. "Don't I?"

"The hell with the wash job this time!"

"But they're expecting—"

"I'll tell them we're too busy. That we can't find a wash boy. We can't let Joe rot during the racing season."

"They'll be mad," Ronnie said.

"The hell with 'em. Come on. Let's get on seventy-two. A week from tonight, you're going to be on the track in that stroker!"

"Hot damn!" Ronnie exclaimed. "Let's get rollin'."

"Get moving, Toad," I said.

Toad answered in a low whine. "I'm too old to work night and day."

"But you will."

Then we closed on the red-and-yellow Tudor, and the night grew old. And once, when I paused for a cigarette, I had a sudden mental picture of Herpgruve, fat and insolent and triumphant, behind his little table in the pay shack.

CHAPTER 22

THE PITS AGAIN. THE TRACK LIGHTS ON, the crowd filing in, the song of engines, the smell of gas fumes, hot oil. The prerace tension. Who would win tonight, who would roll? Who would smash a new hole in the fence, leave skin and gasoline on the track? Half a dozen cars on the track, turning slowly. The water truck, that I'd rented at a killing rate, making its rounds. I had been on the truck all afternoon. Now Toad making the final laps with it. The track announcer kept calling the pits for more cars to get out and iron out the track.

"Let's get those cars out . . . If you boys don't want to run on a heavy track, you'd better get out there now. Time trials start at eight, no matter what the track is like. Let's get those cars out . . ."

Another race night. The same . . . and different. Tonight we ran. Tonight there was a ghost in the pits. A red-and-yellow Tudor with a three-eighths stroker, a cam, and a nitromethane-methanol mixture in the pressure tank. No hood. A protective framework of heavy pipe in front of the radiator. No fenders. Big lug tires on the rear, a small left front, and a medium-sized right front wheel.

Ronnie was ready. Pale, eyes big, jaw muscles rigid. I knew the turmoil that he felt. It wasn't something that ever went away. It was there at the beginning of every race. His hands shook as he lit a cigarette. He was wearing clean denims and a red flannel shirt. Inside the car, a white helmet and a pair of goggles hung from the rearview mirror. Bill's hat and goggles. The flannel shirt had been Bill's, too.

Ronnie paced. He checked the tires, the fuel tank, the radiator, the chains on the doors. "Shouldn't I ought to get out and help work the track down?"

He stood next to me, shivering.

"There's time," I said. "Take it easy."

He threw away his cigarette and lit another, sucking hard.

He moved his shoulders like a fighter getting ready for the first round. "How do you think I'll be, Ace?"

"Like I told you," I said. "We don't want to wreck the car the first night. Don't try to win anything. Just learn how to get around in traffic."

"Okay, Ace. How about my going out now for a few laps?"

I figured he'd be better off driving than standing around being nervous. "Okay. Get in and start her up."

He climbed in through the top and dropped into the bucket seat. The first thing he did was snap his safety belt. Then he put on his helmet and goggles. His fingers shook so hard he almost couldn't get the strap secured.

"You look like a real pro," I said. "Kick it in."

He started the engine. At low idle, it sounded like a pile of junk, barely able to turn over. I gave him the signal for more revs. The higher they climbed, the smoother the engine sounded. It was a dream. He backed off at my signal, and the engine clattered noisily in its idle.

"Slow and easy," I said. "You want to pack the track, not dig it up. Watch me for your signal to come in."

I stepped back. This was the way it started. The first race. Then the second, the third . . . and a guy was hooked. Forever after. Ronnie gave me a last, long look, and then bending over his wheel, he shifted into low and eased out toward the track. In a few seconds, the red-and-yellow Tudor was making its circle, spitting and barking at the low speed. A laugh went up in the crowd as Ronnie passed. They'd seen the name we painted on the back of the car. THE TORQUEING DOG.

I watched him go around. The car handled well, and he handled it well. And he was obeying instructions. One after another, other cars pulled up alongside him and then shot past, trying to tease him into a spurt. But he held to his low speed, and kept to the outside, and remained an unknown quantity.

A slight figure in denim pants and a light jacket ran across the track into the pits. I knew who it was even before I saw the brown eyes and the red lips. Sandy, with a scarf over her head to protect her hair. She ran easily, like a child, almost skipping. My heart went out to her, and I walked toward her so she would see me.

"Surprised?" There was a look of mischief in her eyes.

"You don't belong in the pits."

"I thought you'd be glad to see me."

"After the race. It's no place for a woman. You know that."

"I thought I ought to come and help keep an eye on Ronnie," she said. "And see what it's like down here."

"Let me warn you in advance," I said, turning slowly to watch Ronnie's progress around the track. "The first couple of races will scare the bejeezus out of you. But no matter what happens or seems to be happening, keep your shirt on. Don't ever run out on the track. No matter what. It's a good way to get clobbered."

Sandy nodded. She was looking around curiously. "My rival doesn't seem very glamorous," she said, taking in the stands, the pits, the track.

"Not much for looks, but you should see her in action," I said, grinning. "You have to hold on with both hands."

"Ace!"

"You'll see."

We watched Ronnie square through a turn, his rear wheels spraying dirt as he drifted too high. Sandy grabbed me and made a frightened sound as Ronnie slid toward the fence. But he came out of it the way I knew he would and went on around without any trouble.

"Let's knock that stuff off right now," I said. "You're going to see a lot of hard driving, and if you're going to scream and grow faint every time somebody spins a wheel, maybe you'd better stay home."

"I can't help feeling scared," she said. "After what happened to Bill. Knowing it could happen to Ronnie."

"You're going to be a lot of fun to have around, aren't you?"

She looked at me for a long moment.

"I'm not trying to be nasty," I said. "I'm just trying to get Ronnie ready to race. I've got a lot of things on my mind, and it doesn't help to have you stand around looking worried."

"I have things on my mind, too." she said. "I've always been afraid of the track. I don't know if I can learn to live with it or not. In a way, it isn't as bad as I thought, and in another way—"

"Sandy," I begged, "honey . . . let's talk about that after the race. I'm trying to figure out which tires we ought to run."

"And I'm trying to find out if we can bury our dead," she answered.

"What dead? I don't have any."

"You have Thelma," Sandy said.

"That's over and done with," I said shortly.

"Is it? She looked at me curiously, almost coldly.

"I don't understand you, Sandy," I said irritably. "I'm proving it's over. I've quit the track as a driver. I want to marry you. What more do you want?"

"What she still has," Sandy said.

I shook my head. "Of all the times to stand around and talk in riddles. Just before a race."

"I'm trying to forget what happened with Bill," Sandy said. "I'm trying to get rid of my ghost before I marry you. But I don't want Thelma in our marriage either. You quit racing because of her. Is that why you won't drive again, even if you wanted to?"

"Let's talk about it after the race . . . Please . . ."

"The race," Sandy said. "Always the race. If I closed my eyes, I could be talking to Bill again."

"For God's sake, Sandy," I exploded. "What do you want? Do you want me to drive again? To get caught in it like Bill was caught? I'm trying to stay away from the wheel for your sake."

"Are you? I'm just trying to find out, Ace. I have to know how much racing I can take with my marriage. I have to know if it's going to be like it was before. Racing before everything else. What if it's the same old life all over again?"

"Well," I said, "what if it is?"

"I don't know," she said. "Maybe I'd know how to live it this time. Maybe not. That's what I have to find out, Ace. Before it's too late."

"All right, Sandy," I said. "Whatever you say. But *please* let's let it ride until after the races!"

Ronnie was looking for me. I gave him the sign to open up. Toad was off the track with the water truck, and the way was clear. Ronnie looked back as he went by and waved. He'd recognized Sandy.

The speed and the noise and the action built up as cars challenged each other, spurted, and backed off. The boys were serious now, looking for the groove, trying to find the best way to take the corners this night.

Ronnie sailed down the back chute with his engine singing. He backed off as he came into the turn and brought the car through with spurts of power, turning his wheels into a skid. As he came out of the turn, he floored the gas pedal and shot down the front chute wide open. The second time around, he came in hard, backing off very little. From where we stood, we could see the tense expression on his face and the way he wrestled the wheel as the car bounced and dug in and skidded through the turn. It was very loud, and the feeling of his speed was a little frightening to Sandy.

She turned a worried face toward me as two boys fought each other through the turn, engines screaming. "I didn't know they went so fast!" Her eyes were big.

I put my lips close to her ear. "You haven't seen anything yet."

She watched the cars come around, sliding and screaming, bumping each other. The look on her face was one of perplexity. I signaled Ronnie to come in. He'd accepted a couple of short challenges, and he was getting excited. I didn't want him to be disgraced by piling up during a practice lap.

He was shaking like a leaf as he climbed out through the top of the car. "How'd I look, Sand?" he cried in a shrill, unnatural voice.

"You frightened me."

He laughed, much too loudly.

"What did you find out?" I asked.

He came down to earth a little. "Everything seemed right."

"You getting a bite with those seventy-sixty tires?"

"Yeah. They seem to be biting all right."

"Could you go bigger tires without lugging?"

"Gee, Ace, I don't know."

"Uh-huh," I said brusquely. "I guess you wouldn't."

He turned red and was mad, but he needed it. Toad came over. "How was it, Ronnie?"

Ronnie looked at me before he answered. "All right. I guess."

"The kid did fine," I said to Toad.

I took Sandy by the arm. "Look, honey, you go back up on the judges' stand and watch from there."

"But I thought . . . I could stay. Herbert said—"

"For Ronnie's sake," I said. "You'll make him think about Bill. Besides, I need your help. When Ronnie's in a race, I want you to keep track of his exact position. In case there's a red flag and a restart during the race, we want him where he belongs."

"All right, Ace." She was disappointed, but she didn't argue. She took hold of my arm. "Take care of him, Ace. Don't let him get hurt."

"Don't worry," I said. "He'll be all right. Come back after the races are over."

"Okay," she said brightly. She ran across the track and went onto the judges' stand. She waved, and I waved back. I wanted Herpgruve to be around, so I could laugh in his face. We'd both forgotten that Sandy was a complete human being, and that she had some ideas of her own about what to do when in love with a racing man. If she became a part of racing, she would understand it, and no matter what it demanded of me, she would stick with me, because she would be a part of it too.

The time trials started. I sent Ronnie out with instructions to take the first timed lap as fast as he could without getting in over his head. If he was too slow, I'd give him the speed sign the second time around. If it was decent, we'd let it stand.

When Ronnie came out on the track, the announcer called attention to him and said that this was Bill's younger brother, driving the car his brother had been killed in. On the track for the first time. The crowd applauded. They'd be for him.

Ronnie went into his time lap with his foot on the floor. He went into the east turn hard, but good. But he was trying to do too much at once. He forced in the turn, and he was too green to recover when the rear end slid around too far. Instead of straightening out on the outside, he got scared of the fence and tried to cut away from it. The crowd went "Ooooooooohhhhh . . ." as he turned a complete circle on the track and came to a stop. Then they laughed a little when he couldn't get started. The tow truck drove out, got behind him, and pushed him into action again. When he passed the spot where I was standing inside the west turn, he didn't look at me. He went around and into his second time lap. This time he was too cautious, and the crowd really laughed. He wound up with an official time of 23.47 seconds, a good four seconds slower than the leaders.

Ronnie was disgusted when he came into the pits. He jumped out of the car, swearing at himself and puffed with shame and anger.

"Cool off, boy," I said. "You're not hurt. With your time, you'll be in the front row in the heat. That's when it counts."

Ronnie sat on top of 72 during the rest of the time trials. The slow heat was to be run first, and he was ready and waiting to get on the track. He was in the first row on the outside. I went with him to the starting line.

"You can get the jump on the pole car," I said. "Get out in front and try to stay there. But if somebody makes a clean pass, don't try to fight him off when it's too late. Get in the groove and look for a chance to go past. With this car and a front-row start, you ought to end up at least third. If you do, I'll be satisfied."

I don't think he heard a word I said. I patted him on the shoulder. "Good luck, boy." I felt as though I were sending him to wipe out a machine-gun nest with a bean shooter. The green flag went up, and a dozen engines revved. The flag dropped, and the field moved with a thunderous noise. Only Ronnie didn't move. For a full two seconds, he was motionless. The cars behind him were jammed and tried to pull to the outside to get around. By the time he got going, four cars had seeped past him, and the field was grinding into the east turn, a tightly packed mass of belligerent machinery. Ronnie was somewhere in the middle. I shut my eyes.

A cheer brought them open again. The field was around the turn and coming into the back chute, the red-and-yellow Tudor was moving up fast. By the time the two leaders reached the west turn, Ronnie was right behind them, with the will and the power to pass, but without the knowledge.

He began learning the hard way.

He tried to come around on the outside with his superior power, but the coupe he was tailing drifted toward the fence and shut him off. Tearing down the front chute at top speed, Ronnie pulled to the left, to try an inside pass, and found his way blocked by the second car. He took the turn too close to the pole, drifted out, and lost ground to the others. When he came around again, still trying to pass, I motioned him to the outside.

He went for three laps without being able to get past, driving better than I had hoped. Then the two lead cars, which had been neck and neck, parted company as the car on the outside, a black-and-white coupe, suddenly blew a water hose and coasted to the fence. Now it was a two-car race, with the rest of the field strung out to the rear. Ronnie and the leader, a maroon coupe.

I watched my boy, and I was proud of him. He kept to the outside, riding close, waiting for his chance. And it came. The lead car stayed high a second too long coming into the west turn, and Ronnie cut. The crowd screamed with joy as he got the inside of the maroon coupe, nosed forward, and came out of the turn, gaining ground. With an open track, it was easy. He pulled ahead with a roar and was all alone into the east turn. He looked back two or three times, as though unable to believe he was out in front.

When he came past me again, I gave him the signal to stroke it. All he had to do now was hold his lead. There was no point spinning out trying to increase it. He stroked it, but too much. In the last lap, he sailed around high and easy, never noticing that the maroon coupe was picking up ground. I motioned him on as he came through the west turn, but he was looking for the checkered flag, and didn't see me. I swore as the maroon coupe hit the turn full on, while Ronnie was stroking through high on the outside. The maroon coupe came in tight and hard. He had to drift, but he had Ronnie to catch him. Maroon kept his foot down all the way, and Ronnie was there. The maroon coupe slammed against Ronnie, stopping its own slide as it shoved him toward the fence. Ronnie was taken by surprise. Instead of coming back hard, he took his foot off the gas and tried to straighten out. Another car whipped past him, and he was third to get the flag. Now I could relax and laugh, and Toad laughed with me. It had been a good race. Better than if he had won the first time out. He'd learned more.

Ronnie chugged into the pits with his engine steaming. He had hardly stopped before he was climbing out of the car, mad as a wet bee. "What'd you slow me down for?" he bawled at me. "I had that race. What's the matter with you?"

"I told you to stay ahead, not quit racing," I said in a hard voice. "All you had to do was keep your lead. What'd you do, fall asleep? You kept looking for girls in the stands or something, because you didn't look at me!"

"Chrissake, Ronnie," Toad complained. "All you had to do was stay in front."

"And don't run for your hole the first time somebody bumps you," I scolded. "You quit cold the minute you felt that coupe bump your side. Don't be afraid of the fence. It can't hurt you! Fight back!"

He looked bewildered and wiped the black dirt off his cheeks. The part of his face that had been protected by the goggles looked very white. It gave him a big-eyed, staring look. He was shaking so hard I thought he was going to fly apart.

"That was a pretty good race for your first one," I said in a kindlier voice. "Come on, I'll buy you a cup of coffee."

We walked through the pits to the coffee stand. A score of voices called out to Ronnie, telling him it had been a nice race. He began to unwind a little. It was over, and he had lived through it.

He gulped the hot coffee, spilling it on his chin and his shirt. "I—I was thinking, Ace—"

"Yeah?"

"I wasn't shooting off the corners as good as I should have."

"Put your foot in it. You've got the power."

"My foot was in it. Maybe I ought to try bigger tires."

"All right," I said. "If you think you can do better with them, on they go."

He looked startled. He hadn't expected me to agree just like that.

"You're the driver," I said. "You know what's happening out there."

We went back to 72. We had a big pile of tires near the car. Toad was looking underneath the car with a flashlight.

"We're giving the boy eight hundreds," I said to Toad. "He says he's spinning his wheels and winding out the engine with the small skins."

Toad grunted and got our jack. He raised 72's rear end and started knocking off the right wheel. Ronnie stood by with his hands in his pockets, watching critically, feeling big.

"Ronnie," I said.

"Yeah?"

"Get that left wheel off, boy. You're supposed to work on this car as well as drive it. Snap into it."

He stopped dreaming whatever big-shot dream had been going through his mind and got to work with a lug wrench, sweating and dirty. That's what it took to learn to love a car. Not just driving it. Being with it in sickness and health, for better or worse, on the track and in the pits and in the garage. Mingling your sweat with its grease, your blood with its oil. Knowing the feel of every part in every mood, knowing its soul by its voice. This was no fleeting love affair once flesh and iron had consummated their relationship. It was until death or destruction did you part.

CHAPTER 23

ALL AT ONCE IT BECAME A BAD NIGHT.

The fast heat race started off smoothly, with the big names at the track running their usual fast and smooth race. Five laps with the pack bunched, coming through the turns like a team of chariot horses, side by side, flying wildly.

Then somebody tried too hard, or hit a bad bump, or couldn't hold on. All of a sudden, somebody was coming around the turn sideways, and there was hell to pay.

De Marco hit the spun car full force. It went over on its side with a heavy smash. De Marco's little orange coupe seemed to lower its head like a bull trying to gore a fallen matador. The orange body did a headstand, vaulted over the spun car, and came down with a force that shook the earth in the pits.

The crowd was screaming, but not loud enough to drown the smash of the two cars against the earth, or the crashes that followed.

Jensen tried to pull to the outside, power on. But Towner was trying the same thing at the same time, and there wasn't room for two. The cars tangled. Jensen rammed the fence full on, tearing loose a long chunk of metal boilerplate. He went high in the air, bobbing inside his car like a white cork as it twisted away from the fence and rolled over and over. Towner was thrown back toward the inside and smashed into de Marco's overturned coupe before he tipped and fell on his side. Chip Vann, following closely, did the only thing there was left to do. He took to the infield, sliding sideways on the dirt, scattering pit crewmen until he smacked into a truck.

The other cars in the heat were far enough behind to downshift and turn off the track.

The ambulance came out with red lights flashing and siren going. Everyone in the pits took off on foot at top speed. Policemen ran in from the stands. The crowd was on its feet, trying to see what had happened to the drivers who had crashed right in front of them.

We were nearest de Marco and got to him first. He was hanging head down, his head touching the top of the car frame where it had been bashed in. Ronnie got down on his stomach and pulled himself forward until he was cushioning de Marco's body with his own. Then he rolled over and reached up to unfasten de Marco's safety belt and eased him down until we could get at him and drag him out. The crowd made a sighing, sick sound as they saw us pull out the inert body.

The boy in the car de Marco had hit was being helped out by others. All the skin had been scraped off his left arm, leaving a long ribbon of exposed red meat. When he was helped to his feet, he turned a bloody face toward the crowd and spat out broken teeth. Jensen was on his feet, dazed and dirty, holding one hand pressed against his stomach and limping badly as he tried to leave the track. Towner was standing next to his car, his feet in a puddle of gasoline, trying to light a cigarette. Someone led him away to a safe place and gave him a smoke.

The intern on duty with the ambulance bent over de Marco and gave him a quick examination. There was a bruise on de Marco's neck, but otherwise he was unmarked. His face was white, and his breathing shallow.

"I can't feel anything broken," the intern said. "Load him in. We'll take him to the hospital. The others, too."

The drivers who were conscious protested, but they got into the ambulance with de Marco. All of them seemed to be in a state of shock, and they moved slowly, their eyes staring. The ambulance drove out of the pit gate and disappeared. We could hear the siren wailing steadily as the driver rushed to the hospital.

The tow truck came out, and the work began of prying the wrecked cars apart, righting them, and towing them off the track. The car owners were making quick appraisals of the damage even as they worked to get their cars into the pits.

The announcer's voice came to us on the track. "All right, fellows—let's get those cars cleared off the track so the next race can get underway . . ."

The cars were towed away, the gasoline was fired, and in a few minutes the cars in the middle speed heat were chugging out to line up for their race. In the pits, repair work went on at a feverish pace. Smashed radiators were pulled, bent wheels came off, the twisted bodies were hammered back into some kind of shape, and spare parts were sought.

The next heat race couldn't be run until the ambulance returned, and when it did come back, siren crying and red lights flashing, all the drivers were back with it. Bandaged as they needed to be, revived, cleaned up a little, they were all on their feet and ready to roll. By the time the next heat had been run, Towner's car was roaring in the pits. There was a fifteen-minute delay in running the Australian pursuit to give the top cars a chance. And when that time limit was up, less than an hour after the terrific smash-up, the battered, dragging, misshapen cars of de Marco, Towner,

Jensen, and Vann rolled out to run in the race with their bruised and wounded drivers at their usual wheels.

None of them finished in the money. Steaming, dragging, sputtering, their cars ran a few hard laps and soured out for the night, wheels dragging, engines grinding, steaming, and dying. The Australian pursuit was won by Loren Peale in the crumpled and torn car that had once been his gleaming but never-winning pride.

Ronnie ran again in the semi-main and took second money. He put up a good race. Even a smart one. With fifteen laps to run, he laid back until the field spread out, then worked his way up one car at a time. He had one bad moment when two cars locked wheels and spun in ahead of him as he tried to come around on the outside. He didn't hesitate, but floored the coupe and headed for what narrow space was still left to him between the car and the fence. He squeaked through with the crowd shrieking in excitement, and was on his way around the turn like a veteran, his engine going *rrroooommm . . . roooom . . . rroooommm . . .* as he fed it the gas and backed off in little dabs to get around and in the groove.

Without the fast boys in, the main event was fairly dull. Slow boys fought hard, and a new boy won top money for the first time in his life.

The crowd spilled over into the pits as usual after the races. Sandy came over to our car while we got ready to hook it behind Ronnie's street car. Her face was caked with dust, and she looked tired and pale.

I put my arms around her. "How'd you like it, hon?"

She looked up at me, her eyes wide and uncomprehending. "I don't...don't understand it. Why? Why do they . . . do you do it? What's the purpose? I think it's awful. *Awful!*"

She turned to Ronnie, who was grinning proudly over his showing. "No more of this for *you*, Ronnie! I won't let you!"

"Back off, Sandy," I teased. "Wait until you've seen a few races . . . You'll like it better."

"It's disgusting. It's brutal . . . pointless. Stupid!"

"I ain't gonna quit, Sandy," Ronnie said. "I like it."

"Why? *Why?*" She turned to me, gripping my arms. "Why? Is life so . . . meaningless, to throw it away doing this?"

"The first race always looks worse than it is," I said to Sandy. "You'll get used to it when you've seen more. It was a bad night."

"Never again," she said, her voice low and horrified. "I kept seeing Bill. I know what it was like now . . . In front of that screaming, stupid crowd. . . . An exhibition . . . a show . . . and he *died* for it!"

"Sandy—don't."

"I've had enough."

"Other women live with it," I said. "Other women don't run out. Look around." The curious had drifted away, and only the families were left clustered around the grimy, tired drivers. The wives who looked as tired as their husbands, the weary children. They stood around their broken machines like little groups of refugees. Sandy looked at the drooping women, the fussy, exhausted children. She saw Mrs. Peale, a fading blonde flower in a worn, hand-me-down dress, and the little flock of shabby, neglected children that clung to her.

"Is this what you're offering me?" Sandy asked. "Is this what I'm to share? Is this how our children will live? Until there's another accident and we're abandoned? I don't want to be any part of this, Ace. Not even in the garage. Taking money that ought to buy food for children so some stupid man can race and break his neck! Why? Why do they do it?"

The cars pulled out, the cripples were dragged, towed, and carried. The drivers and their families went past, following the engines and wheels that dominated their lives. Faces swam past, dirty, bitter, frustrated, angry. Hard, tough faces, dark with anger and disappointment, but not one sagging in defeat. Not one.

"Why do they do it?" I said to Sandy, repeating her question. "Because, that's why. Maybe for the same reason, people climb mountains. I asked a climber once why he did it, and he said he climbed the mountain because it was there. Maybe that's the way it is with race drivers. We drive cars because they exist, and on tracks because they're there."

Sandy watched another poorly dressed family trudge out of the pits in the wake of a wrecked coupe.

"Don't the families of race drivers exist?" she asked. "'What about them?"

"They're the same breed that used to follow the old man behind the covered wagon," I said. "It's always tough to be a pioneer. Or a pioneer's wife."

"Not everyone can be a pioneer," Sandy said, "Or a pioneer's wife."

"I guess not," I said. "It takes guts to head into the unknown. Not everybody can face a life that might not always provide three meals a day and a bed at night. Or have some kind of Indian after your scalp. Some women always find a Herbert to take care of them."

Sandy stiffened. I thought it was because of what I'd said, but she was staring past me. Chip Vann was walking past, his ear bandaged, a big cigar in his mouth. He looked toward me and started to say something, and then he saw Sandy. His round face turned pink, and he hurried on. Sandy stared after him, unaware that she was digging her fingers into my arm.

I looked down at her, feeling myself shaking. Why always that? Had Thelma hurt me so bad that I would go through the rest of my life wondering if Sandy had been intimate with every man who knew her? Yet, why Chip's blush, and Sandy's agitation?

I turned Sandy toward me, looking deep into her eyes. "What's the matter?"

She looked away. "N—Nothing,"

"Tell me."

"It's nothing!"

"Don't try to kid me, Sandy. There's something between you and Chip."

She shook her head. "No. Anyway . . . not what you think."

"How do you know what I'm thinking?"

"Your face shows it."

"What is it, then?"

She looked around. Ronnie and Toad were busy with 72 and couldn't hear us.

"He . . . Chip . . . He's the one who . . . the one I . . . hired to . . ." She made a shuddering sound and turned away.

"He spun Bill into the fence?" She nodded. "Are you sure?" "He was the one I . . . paid."

Chip Vann. It was hard to believe, but not too hard. He wasn't supposed to kill Bill. Just put him out of action.

"I'd better go home now," Sandy said. "I've had enough."

"Ronnie can take you," I said. "I'll get our share of the purse."

"How much did he win?"

"Can't tell until we know the gate. But it ought to be about three dollars for third in the heat, and maybe fifteen for placing in the semi-main. On a sixty-forty cut, that would mean about ten dollars and eighty cents for the garage, and a little better than seven dollars for Ronnie."

She looked at me, thinking about the pile-up in the fast heat, the smashed cars, and the wounded drivers. "They do that for two and three dollars? What I saw?"

"Yeah," I said. "And they'll find fifty to spend getting ready to run again next week for the same purse. I told you it wasn't money that brings them out. This is the frontier, Sandy. And it's where the frontiersmen gather." I felt bitter and angry. "Some day, when it's all respectable and clean and safe, these boys will be out of it. They'll be too old. The tracks will belong to the bright young drivers with sponsors, and nobody will even want to listen to stories about these days."

She shook her head irritably, as though shaking off a gnat. "Then why . . . ?"

"I told you once. Because it's there."

"That's not a reason, Ace. That's an excuse."

"Call it what you want to," I said. "We're in it."

"Speak for yourself, Ace," Sandy said, huddling down in her leather jacket. "I've had enough. More than enough." She leaned against 72 and closed her eyes. She looked tired and beat.

"I'm speaking for you, too, Sandy," I said, watching her face. "Maybe you thought you were going to dip your toe in the water and run out if it was too cold, but it doesn't work like that. Maybe you don't know it, but you're like the rest of us. You're up to your neck in it whether you like it or not. So just forget about Bill, and quit looking like you smell something bad, and learn to live with it."

Her eyes opened slowly. "Until when? Until I drag myself to the track with a bunch of kids who don't have clothes or food to watch Daddy break his neck for two dollars—that he'll spend on his *car* if he wins? I don't like it, and if I don't want it, I don't have to have it."

"What can you do?" I asked. "You're already part of it."

"I'll find some way to get Ronnie off the track," she said stubbornly. "And you, too."

"What can you do?" I repeated, wanting to see her whipped right away, so she'd come along without dragging her feet.

She looked at me, grinning at her, sure of myself, sure of her.

"I don't know," she said. "But before I'd let myself get like those other women—" She smiled, but it wasn't pretty. "There's no telling what I might do, is there, Ace?"

It was her turn to stare me down, and the fact that she could needle me with what she'd done to Bill made me shaky inside. I couldn't stand to have a woman needle me about *anything*.

She moved away from 72, and I swear she wiggled her hips. "You know that about me, Ace," she said in a mocking tone. "There's no telling what I might do, is there?"

That was the way she left me.

CHAPTER 24

SEVENTY-TWO WAS ACTING UP. For no reason. It was smooth enough at *medium* rpms, but it wasn't peaking right. I pulled the stack-type air cleaner off the carburetor and revved the engine hard.

"Here's the trouble," I said to Toad, cutting the engine. "The damn throttle valve won't get in a vertical position. File the throttle stop down and adjust it, will you?"

"Now?"

"Of course, now!" I yelled at him. "When do you think? Next summer?"

"I'd ought to git that *Buick* ready . . . feller's coming this afternoon." Toad looked at me quizzically.

"The hell with the *Buick*. We got to run tonight, don't we?"

"If you say *so*." Toad reached into my pocket for a cigarette. "You ain't gettin' enough sleep, Ace. You look beat."

"I don't have time," I said. I lit a cigarette. My hands were shaky. I breathed smoke in and out and looked toward the office, where Sandy was working. For the thousandth time that day, I suppose. It had been like that for a week. We hadn't exchanged ten words since the race night. She'd retreated into a shell, and I was shut out.

"Trouble twixt you and Sandy?" Toad asked.

"I guess."

"We'd ought to leave here, Ace. You and me. You don't want no woman crampin' your style."

I shook my head. "I'm going to marry her," I said. "And make this place go."

"It's goin' now," Toad said. "Goin' to hell. We've already lost business, on account of we don't wash the cars no more."

"We'll get it back."

"Yeah."

"You're a pessimist," I said, pushing him with the toe of my boot.

"I been down this slide before."

"Toad . . ."

"That's me."

"How did Chip Vann put Bill in the fence?"

"Who said he did?"

"Didn't he?"

"I guess I know who I made simple-minded by crackin' his skull with a wrench."

A face came to mind. A face with expressionless blue eyes.

"Duke. Duke Ossman."

"Guess so," Toad said.

I wanted to laugh. Sandy thought she'd hired Chip to do it, and Ossman had been the one. And she didn't know. Still thought she was responsible for Bill's death. I wanted to rush into the office and tell her, but I held back. Not now. If she was coming to me and taking the racetrack life that went with me, she had to come as she was. No assists. Or it wouldn't be right.

"Why didn't Chip tell Sandy he didn't do it?" I asked Toad.

"Well, I guess he sorta thought she knew. But feelin' funny about agreein' to do the job in the first place, he wasn't comin' around to make sure. And you know why I didn't tell her."

"Yeah, you'd have had to admit bashing Ossman. But why'd Ossman take after Bill?" I asked Toad.

"Oh, one of them things," Toad said. "Bill was tryin' to lap him, and Ossman wouldn't pay no heed to the move-over flag. Stayed in the groove. So, Bill put his front bumper against Ossman's tail and pushed him out of the way. Ossman got mad, and when Bill went by on the outside, he just steered into him. Carried him right to the fence and kilt him."

"And you went after Ossman."

"Yup." Toad sniggered. "After I got through, the poor nut was as simple in the haid as one plus one. Been that way ever since."

"You're a sweet guy."

"I aimed to kill him, I did."

I looked at the grease-smeared little mechanic with his thin, puckery face and straggly white hair. He didn't look as though he could hold his own against a sturdy ten-year-old. But he, too, had his loyalties and his hates. I was glad that Toad was on my side.

"Don't you really think I'll make it, Toad?" I said.

"Not a chance."

"Why not? It's a good spot. I want to make it go."

"Yer blood's bad, Ace."

"You just watch, you old shite-poke," I said grimly. "I'll show you."

"I'm watchin'," Toad grunted.

— — —

Toad and I ate supper, then returned to the garage. As soon as Ronnie showed up with his car, we'd tow 72 to the track for another run.

I felt lonesome and lost waiting with Toad. When Sandy had first come to the track, I'd looked forward to having her with us every race night. It was a way we'd grow closer and get to know each other better. Sharing. But she'd had enough. Whatever I did with racing now, as car owner or mechanic, would be against her. We had a fine future that way. I *could* give up all connections with racing, but I wasn't ready to.

I heard Ronnie coming a long way off. He roared down the street and swung his black coupe in next to the garage. I looked up when he stopped, and there, sitting in the seat beside him, her scarf over her head, was Sandy.

I didn't know what to think or say. I just looked hopeful. Sandy laughed at my expression. "Come on, Jones, get moving," she said. "We want to get to the track tonight, don't we?"

"You're coming along!"

She nodded, sighing. "I wasn't going to. Not ever again. My mind was made up until after dinner. Then, while I was doing the dishes, I suddenly got kind of restless. I couldn't understand it at first, and suddenly it came to me. Race night. I couldn't wait to get dressed and have Ronnie get me."

I bent down and kissed her, mindless of Ronnie or Toad. "You're one of us, darling," I said.

"If the other women can do it—I can. Can't I?"

"You're one of us," I repeated. "Now you're beginning to know what it feels like when race night comes up. You can't stay away. You . . . just . . . can't."

"Let's go, then. Get in gear, Ace!"

Sandy left us at the pit gate and took her place on the judges' stand to keep a lap count for us. We unhooked 72, unloaded our fuel and extra tires, and got ready to run. I hummed aloud.

"You sound cheerful," Toad grunted.

"Why not? You see how it is with me and Sandy now."

"I see."

"You don't sound very happy about it."

"Why should I? It ain't nothing to me. I was hopin' we'd git to the big time, us two."

"Toad, this is the big time for me. Being with Sandy."

"What are you gonna do when the garage goes bust, and you got her on your hands?"

"I'm not going bust." I was annoyed by his pessimism. He made me think of Herpgruve's complacent belief that I would ruin myself. He made me feel unsure. "You talk like that anymore, and I'll run your tail out of the garage," I said. "I mean that."

Ronnie came up, impatient and jittery. "What's holding you guys up? I want to get out and take my slow laps."

"Watch me every time you come around tonight," I said. "And you run where and how I say. Understand?"

"I guess I know what to do, Ace. After all, I'm on the track, and—"

"You won't be if you don't do what I say. Now get out there and feel out the track. And for God's sake, have something intelligent to say when you come back in."

Ronnie drove onto the track, leaving the acrid smell of his fuel mixture burning our nostrils.

"You better watch out," Toad said. "That boy's beginning to feel his oats, now that he's raced. He'll deck you again if you sass him."

"We'll take care of him tonight," I said.

"Yeah?"

"The boys have been holding off on account of his being Bill's brother. I think he ought to get the same welcome out here anybody else would get."

"Might cost us a smashed car, too," Toad complained.

"It's worth it if he doesn't get a swelled head. He needs toning down."

When Ronnie had run his time trials and managed to get in the Trophy Dash, I went to see the other boys who would be running against him. They weren't too cordial, in spite of the fact that I had worked on the track. They remembered my sneering at them as small-time country drivers, and it rankled.

"Ronnie's in the Trophy," I said to de Marco, who was sitting alone in his orange coupe.

"So what?"

"He thinks he's pretty hot."

"He ain't the only one."

"You'd do him a favor if you treated him the same as any other newcomer out there. He needs it."

De Marco gave me a sullen look. "He'll get treated the same. We've got no love for your car, Jones. Or your boy."

"Okay," I said. "That's all I want to know." It was all right. Ronnie wouldn't get any favors.

I went back to Ronnie. "You're in the Trophy Dash tonight," I said. "It's going to be rough. Don't get scared, or mad, or lose your head. You'll get passed, so don't worry about it."

"Maybe I'll get passed," Ronnie said confidently. "I learned something last week. The way those guys kept me from passing. I can do that."

"Don't try it with the fast boys," I said. "Believe me."

"Get off my back, Ace," Ronnie said tiredly. "Either I'm the driver or I ain't. If I ain't, you get in and drive for yourself."

"All right, kid," I said. "Calm down. I'm just trying to help you."

He nodded nervously. "Okay. I know. I'm okay."

He was in the second row on the outside for the Trophy Dash. When the green flag went down, he cut to the outside and went into the turn high. He thought he was doing fine, but the fast boys were coming up through the traffic after him, and although he didn't know it, he was running on de Marco's favorite track.

Into the west turn, Ronnie was out in front, but the next time around, both de Marco and Jensen were on his tail. Ronnie bent over the wheel, pushing, apparently thinking they were trying to pass. But, of course, they didn't want to pass. They wanted second money, and they were keeping him out in front.

But he couldn't go fast enough. He didn't have enough savvy

to set a pace. He was slow. And that gave another car a chance to slide past de Marco and Jensen and Ronnie before Ronnie knew what the score was. Then, Ronnie was in the way for anybody who wanted second money.

De Marco tried the first pass, and Ronnie drifted high in front of him. Just like it had been done to him. When he drifted high to block de Marco, Jensen breezed past on the inside. De Marco cut to the left, and Ronnie blocked him again.

They came up the back chute fast, with de Marco's front bumper nerfing Ronnie's rear bumper. Each time he was bumped, Ronnie looked back, nervous and scared, and not knowing what to do. So, he tried to stay in the groove.

They went around the west turn with de Marco's car touching Ronnie's. De Marco could have spun the kid out of the way without half trying, but he was easy on Ronnie. Around the turn, de Marco made a pass to the right. Ronnie gamely pulled to the right, but even as he did, de Marco was moving toward the left, and he went by on that side, squeezing Ronnie in close to the fence. He held Ronnie out until they reached the east turn, then de Marco dropped down into the groove and skated around in hot pursuit of Jensen, while Ronnie rode the rim, sliding and churning in the loose dirt at the top of the track. By the time he was back in control again, he was running last, and that was how he finished.

"Smart, weren't you!" I bawled at Ronnie as he cut the engine in the pits. "Going to show the big boys how to play their own game. You see where it got you!"

"What am I supposed to do? Let everybody go past? I'm willing to mix it with anybody out there. That's the only way I'll learn!"

"Run the way I tell you!"

"Maybe I don't want to. Why do you always have to be right?" He was shaking mad. "What do you know about it? You're just a mechanic!"

We went at it so hot and heavy, we didn't hear the PA system. We did hear the crowd roar at something. Toad had heard. He was laughing and coughing with a kind of mean delight.

"What's so funny?" I yelled at him. "What's going on? What are they calling our number for?"

Toad grinned at me. "Special race coming up. Special extra race presented by Herbert Herpgruve, owner and operator of Town Raceways."

"What kind of special race?" I was aware of other drivers coming our way, their faces twisted in amused but spiteful grins.

"Why," Toad said, "it's a mechanic's race. And since I can't see good enough to walk, let alone drive, it looks like you're it."

— — —

No thanks, none for me. I don't touch the stuff anymore. I only get behind the wheel to drive to church on Sunday morning. Nobody could force me to drive anymore. Nobody, except a guy named Herpgruve.

Maybe Sandy had told him about the kind of crazy driver I'd been, and he'd hoped my long layoff would finally kill me once I started to go for the other drivers out there on the track. Or probably it was just that he knew my kind. He knew that once I got on rubber again, I wouldn't quit. That I'd let everything go to hell so I could keep driving—including Sandy. And he'd be right there to tell her . . .

"You want to wear my helmet, Ace?" It was Ronnie, fumbling around, trying to be helpful.

I shook my head. "Scratch seventy-two. I'm not racing."

"You have to, Ace. They'll say you're yellow."

"The hell with 'em."

"But nobody will come around to the garage anymore," Ronnie said. "Not even the passenger cars. People are funny around here about things like this. The race is for you. You're a stranger."

"Hey, Jones!"

It was Loren Peale. He'd changed since his car had been wrecked. He didn't shave before the races anymore, and his mustache was getting long and ragged. Once that beloved car of his had been smashed, he seemed to turn into a real wild man.

"You been talking mighty big around here, Jones," he taunted. "Telling everybody else how to run. Suppose you show us how it's done in the big time. We want to hear, don't we, boys?" The others were getting a good, vicious laugh out of every word.

Then Ronnie stepped away from our car toward Peale. "Shut up, Loren, or I'll smack you."

I grabbed Ronnie by the shoulder and pushed him against our car. "I don't need you to front for me with these hyenas!"

"Then drive!" Ronnie pleaded. "You gotta drive, Ace. You've talked enough now. You got to show 'em you've got the guts."

Toad was leaning against the side of 72, squint-eyed, a slight smile twisting his lips. "Toad," I said. "What do you think? You know what will happen if I start driving."

"Guess I do."

"That's not all," I said. "Somebody will get hurt. I can't tell you, but somebody will get hurt."

"Somebody usually does," Toad answered.

And then I knew I had to go through with it. I put on the crash hat and goggles and climbed into the bucket seat. I turned the key, and the engine barked to life. The fumes drifted into the cockpit and into my nose. Moving out of habit now, I took a handkerchief from my pocket and put a corner of it in my mouth. I held it there to keep out the dirt and to wipe my goggles if I got splattered.

I was on the track. The car trembling as the engine labored at low rpm, the track moving back under my feet, exposed by the ripped-out floorboards. The other cars coming out, the chorus of engines, the flagman waiting on his platform, the starter motioning us into position.

I was in the third row, on the outside. I drove into my spot, and out of habit, I looked toward the crowd. Looked for Thelma. And when she wasn't there, the old pain came back, and the old sickness of hate and disgust.

Until I looked up at the judges' stand and saw Sandy staring down at me through the wire screen.

I shut off my engine, unsnapped my safety belt, and crawled out to meet her as she ran down the steps to the edge of the track. I grabbed her by the shoulders. "This wasn't my idea, Sandy," I said, hoping she'd believe me. "It's a trick of Herb's. You know I don't want to drive. I got sucked into it."

"It's all right, Ace," she said. There was something strange about her calmness.

"I know you have to drive."

"You could stop me. You're the owner."

She shook her head slowly. She looked as though she were getting ready to jump off a high diving board and wasn't sure she could swim. "I wouldn't humiliate you like that, Ace."

"If I start to drive, I might not be able to stop," I said. "I might get like Bill. You know that."

"Yes," she said. "I know that." She looked me full in the face. "You don't understand, Ace. I want you to drive. The mechanic's race was my idea."

"*Your* idea!"

"I told you I've been doing a lot of thinking about us."

"Do you have to kill me too?"

She didn't answer for a moment. Then she asked suddenly, "Do you want to marry me?"

"You know damn well I do."

"All right, then drive! You've been running from Thelma long enough. I won't have a man whose life is run by the memory of another woman. You'll have to get rid of her on that track."

"What if I can't?"

"You shouldn't have asked me until you were sure you were free. But you did. And now you've got to make sure you're free."

The homey type. The wife type, the broom-and-dust-pan type. Pretty, sweet, comfortable. That's how I'd had her figured. And now she'd come up with her answer—one live husband all to herself, or one dead lover to share with Thelma. And I thought I was tough.

The flagman above us leaned over the railing of his platform. "Let's go, Jones." I turned away and walked back to my car, and climbed into the seat again. Sandy had to know. All right, she'd know, and maybe she wouldn't like it.

I started my engine, shifted into low, and held the clutch down, revving the engine. I had the handkerchief in my mouth. The starter poked his head inside the car to see if my safety belt was fastened. "Nine laps," he yelled. "No restart unless the track is blocked."

I nodded, looking straight ahead at the car in front of me, already planning which way I would cut and how many cars I'd try to pass before we were through the east turn.

My heart seemed to swell to ten times its size and break loose from its moorings, rising until it bumped against my throat, shutting off my breath. I was biting down on my handkerchief with all the strength of my jaws. My muscles were tensed to the snapping point. I risked a fleeting glimpse toward Sandy. She was standing under the flagman's platform where I had left her, hands under her chin, fingers locked. Her eyes were wide, her face pale. She was biting her lower lip.

I listened to the racket of engines around me and felt the tears come out of my eyes and spread on the rubber flanges of my goggles.

This was how the dream ended. In a gag. In a comic competition, a burlesque race. That would be very funny until I killed somebody.

In the movies and the books, a man's last race is always the big one, in front of big crowds, with a big meaning. Win or lose, it is a race with drama and dignity. Dignity.

Dignity . . . Ace Jones, once one of the greats, running his last race against a handful of grinning, nearsighted country mechanics, in a tin jalopy, on a homemade track, in front of a hooting crowd.

What a way to lose everything. I'd felt so safe, so secure, so *sure* I'd never drive again. All I wanted was to have my garage, and my girl, and a dot on the earth I could call home. All I wanted was to work on the racers, and be around the track, and let my young driver take the thrills.

And now I was behind the wheel again, ready to race, and the old red haze was on me. The way it always came. The engines screamed, and I wanted to scream with them. Thelma was gone . . . *Where?* I had to go, had to get around, had to finish in a hurry. Had to smash through the cars. Smash through the drivers who were laughing at me. My crazy hatred revved with the engines. I wanted the flag to drop so I could go and kill. And I was afraid. I wanted to let go of the wheel and hide my face and let them go on without me. Afraid because this wasn't a race, but an attack. Hurl myself against all those grinning faces that had made a fool of me. And kill them!

The mechanics were grinning all over the place as they waited for the flag. Cigars stuck in their faces. Revving their motors like mad. Having a big time. Laughing. They knew . . . they knew . . . I'd kill them for it . . . Oh, God. I was scared . . .

There was a blur of moving green and a sudden sound. A deafening roar of engines that rose from the ground like a tidal wave of sound. Before I knew in my head what had happened, my left foot was coming off the clutch, my right foot was feathering the gas pedal. I had swung sharply to the outside, and I was moving.

My race was on.

CHAPTER 25

The race was on, and it was the same. I drove into the traffic on the first corner like a maniac, struck at the other cars like a hurt snake that attacked anything that moved.

I was caught in a maelstrom of dust and fumes and flying clods, and I didn't drive through. I clawed my way through. I felt the shocks as I hit other cars, heard the grind of tearing metal, and was dimly aware of the spark showers that flew up from the wrestling fenders.

They were mechanics trying to drive, and they were headed in every direction as they skidded through the first turn, and I smashed through them, shaking them off, spinning them off, ramming them off. And even as I broke through, into the clear, and put my foot all the way in, I knew that no matter what happened, my only trophy would be ridicule. And I had to go. At top speed. Even if it killed me. I had to *go*!

They were lucky. Because they were inept and clumsy, I blasted through them on the first turn, and I was all by myself on the back chute, going like hell, tearing the guts out of 72 as I roared toward the west turn.

I sat hunched over the wheel. My lips peeled back, and my mouth felt like it was going to split at the corners, eyes staring so hard they popped out of my head. I held the gas pedal down and threw 72 into the corner. It was rough, and I should have backed off, but I couldn't lift the gas foot. The tires screamed like sirens as they took the force of the turn on the sidewalls and pulled away from the rims.

I could feel the left side of the car lift off the ground, and steered right, into the skid, holding the gas pedal to the floor. I was up on two wheels, heading for the fence, headed for a power-on roll, and I hung on to the wheel, turned my front wheels into the dirt, and poured on the coal. I hit back on four wheels again with a jolt that almost broke my back and had to wrestle the wheel to keep 72 from spinning into the wall. I was on the front chute, blasting ahead, with the rear end of 72 threatening to take off by itself any moment and throw me.

There weren't any brakes. Just power to cut as the world stopped spinning and rocking, and I went into the next corner with 72 still trying to break loose. My muscles ached, my back ached, my neck was sore, and I was shaking so hard I could hardly steer. *What had I tried to do?*

I'd been all alone and had gone into that turn in a way that should have killed me. And in the middle of it, when I was half in the air and half on the ground, when it looked like I was gone, what had I felt? Not fear, but the wildest, craziest peak of hatred I had ever known. A great wave of kill fever as if I'd gone all the way at last and discovered something that had me cold and shaking.

Bomb and target were the same.

I had target hypnosis, and I drove to kill, but my targets weren't in the other cars. The target was in my car. It was me. Now I understood why I had to smash ahead with my foot down even when I was alone on the track. The real reason why I was afraid to drive.

The hatred of the woman who betrayed me, of the drivers who mocked me, of the officials who banned m——that hatred was a mask to hide the face of the one I really hated.

Myself.

I was burning up the track now and couldn't stop. My foot was down, and I was beating 72 to death, and I couldn't stop. I'd found my target. Ace Jones.

I didn't hate Thelma for being unfaithful. I hated myself for being the kind of man a wife could betray. I didn't hate the man who had seduced my wife. I hated myself for playing the fool's role, and not the seducer's. I didn't hate the drivers who had laughed at me. I hated myself for being the one they laughed at.

The crowd went up on its feet as I tore through another turn, slammed against another car, and bounced toward the infield. But I kept going hard, bore-sighted on my target. Ace Jones, a guy who had started out with big plans, big schemes, big dreams—and wound up being a fool and a failure. Every time I saw his face in the mirror, I wanted to spit in it. Every time I got him on the track, I wanted to kill him.

And I tried. I tried to hold the wheel straight and go for the fence, but somehow my hands and feet wouldn't listen to my crazy brain. I'd caught up with the guy I'd been chasing, but I couldn't kill him. I couldn't.

And then I came down the front chute, trying dully to keep on target, and I saw Sandy standing on the platform, and I saw her wave. And suddenly Thelma was in a grave as deep as Bill's, and I wanted to live again and race to win, not die.

I hit the next corner fast and hard, but happy. I started to spin because suddenly 72 wasn't reacting right, but I drove myself through and began lapping the other cars with a feeling of pleasure and satisfaction I hadn't known in a race for a million years. I was me again, and I was back in action, and I didn't hate, and I didn't have to be scared.

Hell. Ace Jones was *somebody*!

Now I enjoyed the speed, the slam of the corners, siren-like screech of rubber against the hardpacked earth. Now I could feel every bump in the track in my fingers, the sudden tilt, like a fast turn in a plane as the track banked suddenly before the curve. And I would race again. I'd fix the things that were wrong with 72. Things I had to feel in a race to know. She didn't track right and had a tendency to tear loose on a hard corner, and was hard to control somehow. Not precise. That could be dangerous. But I was sure it could be fixed later. Now there was a race. A wonderful race to run.

It was like a kiss to hurtle down the chutes, like a quick hug to throw the rear wheels into a corner and bring the Tudor around with the gas pedal, controlling with power. I hung on to the wheel, leaned into the turns, and gave it all I had. I needed speed, and I fed it to myself in great chunks. I was lapping the field, but it didn't mean anything. I *flashed* past cars on the chutes, the turns—any place I caught up with them. Again and again, I felt the push of the track under me as I hit into the banked turns, went through them sideways, rubber screaming, bouncing over bumps and holes, going flat out down the chutes. The wind in my face, the dirt, the stink of my exhaust were the flowers and shoes and rice at this new wedding with racing.

It seemed only seconds passed before I got the white and then the checkered. I went around again, slowing reluctantly. I wanted to keep on running, around and around and around. I'd left the past and Thelma behind me like hot rubber on the turns. Sandy had gambled and won.

I turned into the pits, but the announcer called me to the judges' stand. I went across, carrying my helmet in my hand, shaking like a leaf, but happily. Too happy to notice whether Toad and Ronnie had been there when I stopped the car.

Sandy met me first, under the flagman's platform. I didn't have to tell her. She could see by the way I walked with my head up, by the look on my dirt-smeared face, by the way I carried my shoulders. By the way I had raced.

"You did it, Ace! You did it!" Her face was dirty too, streaked where the tears had run.

"Nothing to beating a bunch of mechanics," I said. "But you were there. That's what counts, Sandy. You were there! Let's get married right away. We don't have to wait anymore."

She kissed me then—soft, warm, loving. "Go up on the platform, Ace. They want to talk to you."

I got a big round of applause when I showed on the platform next to the guy on the PA system. He was one of the announcers at the local radio station.

"How about a big hand for Ace Jones, folks!"

We waited until the big hand was over.

"That was quite a race, Jones. In fact, you set a new track record for nine laps. What do you think of that, folks? Looks like we've got some hidden talent here. Ace Jones, who's helping run the Richards' garage."

I didn't say anything. I was anxious to get back to Sandy.

"Have you ever driven before, Jones?"

I stared at him. He held the mike toward me. "Yes," I said. "A little."

The crowd roared with laughter.

"I imagine we'll be seeing more of you on our track. I'd like to see you out there against Jensen and de Marco and some of the other good boys we have here."

"I don't plan to drive," I said. "I'm just a mechanic."

A roar of protest came from the crowd. The announcer chuckled. "Don't worry, folks," he said. "He'll drive again. Let him hear how much you want to see him in some real action."

He got the roar he was after. I shook my head and looked at Sandy. She motioned toward the crowd and shrugged. Her face had a happy, excited look on it. She wanted me to race again. She and the crowd. And Herbert Herpgruve, who was sitting in a chair ten or fifteen feet away, puffing on a cigar and smiling. Herbert, too.

"I guess maybe I will race again," I said into the mike. "Once in a while."

"Thanks a lot, Ace Jones." The announcer let me go. I went over to Sandy, hearing the announcer giving the crowd a pitch about coming back again to see the excitement, and giving me a build-up. I was somebody new, and good, and that would bring the people out.

"You see what you did," I said to Sandy. "I'll have to race again."

"You want to, don't you?"

"Well . . . yes, I do."

"Then I want you to. You don't have to be . . . afraid anymore, do you?"

"Not anymore. I'm happy out there now. It's good again. Because of you."

"Then race all you want to. I won't mind."

"Will you do something for me? To help me?"

"Anything to help you."

I stumbled a little over the words, trying to say it. "Would you come to the track whenever I do?"

She stiffened a little. "Are you afraid, Ace? Afraid to trust me out of your sight? Like . . . the other one? Is that why?" There was almost contempt in her voice.

"I don't know what it is," I said. "Only, I'd feel better if I could see you here. Maybe . . . I'm afraid Thel—the other one, might try to get on the track with me if you aren't around."

"That's not a very flattering reason."

"More than that," I said. "Tonight you were there when I started, and I ran a good race. I want you at the start every race."

"Ace! You're not *superstitious*!"

I laughed. "No. I mean, I don't like green around the pits or to have anybody whistle, or eat peanuts, or take my picture before a race, or have a stranger in my car, but I'm not superstitious. It's just that I'd feel better if you blew me kiss when the green flag dropped."

"All right, honey," she said. "If I helped you—and can help you—that's what I want. I guess it means you must love me."

"It does," I said.

The look in her eyes showed she believed me, but I was beginning to feel sick inside. Sure, I'd got Thelma out of system, but her old space wasn't empty. Sandy was in it now. And how long would it be before Sandy had me crazy again? She had me right where Thelma had had me. Maybe all I'd done was change keepers.

And there was still the problem of making the garage pay so that I'd have enough to keep Sandy and make Herb swallow that damned cat-and-mouse grin, make him know he'd wait till it snowed in hell before he'd get his filthy hooks on my girl. And in back of everything was a nagging worry about the way 72 had—or rather hadn't—handled.

I was a long way from free. A long way from safe.

CHAPTER 26

I WENT BACK TO THE PITS TO GET THE CAR READY for Ronnie's next race. I knew I would race again, but that would be some time in the future, when I could take the time.

Toad was sitting on our pile of tires, and Ronnie leaned against 72, a disconsolate look on his young face. Ronnie looked at the ground when I came up, but Toad lifted his head and snickered.

"We showed 'em," I said. "You got everything ready for Ronnie to run?"

"Yup. Who was you after, Ace? The way you tore up that track!"

"I needed the exercise," I said. I grinned. I was feeling pretty good. A new track record for nine laps, and my first time out. "We'd better put bigger tires on for Ronnie. There's not enough bite to shoot off the corners like we should."

Toad rubbed his nose. "Anything else? Engine arc all right?"

"Yeah," I said. "But she's not handling right. She's got plenty of dig and all that, but she doesn't always go where you point her."

"Could be the frame is shot," Toad said. "Funny, Ronnie never complained."

"He wouldn't know good from bad," I said.

"He'd know that," Toad said. "He ain't that green."

"Don't be so damn lazy," I said. "If we have to get a new frame or chassis for the engine, we will."

It had to be the car. A guy couldn't run a good race in car that wandered all over the track and drifted too much and was slow to respond. He'd be in crack ups all the time if he tried to run in front with a car like that.

We were changing tires when the others came over—Jensen, de Marco, Towner, Vann, and others, with some of their crews. Jensen had evidently been chosen as their spokesman. He came a step closer than the others, looking neat and professional in his white coveralls. He was a rugged, good-looking boy who spoke softly.

"That was a good piece of driving, Ace."

"Thanks," I said.

"You were a little out of your class, don't you think?"

"I've driven," I said. "I don't have to tell you."

"It's one thing to win over a bunch of mechanics," Jensen said. "It might be another thing to match wheels with us."

"I'll drive against you some time," I said.

"How about tonight?"

"I can't. Ronnie's my driver."

"Don't give us that kind of crap, Ace," de Marco said, moving up next to Jensen. "You've got the crowd thinking you're pretty hot stuff, whipping the amateurs! While everybody's here, we want you to come out again tonight. Against us."

"Well, see here," I said. "I won't push my driver out just because you say so."

"They only have the mechanics' race once or twice a year," Chip Vann drawled. The others laughed. But they were waiting. They didn't like me, and they wanted a chance at me, after my big build-up and flashy showing against the amateurs. I didn't blame them.

I turned to Ronnie, who was still leaning against 72, looking sad. "Can I have the car for one more race tonight?"

"Why ask me?"

"You're the driver."

"Sure. Go ahead."

"We're in the Australian Pursuit and the Main," I said. I looked at the other drivers. "I'll take the Australian."

There was a chorus of satisfied grunts. That was the right one, and the rough one. We'd start in a single line, with the fastest cars at the rear. Ronnie's time in the trials had won us fourth spot in a field of ten. It was the race where a car has to be completely passed to be eliminated. I'd have all the fastest boys lined up behind me.

The others drifted back to their cars.

"That all right with you?" I asked Ronnie.

"Take 'em both," he said. "You ought to be driving, not me. I feel like a fool after what you did."

"Nuts," I said. "Give you a little time, and you'll be twice as good as I am. Only, from now on, maybe you'll listen when I tell you what to do out there."

An embarrassed grin curved his lips. "Yeah, Ace. I guess I'll listen from now on."

"Good. Now let's get these big skins on. We'll show those guys how to run."

When we were called out for the Australian, the crowd applauded my name. I didn't like it. I knew every other driver in the race would be after my scalp, and I could wind up looking pretty sad if they ganged up on me. Which, I suspected, they would.

We lined up Indian file. Loren Peale, Red Merwin, and Rawlins were in front of me. Chip Vann was behind me, then two other cars, and then de Marco, Jensen, and Towner, in that order.

Peale led us slowly around the track to get into the running start. But somebody crowded and got out of line, and we had to go around again. Sandy was waiting under the flagman's platform. She would blow the kiss when the green flag dropped. The butterflies in my stomach folded their wings.

Around we went, rumbling, revving up, and slipping clutches. Blue smoke rolled out of our engines, exhausts fired, and cars moved nervously as each driver tried to be in a good position for the start.

This time, the flag dropped.

We were already moving pretty fast when we got the go sign, and we all floored our cars as we raced into the first corner.

Traffic was thick. I had pulled to the outside to get around Rawlins, but my radiator was only even with his rear wheel when we went into the turn. He knew I was coming on outside and pushed in front of me. At the same time, Chip Vann squeezed in on my left, bumper to bumper with Rawlins, and Towner's stubby little GMC sang at my right rear wheel as he took the outside of me.

We went through the turn in a blinding cloud of dust, smacking into each other, grinding bodies together, hitting wheel against wheel, knocked to the right by one impact, knocked back to the left by another.

The only thing to do was to feed power, hang on to the wheel, and charge into the dust and mass of cars, hoping the size of the jam would keep others from passing you. Hoping your speed and power and thrust would get through and past somebody else, whether you skirted him or pushed him out of your way into someone else's path.

They all wanted me, and everybody knew it. Even the crowd. But it was no excuse to say you were bottled. The crowd expected a bottled driver to kick out the cork.

I came out of the turn riding on Merwin's bumper, feinting from side to side to get him out of the way and keep anyone else from passing.

But Merwin was fast enough to hold the little lead we had over the other cars. I stuck with him, planning to take him at the next corner.

We roared into the turn with the pack breathing down our necks, and with Peale still in front. On the front chute, Merwin didn't put his foot in it, and when I tried to go left, Vann was right there to keep me behind Merwin. And leaving room for the others to go by.

There was only one way out. I floored my Tudor and came in hard on Merwin, aiming for the little bit of daylight between the nose of Chip's car and the left rear wheel of Merwin's. It wasn't big enough to get through, but it could be stretched.

I headed into that hole as hard as I could. I caught Merwin and Chip at the same time, spinning Merwin to the fence, and out of my way, and driving Chip to the inside, where he blocked the cars behind us that were planning to shoot by.

By the next turn, Merwin had been passed, and Chip and I were being chased by Jensen and de Marco, who had managed to chop the other cars in front of them. With a more open track, it was easier to run. Rawlins and Peale were still in front, with Rawlins trying to take Peale and Peale fighting him off. I sneaked up on them and went around them both on the outside when they got in too close to the pole.

But I went too far out, where it was heavy, and my big tires lugged when they should have been pushing. Jensen and de Marco swept in after me, and we went up the back chute three abreast, fighting for position as we came up on the third corner.

We came around together, touching, rubbing fire as metal scraped metal. Still on the outside, I kept my foot down harder, holding my nose to the left, crowding Jensen in against de Marco, who was on the pole. And down the front chute, doing better than sixty-five, with our wheels grappling like wrestlers. And into the next turn like that. Nobody willing to give. And up the back chute, shoulder to shoulder. And screeching through the east, turn the same way, rocked and bumped, shaken, heeling over, but fighting.

Coming out of the east turn, it happened. With front wheels being twisted left and right, it had to happen. All our wheels tangled at once. I hooked Jensen, and he hooked de Marco, and in another second, we were sliding around in a big tangled spin, with our cars trying to climb each other like wild horses in heat, and the tearing sound of splitting metal and ripped running gear taking over when our engines died.

So we slid to a spinning stop on the side of the track, and Bob Turner went by in his little GMC, the winner.

We pulled ourselves out of our cars and began inspecting the damage. The broken spindles and bent wheels. De Marco lit a cigarette and ran his fingers through his black hair. "You can play rough," he said, giving me a mirthless grin.

"If I have to."

"You still think we're small-time?"

"You haven't moved since the last time I saw you."

He looked at me through narrowed eyes. "You come back some-time. Anytime. You'll get your belly full."

"We're in the Main together," I said. "See you then."

We got the cars separated. Toad bawled me out while we put on a new left front wheel. "What's the matter with you? You could have kept wide and stayed. You got the engine and the bite. You asked for what you got."

"I know," I said. "And that's the way it's going to be for a while."

"Oh, hell," Toad complained. "We'll be rebuilding this dog every week."

Ronnie looked up. He was at the wheel, helping Toad. "I'm run-ning the Main, ain't I?"

I shook my head. "Not tonight. It's grudge night."

"But Ace—"

"Next time," I said. "I've been invited in tonight, and I don't want anybody to think I'm looking for a way out."

"Okay, Ace." He lapsed into a hurt silence.

There was a lot of excitement in the stands when we rolled out for the Main. But it didn't last long. We all got around the first turn all right, to make it a start, and then the roof fell in. When we got into the west turn, a dozen thick, I felt like the first duck over the marshes on opening day of the hunting season. About six cars came into me at once, falling all over themselves to get in a lick. I cut power, hung on to the wheel, and pulled in my head. When the dust cleared, I was hung up on the fence with Loren Peale on one side and Chip Vann on the other. And that was all for me that night.

But there would be another time. Soon.

CHAPTER 27

THREE WEEKS PASSED IN A HURRY. Somehow, Sandy and I didn't get around to the marriage. We were too busy. I was, anyway.

It was rough at the track. Every time. The way we had it worked out, I drove 72 in the time trials to get a good spot. Then Ronnie drove the Trophy Dash and the heat race. If we had the fastest time of the night, with tail spot in the Australian, I drove, because nobody could get at me unless I tried to pass. And I could hang back until there were only one or two cars left before I made my race.

Then I drove the Main. By that time, we'd made a little lap money. The other guys gave Ronnie a fair shake. It was when I came out that it got rough. In three weeks and six race nights, I had yet to finish a main event.

I always had a fast time and started toward the back. That meant I had to come up through traffic. It's never easy. Guys fight like mad to keep you back. Any way they can. You go around when—

and if—you can. I got by a lot of them, but never passed them all. Somewhere between the first and the twenty-fifth lap, I'd be shouldered into the fence, dragged to a stop, or spun out.

Somebody riding my tail through the turn would nudge my rear bumper at the right moment, and I was in my spin. They must have planned it all before each race, because in the old days, nobody got away with that crap. Sometimes I came out, and got in the race again, and picked up a few bucks. But most of the time, I ended up with bruises for my purse and a smashed car for a trophy.

After which, we would return to the garage and go to work. A new radiator, new coil, distributor if needed, new driveshaft, a new rear end, new wheels. One night, the throttle valve screw wasn't peened properly and fell into the air stream, and into the engine, and the mill blew up. So we found another engine to bore, and stroke, and install.

It took time and money. More of both than we had. But I was racing again, and I had to be on the track when the flag dropped.

The crowds were bigger now, and the purses were larger. As a result, we were getting drivers from other towns and running as high as forty cars. And race nights, Herpgruve paid out real money. Even our share was pretty good for what we usually made in the preliminary races. But Herpgruve could look at my haggard, dirty face, and my red eyes and shaking hands, and laugh as he handed me my money, because he knew it was spent and more, to keep me coming back.

It was a good thing the garage's percentage take from the track grew, because business had fallen away. More than fallen away.

Toad and I were putting the new engine in 72 one day when Sandy came out of the office to see me. She hadn't missed a race night, and she always blew me the kiss I needed, but she was look-ing thin and weary.

She watched us working on the engine. "Ace . . ."

"Yeah, honey?"

"What did you say to Marchfield?"

"Who's he?"

"That farmer. You know. The one whose car you fixed the first day you came here."

"Oh—him."

"What did you say?"

"He wanted the front end aligned. That takes a lot of time."

"The garage is empty, Ace. We don't have any other cars to work on."

"We've got seventy-two," I said. "If I fool with that front-end job, we'll never make the next race."

"Did you turn him down?"

"I told him to come back some other time."

Sandy looked around the garage. Tools, machines, and one car in it. Our racer. I hadn't wanted to send Marchfield away. Or any of the others. But I couldn't do their work and mine, too. And I couldn't be among the missing when the cars were called from the pits. So, I had to discourage the civilian trade for a while. Until 72 was racing again.

"You've found time to work on other racing cars."

"They'll pay us for that," I said. "What difference does make who we work on, if we get paid the same money?"

"*If* we get paid."

"Look, dear," I said. "If I don't help the other guys, they'll think I'm afraid to run against them."

"We're not taking in enough to meet our expenses, Ace."

"We will." I went to her, taking a bulky envelope from my pocket. "The last husband you had bought his insurance from a Texas mail-order house," I said, handing her the envelope. "Here's a ten-thousand-dollar policy made out to you. If anything happens to me. Happy?"

"I don't *want* to collect it. I'd be happier if we were both here to earn it the right way. We had such a good start, Ace."

"I didn't want to drive," I said. "Now I'm hooked. I can't back out now. But we'll make it up in the winter. After the racing season. Meanwhile, hang on to that insurance policy. That's no Texas fraud. I got it with the best little old insurance company in New Mexico."

I thought it was funny. She didn't, and turned away, walking slowly back to the office.

"I wish I could make her understand," I said to Toad. "I know the other guys are out to get me, and that's why I can't turn them down when we spin out together. They'd think I was trying to keep them off the track. I owe it to them to keep them running."

Toad knocked off to take one of my cigarettes. "Wasn't you two supposed to git married?" He coughed into his hand.

"You think we won't, don't you? We will."

"Sandy ain't very happy about the way things are going. You're goin' to lose this damn place if you don't watch out."

"We'll hang on somehow," I said.

"You'll lose her, too. Then you and me can head out for the big time."

"Not her, Toad. She's mine."

"You're pretty damn sure about her, ain't you?"

I grinned. "You watch her a couple of hours before the next race date," I said. "She's hooked, Toad. She doesn't know it yet, but she's hooked too. She gets so nervous before race time, she just about explodes. Paces up and down that office, chomping at the bit until we load up and head for the track."

Toad explored his sinuses with a dirty fingernail. "I was right," he said. "You're a worser bastard than Bill. He went to hell, but he left her up on earth. You're gonna ride there on her back."

"Yeah," I said. "I guess so. But that's the way love works, Toad. It makes you do the damnedest things. Like my getting that insurance policy. Like her knowing things are going to hell with the garage and sticking with me all the way down."

"What happens when you hit bottom?"

I shrugged. "I'll tell you when we, get there." I picked up a wrench. "Maybe find a way to fix cars for farmers." I spat. "What the hell, Toad, people go broke trying to be lawyers and poets and hardware dealers. There's no disgrace going broke trying to stay with the racing game."

"No disgrace," Toad said. "And damn few meals."

"Two can starve as cheap as one," I said. "Sandy and I are going to get married, come hell or high water. If we make out here, we make out. And if we don't—"

"Yeah?" Toad said.

"If we don't, she'll still have me," I said, grinning.

"She don't look very happy about it," Toad said.

"You know women," I said. "They get scared at the idea being broke. It would do her good to see how we could go bust and still find a way to live. Toughen her a little."

"This place means a lot to her," Toad said. "It's her home.

"Her home will be with me," I said. "And I don't give a great big damn about this place. If I keep it—fine. If I don't . . . Hell, Toad, I'm driving again. You and me, and Sandy could move up to the big time if we didn't have this place around our necks."

"You and me, maybe," Toad said. "Not Sandy. What would she do if you get creamed, with no home or nothing?"

"Look for another husband," I said.

"She ain't getting no younger."

"She'd just have to look harder."

Toad spat on the floor and rubbed the place with a greasy shoe. "I've knowed Sandy a long time," he said. "Damn it! She deserves better'n you!"

"I'm her kind," I said. "As long as I'm around, she'll stick with me. No matter what happens."

We worked in silence for a few minutes. Our talk had revived some disturbing thoughts in my mind. I was almost ashamed to tell them to Toad, but he was the only one I could talk to.

"Toad . . ."

"Uh-huh." He was under the car.

"Do you think anybody is out to get me on the track?"

Toad coughed. "What makes you think that?"

"I ought to be running in the money, but I'm not. I'm in every damn pile-up every time. The guys might want to spin me out a couple of times to show me they can't be shoved around, but nobody wants to run out of the money all the time just to be nasty. As good as I can drive, I shouldn't be getting clobbered *all* the time. Not unless somebody's after my scalp."

"Name anybody," Toad chuckled.

And it could be. Any driver. Peale, Herpgruve would like to see it, Sandy had hired it to be done once, and things were going to hell again . . . That was the trouble. It could be anybody.

"You ain't always in it with the same guys," Toad said. "They cain't all be after you."

"That's what doesn't figure."

"Mebbe they're all out of step but you."

"You're nuts. I'm as good as I ever was. Maybe better. I know my own driving, don't I? What the hell are you trying to say? That I'm gunning for the other guys?"

"Fergit it," Toad said. "I was just talkin'."

I couldn't forget it. Toad didn't talk just to be talking. But I didn't feel mad anymore when I drove.

Ronnie came in carrying a box of colder spark plugs than we'd been using. He was excited and a little upset. "I want to ask you a favor, Ace," he blurted out as he gave me the plugs.

"What? If it's money, we don't handle it here."

"Not money." He squirmed a little and blushed. "It's— Well, the Square Deal Service Station wants me to drive their car in the races that you run ours. They got that little silver coupe that ain't done so good this year."

Toad crawled out from under the Tudor. "Run against Ace? Haw!"

Ronnie's blush deepened. "Why not?"

"You can do it, kid," I said. "But I thought you were happy with us."

"I want to drive ours when you don't," Ronnie said earnestly.

"Only—" He stopped, afraid to go on.

"Only what?"

He scuffed his toe against the floor. "You treat me like a kid. You never let me run hard. Always telling me to lay back and take second or third. I want to win!"

"Do you think you will, against me?" I asked softly.

He lowered his head. "It's been done. Maybe I could, too. At least I could try. You don't let me *try*."

"I do it for your own good, Ronnie," I said. "Sandy and I want you to race, but we don't want you getting hurt. Besides, if you piled up in seventy-two, I couldn't run."

"That's why I want to drive the silver coupe when you run. You wouldn't have to be afraid of getting our car hurt by anybody else."

"Okay, kid, okay," I said. "If that's the way you feel, go ahead. Just remember this. All friendship ceases when that flag drops. I won't be any easier on you than I am with the others. You'll have to work for any wins you get over me. Even if you drive our car in the next race."

"That suits me," Ronnie said. "And it goes both ways."

Now he could look at me. Head up, dark eyes steady. Man to man. Not boy to man, but man to man.

I patted his shoulder. "Just don't forget what I taught you, and you'll be all right. And don't ever quit trying as hard you can."

He nodded. "Thanks, Ace. Thanks a lot. Can I tell my bro—Sandy?"

"Yeah," I said. "You can tell your brother's wife."

He walked away, and I felt a sense of loss, of loneliness. This was what it was like when the kids grew up. This is how you felt. Old and lonely and envious. I felt tired. I wanted to sit down and rest, to ask the world to please stop turning for a little while, until I was refreshed, and could catch with it. But it wouldn't stop. There was no catching up. No restart once you had made it around the first turn, and I had done that a long, long time ago.

Toad's little hammer tapping at metal was no comfort. It was like a knell.

CHAPTER 28

IT WAS A LOUSY NIGHT FOR THE RACE. One side of my mind wished that the low-hanging clouds would spill out rain and break the sultry heat. The other side prayed for the rain to hold off, so the races could be run. Toad and I waited at the garage for Ronnie to come pick up 72. He would still do that for us. We were soaked with sweat, our clothes smeared with dirt and grease. Our faces were unshaven and grimy in the wrinkles. But 72 would run.

I rubbed my eyes. "What's keeping Ronnie?" I complained.

"He's comin'," Toad said. "I can hear him."

I waited a few seconds that seemed like hours. "You're sure a talkative old shite-poke tonight," I snarled at Toad.

"Ain't got nothing to say."

I rubbed his head with my hand. "You're tired. I ought to be kicked in the rump for keeping you up night and day. How old are you? A hundred?"

"Almost." Toad reached into his pocket and got a sack of tobacco and a package of papers. I looked down at my shirt pocket. I had cigarettes left. I felt offended because he hadn't taken one of mine. And inadequate, like a flat-chested stripper. But if Toad didn't want to talk, I wouldn't push him. The poor old man looked like a corpse. Just too tired. It was the heat. The oppressive heat.

Ronnie drove up and backed around to hook on 72. Sandy was in Ronnie's car. I don't know why, but I was surprised to see her. I walked around to the side of the car and stood there, like an old hound dog wanting his ears scratched.

Her face was in the shadow, and I bent over and kissed her cheek. A muscle along her jaw twitched.

"Hot night," I said.

She turned to look at me, and I saw in her eyes what I looked like. Felt how filthy, how unkempt I was. She looked away. "There were more bills today I couldn't pay."

"They'll bill us again. They always do."

"Not these. Western Supply is threatening a court action."

"That takes years. We'll have the machinery all worn out by that time, and they can take it back."

She closed her eyes. How weary she looked. It was like the terrible weariness of the other women at the track, after the races were over, and their men had lost again. She turned her head away from me.

"All set," Ronnie said, getting behind the wheel. "Let's go."

Toad and I climbed into the back seat, and Ronnie drove off. No one spoke. There didn't seem to be anything to say.

Ronnie stopped at the pit gate to let Sandy out. I got out with her. I wanted to walk to the judges' stand with her. We walked silently, and I saw her glancing at the cars that passed, doing their slow laps. And at the splintered fence, where cars had hit. She seemed to droop a little.

"Sandy," I said. "I ought to tell you something."

"I know what it is. Toad said you and he had been talking about pulling up stakes. You're tired of the garage . . ."

"Toad's talk," I said. "What's he trying to do, break us up? I ought to clobber him for that. No, it's about Bill," I said. "You ought to know. It was Duke Ossman who put him on the fence. Not Chip."

She stopped in her tracks. "You're just saying that."

"It's true. Ask anybody."

She walked on again. Her voice remained flat. "I'm just as guilty. I paid—"

"You were cheated. Ask Chip to give you back your money."

"What an ugly thing to say."

"I'm an ugly guy. I spin ladies out of their garages and run girls into the fence."

We were on the platform. She sat down next to the timer and opened her notebook to check lap positions.

"Oh, Jones."

Herpgruve took me aside. He was dressed in a light tan nylon cord summer suit, Palm Beach tie, nylon shirt, and brown sandals. His cigar smelled more expensive than the old ones used to.

"Another full house," Herpgruve said, blowing smoke in my face. He looked me over from head to foot and smiled. "Give them a good show tonight, Ace. A lot of them are here to see you. I'll expect a good show—while you last."

"What do you mean by that?" I stepped toward him.

He stood his ground. "You're done at the garage. You blew faster than I had ever hoped. Just like I said you would. You're finished, man."

"Maybe not."

He looked at his cigar ash. "Don't bother to stop and say good-bye to Sandy when you leave. It will be easier that way."

"I'm not leaving."

"Okay, Ace. If you need another foot of rope, you can have it. But I'm buying Sandy's garage as soon as it's foreclosed, and I don't think we'll want your trade. So don't get in any wrecks."

I went to the pits without speaking to Sandy. What was there to say?

I ran the time trials, and when I got back to the pits, I sat in the car. Toad checked to see that everything was all right, and then came up to snuffle in my ear.

"You're all set," Toad said. "Mind if I see how Ronnie's doin'?"

"Why should I mind? Go ahead."

"The kid's first race alone, sorta," Toad said. "I ought to git him started right."

"Go ahead," I said. "You don't have to ask my permission. Go on."

"Don't have to git huffy about it," Toad said.

"I'm not. I'm just going to show you how to win tonight. You think I'm slipping . . ."

Toad went over to talk to Ronnie, who was standing by the silver coupe. He stayed with him until we were called out for the Trophy Dash. It was all right with me. Ronnie needed him.

Still, it was funny not to have Toad give my car a final touch for good luck before a race. As I drove out to the track, I saw Toad's shabby little figure trotting toward the inside of the east turn, just past the finish line, where he'd take up his station to give me my signals in the race. I smiled at him. Good old Toad. With two chicks to look after now.

I was in the last row on the inside, with de Marco on the outside. Ronnie was on the inside, too, about three cars ahead of me.

The starter came up between the cars, checked us, and ran back. The engines picked up in his wake, roaring their machine-beast noises. I adjusted my goggles and chewed on my handkerchief. De Marco would cut to the outside. I'd cut to the inside.

The flag went down, and we were off. I took the pole and shifted into second, hooking my gear-shift lever to the dash. As I went by the judges' stand, I looked at the spot under the flagman's platform where Sandy was supposed to wait with my lucky kiss. She wasn't there.

Where was she? With whom!

I plunged blindly into the traffic at the first turn. I felt myself ramming other cars, choked in the dust that filled the cockpit, and winced as clods of dirt and small stones flew through the open windshield and struck my face. My foot was all the way in. I had to go fast. I had to get around right away, so I could run and find her, to see what she was doing.

Where was she?

She was standing inside the east turn, with Toad, and when I slid past, wheel to wheel with de Marco, she blew me a kiss.

The next time around, I had worked my way up in traffic and was trailing Ronnie. Toad was waving his arms wildly, motioning me in. So was Sandy. I couldn't understand why. I was running fine. I'd know if anything was wrong. I passed Ronnie on the front chute, and it was easy. He knew I was coming, but he stayed over and let me slide past.

"Fight!" I yelled as I went by.

He turned and yelled something at me, but I couldn't hear him any better than he could me. But he did pick up speed and followed me through the traffic on the east turn.

Toad and Sandy were still waving their arms when I came around again. I shook my head at them, and suddenly I saw that I was wrong. They were waving at Ronnie.

I got it. I was going like hell, and Ronnie was on my tail, and they didn't want us to race against each other. They were afraid. But it had to be. I'd have done the same thing in Ronnie's place. He was out to show me that he could match wheels with me.

"Come on, cub," I said, watching him in the rear-vision mirror. "Stay with me if you can."

I floored the Tudor and went deeper into the next turn than I'd ever gone before, power on. I threw the Tudor into a slide, still with my foot in it. Rubber howled as the tires lost their grip, and I slid toward the outside. I came up hard against Peale's battered coupe, which was taking the turn ahead of me, and hitting him checked my slide. I poured the coal to 72 and was streaking down the back chute before Ronnie was through the turn. Stay with me, would he!

I bulled my way through traffic, setting a pace that almost pulled the wheels off my car. But it held together, and by the seventh lap I was lapping the slowest cars, swearing at them because they wouldn't obey the orange flag and pull to the outside so I could go by. Ronnie was three-quarters of a lap behind.

I came into the last lap with my radiator steaming and the engine winding out. There was no money for this win, just a trophy, but I had proved that I could win. That I wasn't slipping.

I roared under the green flag with my foot all the way down, looked to the left, to where Toad was standing with Sandy, just inside the east turn. I'd showed him! I looked, and Toad was giving me the go sign, and Sandy was looking back down the track where Ronnie was coming in behind me, trying to flag him down.

What the hell? I thought. *What the dumb hell!*

I looked back. A fraction of a second, but too long. Ahead of me, Loren Peale's tarnished jewel had hit a bad bump, and he was seesawing madly in an attempt to straighten out. I knew just where he'd be when I caught up to him, and all I had to do was aim at the outside. Reflexes would do it.

We touched lightly. Not hard enough to make another dent in our battered cars. But suddenly we had to hit again. Hard. His car seemed to swim at me, and I pulled my head down between my shoulders. The moment we hit, I covered my face with my arms.

I was thrown forward, my safety belt tearing at my stomach. My head smacked against a roll bar, and my left arm went numb. And I was in the air. Turning. Until I hit upside down.

I'd hardly come to a stop when I had my safety belt unsnapped with my good hand and was crawling out through the top of the car, which now lay on its side. I heard the crowd screaming, and at the same moment, my senses came back enough to make me claw wildly to get away. Peale's car was in the middle of the track ahead, just short of the turn, upside down and on fire, and he was still inside.

I tried to run toward his car, but what had been my left leg wouldn't hold, and I fell down. I grabbed hold of my car and dragged myself up again, holding on, standing on my right leg, screaming at Peale to get out.

I heard someone coming down the track flat out. It was Ronnie, in the silver coupe. The damn fool had his foot in it coming to the finish line.

I saw Toad run onto the track, toward me, waving Ronnie to the outside. Toad's face was a picture of agony and terror.

"Run!" he screamed at me. "Run!"

And I saw why. Ronnie wasn't going by. I stood between him and my own overturned car, helpless. An easy target. And he had me boresighted. *Ronnie was coming in to kill me.*

I had a working right arm and right leg. I threw myself on the wrecked Tudor and slithered across it, falling to the track on the far side. Then I rolled over and over, on good side and broken side, as far away from the coming impact as I could get.

I saw Toad moving between Ronnie's car and mine, flailing his arms. Then I rolled again, and Ronnie hit, and the terrific smash sent pieces of broken metal down on me.

But I was safe, and I lay on my back in the middle of the track, a mass of pain, seeing the bonfire of Peale's car light the dark sky, feeling the heat of the yellow flames, hearing the screams of the poor dude trapped inside. And the crowd screams, and the ambulance screams, and all the terrible sounds.

And I heard someone running toward me. Ronnie running like a tackler in his heavy boots, his helmet and goggles still on. Ronnie running to be first to my side. And then he was on me, with his hands around my throat, squeezing.

Then I couldn't feel his fingers anymore, and I slipped away into the darkness, thinking, *"Why, kid, why?"*

CHAPTER 29

I CAME TO IN THE AMBULANCE, with the siren blowing the top of my head off. I wasn't scared. You can't race for ten years without taking your share of rides on your back. Before I opened my eyes, I took what inventory I could.

I cautiously filled my lungs with air. Sore muscles, but no stabbing pains. No splintered ribs sticking into anything. I moved my knees slightly and wriggled my toes. The left knee was banged up, but the spine was all right. No broken back, as far as I could tell. My left arm was numb, but my right was in good shape from shoulder to fingers. I counted my teeth with my tongue. I had all I'd had when I started the race. My neck was sore. Ronnie.

The ambulance scalded a turn and almost threw me off the litter. I opened my eyes. "Tell the driver to take it easy," I said to the person sitting near my head. "I've had my crackup for the night."

The person bent over me. Sandy's anxious face looked down at me. She looked pale and shaken. "Ace . . . Are you . . . How do you feel, honey?"

"Scared," I said. "Tell that goofball who's driving to slow down and turn off that damn siren."

She did. My neck was too sore for me to lift my head. "We alone?" I asked Sandy.

"Yes,"

"Toad," I said sharply. "Where's Toad?"

"In another ambulance," Sandy said, stroking my forehead with her fingers.

"Why not this one? He ran in front of Ronnie. He can't wait until they send another ambulance."

Sandy's fingers rested lightly on my head. "He can wait, Ace," she said, her voice choking out. "He's . . . dead."

"Honey . . ."

"What is it, Ace?"

"Ronnie tried to kill me, didn't he?"

"Yes," she said in a low voice.

"What happened?"

"I pulled him away from you."

"*You?* Where'd you get the beef?"

"I had it."

"Where's Ronnie now?"

"I don't know."

"It doesn't make sense, does it?"

"It does when you know."

"Know what?"

"He thought I was pregnant and you were going to run out on me."

I tried to rise up and groaned. "Where'd he get *that* idea?"

"I'll tell you later, when you feel better."

"Tell me now."

"You'll be shocked."

"Oh, hell," I said. "I've been run out of business, wrecked, choked, and beat-up. I guess I can stand a shock."

"Toad told him."

"No," I said. "That's crazy. Toad knew I was going to marry you. He's the only one who did know how set I was on that. Why, Toad and I were . . . we were . . . close, honey. Close."

"I'm sorry, Ace."

"Don't be sorry," I said. "It's not true. Something's mixed up somewhere. Toad tried to save me out there. Why'd you say it was Toad? He's dead. He can't talk. You can't do that to him."

"Ace . . ."

"Don't," I said as she started stroking my forehead again. "Don't do that. I'm beginning to feel . . . sick."

- - -

I was sitting on the couch in Sandy's living room, my left arm in a sling, and my taped left leg stuck out in front of me. I looked at my watch. The fancy, multicolored watch with a dozen different hands that told everything from the time of day to the angle of the moon.

Toad.

It was making sense now.

Sandy came out of the bedroom wearing a black dress.

"I was just thinking," I said. "What a scene it must have been. Everybody watching Loren burn, and nobody but you seeing that Ronnie was trying to wring my neck."

"I had to stop him," Sandy said. "I knew what he was trying to do, and I had to stop him."

"Good thing you did," I said, feeling my neck. It was still sore. "Or they'd be laying me away alongside of Toad and Peale."

"I still don't understand it," Sandy said, coming over to sit next to me. "It doesn't make sense to me."

"It did to Toad," I said. "I wondered why he was always after me to pull up stakes and shove. He was trying to protect you, Sandy.

He knew I'd make a mess of everything once I started racing. He told me once that Bill went to hell alone, but I was riding there on your back. You know he tried to kill the driver who wrecked. Bill. He wasn't going to wait until I wrecked you before he got me off your back. I even bragged to him that racing had hooked you, too, and you were mine whether you wanted to be or not. When he saw I wasn't going to give you up, no matter how things went to hell, he tried to protect you the only way he knew how. He told Ronnie just before the race that I'd got you pregnant and was running out on you."

"Those two," Sandy said. "One trying to kill you because you wanted to marry me, and the other trying to kill you because he thought you didn't."

"And both damn near succeeded," I said.

"It was like a nightmare," Sandy said. "Just before the race started, I ran to the pits. I wanted to see you and tell you that no matter what happened to the garage or anything, I would share it with you. When I got across you were already on the track."

"That's how come I didn't see you under the flagman's platform," I said. "What a feeling *that* was."

"I saw Toad standing inside the turn, so I joined him. I was feeling very happy, because I'd made my decision about you. I said to Toad that I knew he'd been after you to give up the garage and go back to big-time racing, and that I was going with you. That no matter what you did, I wanted to be with you. That being with you was more important than anything else in my life. I suppose I sounded awful gushy, but I had to tell him."

Sandy leaned over to pick a thread from my jacket.

"I remember how white and tense Toad looked when I said that. Then he grabbed me and started shouting, 'We have to get him off the track! Get him off the track!' I said to let you finish the race, and Toad gave me a wild look and said, 'Not Ace! Ronnie! Get Ronnie off the track!' I didn't know why, but I'd never seen Toad

so upset. So I joined him, trying to wave Ronnie in. And then . . .
it happened."

"It sure did," I said.

"Poor Toad," Sandy said. "He ran in front of Ronnie, trying to
stop him. It won't be the same without him. He wanted so much to
go back to the big time with you. And he could have gone with us.
Now that we're losing the garage."

I grimaced. "That's the bad part of it," I said. "We won't be
going."

"I want to, if you want to," Sandy said earnestly. "The garage
doesn't mean anything to me anymore. Or staying in Town. Or
having the same roof over my head every night. You want to be a
racer, and I want to be the racer's wife."

"Sandy," I said, "you know how many pile-ups I've had since I
started racing."

"I know," she said, her voice tinged with anger. "And most of the
time, you were spun out on purpose. If they don't stop, I'll—I'll tie
into somebody!"

Sandy, fighting in the pits. . . .

"There won't be any more, hon," I said. "Not for me."

"You're quitting? Why? You don't have to on my account."

"I've been retired," I said. "I should have seen it long ago. Maybe
Peale would be alive now. I should have missed him, but I didn't.
For the same reason, I was always getting in other pile-ups and
blaming the other drivers. It wasn't always their fault. It was mine."

"It wasn't . . .Thelma?"

"Me," I said. "Toad knew it. He made a crack about everybody
being out of step but me. That should have been enough to make
me quit."

"Your eyes?" Sandy asked, looking at my eyes.

"My reflexes," I said. "I'm too slow. Too many hits on the head,
maybe. I don't know. I mean, I can drive a car on the road all right,
but I'm through on the track. I might as well face it."

"That means—" Sandy looked troubled.

"We have to stay," I said. "And try to hang on to the garage, and make it go. If we can't, maybe I can get a job with another garage. But I'd sure like to have my own. Well, I had the chance."

A car pulled into the drive, and a door slammed. A moment later, there was a heavy fist hitting gently against the front door. Herbert Herpgruve had arrived to take us to the funeral.

"What are we going to do?" Sandy asked me. "If you can't drive, and we lose the garage . . ."

"I don't know," I said. "But when we get to the funeral and you pray for Loren and Toad, add two names before you say Amen."

CHAPTER 30

THE LAST RITES WERE HELD AT THE TOWN MORTUARY, a long frame building painted gray. It had once been a grocery store, but the big front windows were covered by heavy draperies. That made it suitably dark inside, and with the thick carpeting, the indirect lighting, the heavy smell of flowers, the rows of folding chairs, and the caskets up front, and an unseen organ playing a dirge, there was no doubt about this being a real funeral for the real dead.

It wasn't often they had a double ceremony at the Town Mortuary, and the mortician moved about nervously, with the air of professional hush that made him look as though he had to go to the bathroom and didn't know how to ask to be excused.

I sat down in the last row, so I could slip out if I wanted to without disturbing anyone. Sandy and Herbert started to go up front, then changed their minds and came back to sit with me. The minister was sitting alone in the front row, reading the notes for the last words he would soon say.

Toad was going to be spoken of first, and his casket was nearest the side door, with Peale's coffin about two lengths to the rear. Even here, the poor dude couldn't run in front.

The racers and their families arrived. They filled the little chapel like boys fill the seats in a schoolroom on the first day, from the back of the room forward. The undertaker tried to guide the new arrivals to the front, anxiously counting the house, and wondering where he could put more chairs if they were needed.

I felt a hand on my shoulder and looked up. It was de Marco. He looked at me for a moment with his black eyes, showing clearly what he meant. He knew how close Toad and I had been. Everybody knew. They were sorry.

De Marco moved away and found a seat. As the other drivers came in, they too stopped for a moment where I sat with Sandy and Herbert, and with a touch or a look or a word, they let it be known that they shared our loss. There wasn't a man in the room who hadn't some of Toad's sweat on his car.

Mrs. Peale came in with Ossman and her children. Her face was hidden behind a handkerchief, and she sobbed as the mortician led her and her children and Ossman into a little curtained-off side room where the immediate family was positioned, out of sight.

When the place was filled with drivers and wives and the handful of old ladies who went to all funerals to compare services and sermons, the minister got the program underway.

"We are gathered here today to pay our respects to the memory of Frederick Taplinger. Frederick Taplinger was born in Goose Creek, Texas, on September 24th, 1881 . . ."

Toad that old? Over seventy . . . Timeless old Toad, ageless and aged as a rusty bolt . . .

"Mr. Taplinger moved to Town with his parents, John and Mary Taplinger, when he was four years of age, and attended the public grammar and high schools here. After an absence of many years, Frederick Taplinger returned to the scenes of his happy boyhood and once again established his residence among his friends in this community, A lifelong bachelor, Frederick Taplinger was known to many in our community. His willing spirit, his cheerful countenance, his interest in his fellow man made Frederick Taplinger the kind of man about whom it can be said, 'To know him was to love him . . ."

The minister droned on, trying with generalities and quotations to describe the sterling worth of a man he didn't know. And to us. It was like a blind man trying to explain an elephant's appearance to the mahout.

I got up as quietly as I could and went outside. I couldn't sit there and try to mourn for a mythical character named Frederick Taplinger who had been pasted together out of the preacher's book of famous quotations. I sat down on a step and lit a cigarette, and felt tears in my eyes. There wasn't any wrinkled, grimy hand to steal the pack from my shirt pocket.

"Friends," it should have been. "Old Toad won't be around anymore to fix your carbs or grind your valves or doctor up your sick engines in the pits. Let's run the old man around the track a couple of times before we lay him away. He'd like that, because the track is heavy, and it needs traffic to pack it down for the race."

Something like that.

Herbert Herpgruve tiptoed out of the funeral parlor and joined me. His face was red, his eyes bulged. He didn't like to pussyfoot around the dead either.

"They're starting in on Peale," Herpgruve said. "Same pitch. Knowing there's nothing in that box but a canvas bag and some burnt bones." Herbert shuddered and went for a cigar. "It don't seem real."

The fresh air and the sunshine felt good. Herpgruve puffed at his cigar and looked at me with a faint smile on his lips. "You know, Jones, this is the first time I've ever seen you in a suit. When you get out of those filthy khakis, and clean up, you look like a respectable citizen."

"All I need is the cigar," I said.

He took the cigar out of his mouth and examined his teeth marks on it. "Sandy tells me you two are getting married as soon after the funeral as it's decent."

"That's the plan."

"You'll be leaving, I suppose. Going back to race the big tracks."

"Yeah. We're losing the garage. Just like you said we would. Only Sandy goes with me, not the building. You didn't figure on that, did you?"

Herpgruve pulled a white handkerchief out of his back pocket and mopped his face. "I never thought I'd be saying this," he growled angrily. "But I hate to see you go."

"Me or Sandy?"

"You."

I grinned. "I didn't know you felt that was about me, Herb."

"Oh, hell," he sputtered. "I still don't like you, and I never will. But facts are facts, and business is business. The point is, I need that damn garage. Since you've had it, we've had more cars on the track than ever before. And if it shuts down, racing will suffer. That could be the biggest and best garage in this part of the state. With my money and your know-how. What do you say, Ace? I'll handle the financial side, and you run it. We'll work out a deal so nobody gets hurt. A lot better than you'll do ratting around the country driving the tracks."

"I don't know . . ."

"All the independents will be up the crick if the garage goes out of business."

"You could get somebody else to run it," I said. "Why me?"

"Well, to tell the truth, I'd like for you to manage the track, too. You're the only one around here that could do a good job both places."

"Sounds like quite a wedding present," I said.

"Present, hell! Business. I know good business when I see it. Fact is, Jones, I'm getting to be too big in this town to spend my nights in the pay shack haggling with drivers over a two-dollar purse. And all the other bother. I know you could handle the track and the men. So, I'm making that offer too. There's no law a man has to like another man to do business with him. Now, do you want to think it over? The way you feel about me?"

"I don't know any rule that says you have to love your boss," I said. "I guess you don't have to like me in order to finance me, and I don't have to like you to run the garage and the track the way they should be run. I don't see why we couldn't try it, anyway. What's your offer?"

"What do you think you're worth?"

"You can't afford that," I said. "You asked me. You had some idea of what you wanted to pay."

"Well, I'll tell you." Herpgruve licked the end of his cigar and sniffed. This kind of thing was right down his alley. He'd rather talk business than go to a funeral any day. "The standard labor charge in garages here is three dollars an hour. That's supposed to include the profit, of course. But I'll pay you three dollars an hour for a forty-eight-hour week. No overtime, naturally, and no checking to see if you put in less than that."

"Big chance of that," I said.

"That's a hundred and forty-four a week, Jones. That's damn good money in any town."

"How much for Sandy as bookkeeper?" I asked. "I can get all I want for thirty a week. Good ones, that is."

"She'll have to decide on that," I said. "How much to run the track?"

"Five percent of whatever the purse is. Minimum fifteen dollars a night"

"Ten percent of the purse," I said. "Minimum of twenty-five. Including nights we're rained out and can't race."

"You'll be making more than ten thousand a year," Herpgruve blustered. "Where do you think you are?"

"I'll be worth it," I said. "If I'm not, we don't have anything to talk about. You'll make money on it. *If* you take my terms. And I'll be looking for a raise next year."

"Good enough," Herpgruve grunted. He stuck out a pudgy hand. "Shake on it?"

I looked at his hand and didn't move. "Let's not tamper with a beautiful relationship," I said. He glared at me for a moment, then he laughed and threw away his cigar. "They're coming out now," he said. "Let's go."

I thought he was going to give me a hand up, what with my bad leg and all, but he walked away and let me figure my own way to my feet.

— — —

Toad and Peale lay the same at the cemetery as they had in the funeral parlor. Toad was laid away first, and then we all moved over to Peale's spot, and his box was lowered. Then it was over.

The crowd broke up in a hurry. Some of the boys were going down to Shelden to race that night, and they had work to do.

I saw Ossman helping Mrs. Peale back to their car, with the kids straggling behind them. His arm was around her, and she leaned against him, her blonde hair against his dark jacket.

"What will become of that family now?"

"What about them?" Sandy said in a worried voice.

I shrugged. "What do all the others do? They'll get along—or they won't."

"Those poor children . . ."

"All over the world. Don't worry," I said to Sandy. "We'll do something for them. The drivers have been talking about getting up a purse. Jensen and de Marco bought the shoes the kids were wearing. We'll do something."

The funeral parlor car drove away with Mrs. Peale still clinging to Ossman in the back seat, and the kids looking out curiously, like little animals, the way they did at the track when Peale used to drive in with his old Buick.

I looked back at Peale's grave. It was still open. The workmen were covering Toad first. I limped to the side of Peale's grave and looked in. The poor dude. If only my reflexes had been faster. I fumbled with my left wrist and unsnapped the fancy watch he'd given me to pay for engine parts. Then I dropped it in on top of him. The poor dude needed to have something he'd loved and was still his.

— — —

Herpgruve dropped Sandy and me off at the garage. We wanted to talk about our future, and we both wanted to talk about it there, where we had first met. With her sitting in the chair and me sitting on the desk.

It was quiet there. Quiet and empty. We both kept listening for the shuffling sound of Toad's feet on the garage floor. I was too restless to stay parked on the desk. I got up and limped into the main section of the garage. The red-and-yellow Tudor was in its old corner, one side smashed in, the radiator hanging. The distributor would be cracked, too. It always was when the radiator got it bad. Another thirty bucks. There was a bent drag link. And . . .

I sat down on a GMC block we were working over for Bob Towner. A couple of flies buzzed happily in the large room. It was right about here that I'd been standing when I saw Toad. The day he'd come back from lunch with Ronnie.

I heard the car coming again. Ronnie's car. Backfire and all. And then I heard steps. Ronnie's, and somebody *with* Ronnie. They were coming in. I was afraid to look.

"Ace . . ."

I had to look up. Ronnie stood in the doorway, wary, penitent. Joe was with him. Little Joe, with his pale anxious look, and my old Hudson. Both boys were wearing new engineer boots, new Western-type denim pants, and black leather jackets.

"Where were you?" I asked.

"I couldn't go," Ronnie said in a low voice. "I couldn't."

"You should have been there."

"I couldn't." His face looked drawn and haggard. "I keep seeing it again. All the time. I keep seeing it."

"Forget it," I said harshly.

"I didn't mean to . . ."

"Everybody knows that. Toad ran on the track in front of you. You couldn't stop. Things like that happen when people get careless. Toad should have known better."

"That's right, Ronnie," Joe squeaked. "It wasn't your fault."

Ronnie looked at me, and I looked at him. It was all over. Done with. If he'd killed me, it would have been murder. Toad ran in front of him, and it was an accident. That's the way things happened. "Next time there's a pile-up on the track, back off," I said. "Let that be a lesson to you."

Ronnie nodded.

"And be at work early tomorrow," I said. "We're going to wash cars again when they're in for repairs."

Ronnie stared at his boots. "I won't be here, Ace. I want to . . . I'm quitting."

"You don't have to," I said. "The past was buried today. Everything."

"Even so."

"You don't want to quit now. I've quit driving. You'll be able to run seventy-two all the time. Wouldn't you like that?"

"I gotta quit," Ronnie said, his eyes desperate. "I can't drive for you. If I do, you and Sandy will be on my back all the time. Making me be careful, and lay back, and worrying, and not letting me run with the others."

"Who are you going to drive for?"

"He's going with me, Mr. Jones," Joe broke in. "I can't drive your Hudson like it should be drove. So I asked Ronnie to drive. We already got a guarantee for expenses from a couple of tracks. With luck, we ought to be getting in the real big time."

There they stood. With all the big tracks and big races in the world waiting for them. First, the pumpkin fairs, then the state fairs, and the big stock car deals. Maybe the Mexican Road Race, or a chance at some of the famous European tracks. Maybe into big cars and Indianapolis. Where my trail ended, theirs began. I would stay, but my car would roar on the tracks again, with youth at the wheel.

"All right, son," I said. "Take the Hudson and do your best. You've got the stuff for the big time. You can make it."

Ronnie came forward slowly, wiping his right hand on his pants. "Thanks. Ace."

"It won't be easy," I said. "You're going to be up against guys who could take you out on the track now and whip your tail driving against you on a tricycle. But you'll learn. And any time you need us, we'll be here."

He wiped his nose with the back of his hand. "Okay, Ace," he said in a thin voice.

"And for God's sake, don't forget to write once in a while!"

"Yeah, Ace."

"And say goodbye to Sandy."

"Okay, Ace."

Joe called out plaintively, "Let's go, Ronnie. We got to get moving if we're gonna get to the track tomorrow."

I didn't want to say it, but it came out. "And be careful"

Suddenly, Ronnie grinned. "I'll do everything you say, just the way you say it, you nosey old shite-poke."

I didn't answer. It seemed to be the thing to do, to reach forward and take the pack of cigarettes out of his pocket. I put one cigarette behind my ear, and one in my mouth, and gave the pack to Ronnie. He looked at me for a puzzled moment, then reached out slowly and took back the cigarette that was tucked behind my ear. He got out a book of matches, lit one, and put it to the cigarette in my mouth. Then he walked out, and Joe fell in behind him. And I sat on my tail in the middle of the garage, on the GMC block, and I couldn't see the boys leave for the smoke in my eyes.

ABOUT THE HOT ROD SERIES

Originally published in the 1950s, this series of six popular rodding books sold more than 8 million copies. Immensely popular with young readers in its early days, the books are wildly entertaining cautionary tales meant to keep speed-hungry teens safe on the streets. In limited circulation for the past decade, Octane Press has created this fantastic new edition.

The Hot Rod Series by Henry Gregor Felsen includes:

HOT ROD
ISBN 978-1-64234-089-1

STREET ROD
ISBN 978-1-64234-104-1

CRASH CLUB
ISBN 978-1-64234-131-7

ROAD ROCKET
ISBN 978-1-64234-132-4

FEVER HEAT
ISBN 978-1-64234-133-1

RAG TOP
(originally published as CUP OF FURY)
ISBN 978-1-64234-134-8

www.ingramcontent.com/pod-product-compliance
Lightning Source LLC
Chambersburg PA
CBHW020546020726
47494CB00006B/1934